Berkley Prime Crime titles by Meg London

MURDER UNMENTIONABLE
LACED WITH POISON
A FATAL SLIP

A Fatal
SLIP

MEG LONDON

BERKLEY PRIME CRIME, NEW YORK

THE BERKLEY PUBLISHING GROUP
Published by the Penguin Group
Penguin Group (USA) LLC
375 Hudson Street, New York, New York 10014

USA • Canada • UK • Ireland • Australia • New Zealand • India • South Africa • China

penguin.com

A Penguin Random House Company

A FATAL SLIP

A Berkley Prime Crime Book / published by arrangement with the author

Berkley Prime Crime Books are published by The Berkley Publishing Group.
BERKLEY® PRIME CRIME and the PRIME CRIME logo are trademarks
of Penguin Group (USA) LLC.

For information, address: The Berkley Publishing Group,
a division of Penguin Group (USA) LLC,
375 Hudson Street, New York, New York 10014.

ISBN: 978-0-425-25247-5

PUBLISHING HISTORY
Berkley Prime Crime mass-market edition / February 2014

PRINTED IN THE UNITED STATES OF AMERICA

10 9 8 7 6 5 4 3 2 1

Cover illustration by Nathalie Dion.
Cover design by Rita Frangie.
Interior design by Laura K. Corless.

To my wonderful editor, Faith Black,
who has been a joy to work with.
She has taken my rough material,
smoothed out the edges,
and transformed my words into a coherent story.

Chapter 1

"BETTE, no!" Emma Taylor yelled at the wayward puppy scampering toward the front door of Sweet Nothings. "Don't let her out," she called to Sylvia Brodsky, who was trying to edge her way into the store. Meanwhile, Pierre, Bette's very proud father, slouched in his black-and-white toile dog bed, clearly disinterested in the antics of his progeny. Emma shot him a look as if to say *big help you are.*

Bette was part French bulldog, compliments of her father, Pierre Louis Auguste, and his clandestine liaison with Bertha, part dachshund, whose owner ran the Gallery across the street. Bette had inherited bits and pieces of each parent—a longer than usual torso and a square head with rounded forehead but her one black ear and one white ear unmistakably came from Pierre. Right now, at five months, she was all puppy—full of energy and in constant motion—when she wasn't fast asleep.

Emma sighed in frustration and glanced at her watch. Sweet Nothings, the vintage lingerie store she had helped her aunt Arabella renovate, was due to open at six o'clock for a very special Valentine's Day event. Elegant, printed cards had been sent to the male population of Paris, Tennessee, inviting them to this men-only evening sale where they could eat, drink and shop for their lady loves.

It had been Sylvia's idea. She worked at Sweet Nothings as a part-time bra fitter, a job she'd held at Macy's in New York City before moving south with her son and his wife.

Emma looked around the shop. The very air seemed to quiver with anticipation. Large bouquets of magnificent red roses sat out on the counter adding a pop of color and a delicious fragrance to the room. Emma had rented three small, round tables and draped each with white cloths and a red overlay. One would be for the hors d'oeuvres, which Lucy Monroe, owner of Let Us Cater to You, was bringing at any moment; one would hold a silver bucket filled with ice and several bottles of sparkling wine; and the third was for Bitsy Palmer's designer cupcakes.

"What is that puppy of yours up to now?" Arabella stuck her head around the door to the stockroom.

"Just being a puppy," Sylvia replied from her spot behind the counter, where she was unwrapping a piece of chewing gum. Since quitting smoking, her breathing had improved considerably, and she no longer had to haul around an oxygen tank. Both Arabella and Emma were relieved because Sylvia was known to douse her cigarette with one hand while reaching for her oxygen tank with the other. They were in constant fear of being blown to kingdom come.

"Bette is a little cutie"—Arabella laughed—"but quite the minx, too, don't you think?" Arabella smoothed down her top—a raspberry red silk blouse to complement the Valentine's Day theme. It was tucked into a knife-pleated pale gray skirt and accessorized with a strand of pearls at her neck.

"That's for sure." Emma was getting positively sweaty thanks to her pursuit of the wayward pup.

"Just like her brother." Sylvia smiled. Sylvia had adopted one of Bette's siblings. "Dirk ate the tongue of one of Earl's shoes the other day."

Arabella and Emma glanced at each other. Emma suspected they were both thinking the same thing—*what was Earl's shoe doing in Sylvia's apartment*? Earl and Sylvia had met when Sylvia's children insisted she move to Sunny Days, a retirement community on the outskirts of town, after Sylvia had had several mishaps with both her stove and her bathtub.

"I think I ought to put Bette in her crate for now."

"Good idea." Arabella nodded. "Lucy will be here shortly, and Bitsy with the cupcakes. We don't want to end up chasing Bette down Washington Street. She's a veritable Houdini when it comes to escaping. We've got enough to do as it is."

Emma reached for Bette, who, sensing that her freedom was about to come to an abrupt end, dashed underneath one of the tables. Emma got down on her hands and knees and stuck her head under the cloth.

She could have sworn that Bette actually grinned at her.

Her bright pink tongue lolled out of one side of her mouth, and her head was cocked playfully.

"This isn't a game. It's time for you to go in your crate and get some rest." Emma tried to make that proposition sound wildly attractive by using her most persuasive tone of voice.

It didn't fool Bette. Just as Emma was about to close her hand on Bette's collar, Bette took off again at a brisk trot, looking back over her shoulder to see if Emma was following. Emma backed out from under the table, certain that her dark hair, even though fairly short, was standing on end.

"You little rascal," she shook her fist at Bette which only seemed to excite the puppy more. She tilted her head and looked at Emma as if to say *what a fun game this is*, before taking off again.

"That dog is busier than a moth in a mitten." Arabella reached down and scooped up the unsuspecting puppy. "Got you!" Bette squirmed in Arabella's arms but then gave in and began licking Arabella's face energetically.

Arabella giggled and handed the wriggling dog to Emma.

Bette's crate was behind the counter, where they could keep an eye on her and the dog could see what was going on. Emma tucked her inside and latched the door securely. She stood up and blew a lock of dark hair off her forehead. By the time she turned around, Bette was sprawled over one of her stuffed toys, fast asleep, her chest rising and falling rapidly.

Sylvia gave a rattling cough, one of the remnants of her two-pack-a-day habit. She was dressed for the occasion in a deep red, long-sleeved dress, which hung on her thin frame as if from a hanger. Sylvia was all elbows, knees and cheekbones with a blunt, gray bob that emphasized the angularity of her face. "We still haven't decided what to put on Melanie." She pointed at a mannequin that had been so named because of her resemblance to the character in *Gone With the Wind*.

Arabella furrowed her brow and put a hand to the loose knot of white hair gathered at her neck. "What's our most expensive outfit?" She turned toward Emma, fingering the strand of pearls at her neck.

"The royal blue Lucie Ann, I think." Emma opened one of the cupboards and began sorting through the contents.

"The one I bought at the Porters' estate sale?"

"Yes," Emma said, her head in the closet, and her voice slightly muffled.

"Good idea."

Emma pulled out the exquisite, marabou-trimmed robe and negligee ensemble and waved it in front of Arabella.

"It's perfect."

Emma had just slipped the glamorous bias-cut negligee over the mannequin's head when they heard thumping coming from the back door.

"That must be Lucy or Bitsy." Arabella headed toward the stockroom.

Emma was fastening the covered buttons on the negligee's matching silk robe when Lucy bustled into the room, a large, woven basket in each hand, her apron still tied around her waist. Her froth of white blond hair was teased into a bouffant swirl on top of her head and tucked into a French twist in back.

"It sure has turned frigid out there, and I think it's fixin' to rain." Lucy's face was red with cold. She gestured toward the baskets with her chin. "Emma, darling, where do you want these?"

"Over there." Emma pointed to the cloth-covered table from under which Bette had recently exited.

Lucy's huge diamond ring winked in the light as she pulled several containers from the baskets. Emma knew the diamond wasn't real and that Lucy had bought it herself. She wanted people to think she'd married her husband, Harry, for his money and not because she'd fallen head over heels in love with him. Having made the trip to the altar five times already, Lucy's friends and family found it easier to believe she was after a fortune than that she was willing to risk her heart yet again.

Lucy was searching through one of the baskets. "Oh lordy," she exclaimed, standing up with a hand on one generous hip. "Where on earth did I put them? You can't go having a big event like this without my cheese straws. It wouldn't be right." Lucy began to pull things out of the basket willy-nilly. "They did turn out well, if I must say so myself. I was kind of worried on account of the weather—sometimes when it's real damp out, the dough just doesn't want to behave. But I haven't been making cheese straws for more than three decades to be defeated by a little humidity."

Lucy was Emma's mother's best friend and Emma had grown up calling her Aunt Lucy. No Taylor was allowed to be christened, get married or be buried without Lucy's cheese straws. As a matter of fact, no important event in Paris, Tennessee, was allowed to take place without at least one order of Lucy's most famous hors d'oeuvre.

"Oooh, that looks delicious." Emma glanced at the platter of appetizers Lucy had set out. Emma's stomach rumbled, reminding her that she hadn't had anything to eat since early that morning. They'd all been run off their feet trying to get ready in time.

"I put together a little plate for you ladies. I kind of figured you probably wouldn't have had any time for dinner. I'll bring it in with the next load." Lucy had unearthed the cheese straws and was arranging them in a small glass vase. She handed one to Emma.

"See what you think."

Emma took a bite and closed her eyes in rapture. "Perfect, as always."

Lucy nodded briskly. "I thought so. You've got to be careful not to add too much flour when you're rolling out the dough, or it will toughen them up."

Emma filled the silver bucket with ice, and retrieved three bottles of the sparkling wine from the cooler. She stuck them into the bucket and began unpacking the champagne flutes they had rented for the occasion.

Sylvia came out from behind the counter. "Everything looks beautiful. You sure did a good job renovating this place." She shook her head and her enormous hoop earrings swayed to and fro.

Emma looked around at the pale pink walls and black-and-white toile accents. Quite different from the faded psychedelic colors and pea green shag carpeting she'd started with. "Brian helped, too, don't forget. He built the cupboards and did all the painting."

The thought of Brian made Emma smile. He was her best friend Liz Banning's older brother, and while it had taken Emma some time to get him to see her as more than his kid sister's playmate, he had come around, and they'd fallen

7

hard for each other. He'd promised to stop by later, and the thought lifted Emma's spirits.

"Hey y'all. Can somebody come give me a hand?" a voice drawled from the back door.

Emma scurried into the stockroom to find Bitsy struggling through the door with two enormous platters of cupcakes.

"Let me help you." Emma reached for one of the platters.

"Thanks. I should have made two trips. It would be a tragedy to drop one of these." Bitsy followed Emma into the store. She put the platter of cupcakes down on the counter and looked around. "My, my, everything looks so pretty! The men won't be able to resist buying everything in the place." She smiled at Emma.

"I certainly hope so."

Bitsy, whose real name was Catherine, was anything but at six foot tall, but the nickname, acquired at birth, had stuck regardless. She had golden blond hair, which brushed her shoulder blades, and her enormous blue eyes, ringed with thick dark lashes, gave her a look of wide-eyed innocence. She owned Sprinkles, a bakery and cupcake shop around the corner from Sweet Nothings, and she and Emma had become good friends since Emma's return to Paris.

"Where do you want the cupcakes? I've done your favorite—carrot cake with cream cheese icing—along with vanilla, chocolate and strawberry." She lifted the lid on the platter. "I love the way the strawberry ones turned out— perfectly pink for Valentine's Day."

Emma admired the confections, and it was all she could do to keep from snatching one. She felt her stomach growl again, even louder this time. She motioned to the empty table. "I thought we'd set them up over there."

Arabella bustled out from the back room. She glanced at her watch. "It's almost six. We'd better hurry."

Bitsy organized her cupcakes while Lucy put the finishing touches on the hors d'oeuvres display. They both stood back to admire their handiwork.

"Well, we'd best get out of here before the men begin arriving," Lucy said, picking up her basket. "I'll be by in the morning to collect the empty platters."

"Good luck, ladies," Lucy and Bitsy both chorused as they headed toward the back door.

"Thanks," Emma called over her shoulder. She turned to Arabella and Sylvia. "Let's get something to eat while we can."

THE front door opened at four minutes after six, letting in a blast of cold air. Emma was behind the counter and looked up to see Les entering timidly. He was short and slender with delicate features and a rather meek appearance. He and Arabella had dated on and off but were now off since Arabella had begun dating Francis Salerno, an agent with the Tennessee Bureau of Investigation. Les, meanwhile, had taken up with Sally Dixon, a friend of Arabella's.

He and Arabella greeted each other. "Can I help you with anything?" she asked rather frostily.

"I'm just looking, thank you." Les helped himself to one of Lucy's cheese straws.

Arabella sniffed and whispered to Emma. "I suppose he's here to buy something for Sally although I doubt we have anything in her size." Arabella patted her own flat stomach and preened complacently.

Emma smiled to herself. A woman might decide she didn't want a man, but just let another woman snag him, and the claws came out.

The door almost immediately opened again, and several other men hesitantly stepped into the shop, looking as if they were entering enemy territory. Emma noticed their eyes light up when they saw the hors d'oeuvres and cupcakes. She hoped they would do some business tonight and that the men hadn't come just for the free food and drink.

The door opened yet again, letting in another blast of cold, damp air, and some younger men strolled, in looking much more confident than their older counterparts. Emma supposed they were used to shopping at the national chain lingerie shop at the mall. One of them immediately went to the armoire, where Emma had stacked colorful, lacy camisoles and matching panties. She was about to head in that direction when she noticed Sylvia bearing down on the man with a practiced smile and a gleam in her eye.

Arabella was behind the counter when the door opened again. A man stood there for several seconds and looked around, his hand on the doorknob. Emma could feel the frosty outside air all the way across the room. The man was perhaps a little older than Arabella and very distinguished looking with dark gray hair, hooded blue eyes and strong brows. His topcoat had a velvet collar and was obviously expensive, and Emma noticed a gold signet ring on his right pinkie.

Emma glanced at Arabella whose face registered . . .

shock? Emma looked at the man again. Who was he and why was Arabella looking at him so strangely?

"Aunt Arabella, is everything okay?" Emma whispered.

Arabella turned to Emma. "Of all the lingerie shops in all the towns in all the world, he walks into mine."

Chapter 2

EMMA was about to ask Arabella what on earth she meant and who the man was anyway, when Les approached her.

"Can you help me?" he asked plaintively.

Emma gritted her teeth, and forced a stiff smile onto her face. "Certainly."

Les led her over to one of the mannequins. "I'm very interested in this." He fingered the marabou trim on the robe of the Lucie Ann ensemble.

"This is a very special set," Emma said. "Very special indeed. It's a Lucie Ann from 1950. Lucie Ann founded her lingerie line in 1949, and sold the items from her shop in Beverly Hills where Hollywood stars like Elizabeth Taylor purchased them. Do you remember the show *Green Acres*?"

Les nodded, fingering the thin mustache he'd recently begun sporting.

"Lucie Ann designed all the peignoir sets Eva Gabor wore on that show."

"It's certainly a beautiful set."

Emma continued, "Lucie Ann was known for using bold color and glamorous details like rhinestones, pompons and marabou trim." Emma indicated the feather tipped sleeves on the robe.

"I imagine it's very expensive." Les gave a thin laugh.

Emma nodded and whispered a price in Les's ear.

Les stood back and looked the ensemble over again. He fingered the button on his tweed sport coat nervously. "I'm going to take it, I think. Blue is Sally's favorite color."

"Do you think it will fit?" Arabella had sidled over and was standing behind Emma.

Emma gave Arabella a stern look. Whatever had gotten into her aunt? It wasn't like her to be spiteful. And Emma couldn't help but notice how she was dodging the gray-haired gentleman who had recently entered the shop. He looked like he had money to spend—Arabella ought to be wooing him instead of ignoring him.

Emma removed the Lucie Ann negligee and peignoir set from the mannequin and took it to the counter, where she carefully wrapped each piece in tissue. It really was a beautiful outfit. She wouldn't mind having one like it herself. She wondered what Brian would think, and the idea brought a blush of heat to her face.

"Here you are." She placed the tissue-wrapped bundles into a glossy, black-and-white Sweet Nothings bag and handed it to Les.

He gave a courtly bow and, after shooting a last glance at Arabella, left Sweet Nothings.

Emma edged her way over to where Sylvia was standing. "Have you noticed anything funny about Arabella tonight?"

Sylvia held a pencil between her fingers like a cigarette and nearly brought it to her lips before she realized what she was doing. She shrugged. "You mean like how she's avoiding that man in the fancy coat who just came in?"

Emma nodded.

"Then, yes, I have noticed something funny about her. He looks like he has money to burn. You'd think she'd be all over him."

"Has she said anything to you?"

"Nah, not a word."

Sylvia went off to wait on a young man in jeans and a worn leather jacket, and Arabella joined Emma behind the counter. Suddenly, the mysterious gray-haired gentleman began to approach them. Arabella looked panicked, as if she wanted to flee, but before she could sidle out from behind the counter, he was upon them.

"Arabella," he said in a deep, smooth voice.

Arabella's face registered a wide array of emotions—part alarm, part defiance and part disgust. "Hugh," Arabella said curtly. She held her head high, her chin raised.

The man turned toward Emma and held out his hand. "Hugh Granger."

Emma returned the firm handshake. "Emma Taylor."

"Is this your daughter?" Hugh looked at Arabella, his thick brows raised.

Arabella shook her head. "My niece."

"But you married?"

She shook her head again. "No. I chose not to." The look she gave him would have turned a lesser man into an ice sculpture. "What are you doing here?" Arabella asked. "I would have thought you'd have done all your shopping in Paris or London."

Hugh smiled. "It was time for me to come home—to stop roaming the globe like a nomad. As a matter of fact, I'm giving a dinner dance on Saturday night at the Beauchamp Hotel and Spa to celebrate my birthday and our return to Paris. I do hope you lovely ladies will come and bring your . . ." He looked at Emma questioningly.

"Boyfriend," she supplied, feeling a rush of contentment at being able to apply that word to Brian.

"No," Arabella said abruptly. "Thank you, but we already have other plans."

Emma stared at her aunt, open-mouthed.

Arabella turned toward Emma with a strange look on her face. "You and Brian are coming to my house for dinner, remember?" she prompted.

"Oh, but surely—" Hugh began.

"I'm sorry, but it's just not possible." Arabella turned her back on him and began to fiddle with the contents of one of the drawers.

Emma gave Hugh an apologetic look. "Is there anything I can help you with?"

"As a matter of fact, there is. I'm interested in getting something for my sister, Georgina. She's in a nursing home, I'm afraid." He tapped his head. "Dementia. The staff has told me that things from the era of their youth are very comforting to patients with memory loss. Do you have any gowns from the early 1960s? She would have been a young woman then."

Emma led him toward one of the armoires, casting a backward glance at Arabella, who was standing behind the counter, her arms crossed over her chest and a very mulish expression on her face.

BY nine o'clock, they had closed the door on their last customer. Sylvia already had her coat on and her purse over her arm. "If it's all the same to you, I'll be heading out. My feet are killing me."

"Mine, too." Arabella had slipped out of her pumps and so had Emma.

Bette was chasing a tennis ball around the floor, rolling and tumbling like a pair of thrown dice while Pierre looked on from the comfort of his dog bed. Arabella bent down and scratched Pierre behind the ears. "I remember when you used to play like that, too."

Emma still hadn't been able to ask her aunt about the mysterious Hugh Granger. Arabella had managed to avoid her all evening, but Emma definitely planned to find out who he was.

Sylvia left through the back door and shortly afterward they heard the belch of her ancient Cadillac as she pulled out of the parking lot. Emma was about to lock the front door when someone pushed it open.

"Anybody home?" Francis stepped inside, shaking out his umbrella. "It's raining now, but if it turns any colder, I think we'll get some snow." Moisture clung to his dark hair and his thick, black brows. He was normally based in Jackson, a little over an hour away, but had recently been assigned to a special case in Paris, much to his and Arabella's mutual delight.

Arabella smiled when she saw him. He put his arm around her, and Arabella momentarily let her head drop against his broad chest.

She tilted her head back and looked up at him. "What do you say we all go to my house? I can put on a pot of coffee, and I have a pecan pie waiting that I baked this morning. We've been here all day. It's time to go home. We can clean up tomorrow morning."

Emma was hesitating—she didn't want to intrude on Arabella's time with Francis—when the door opened again, and Brian stuck his head in.

"I was hoping I hadn't missed you ladies." He brushed at the drops of rain on the shoulders of his raincoat. "I was at the hardware store going over some accounts, and I lost track of time. I was glad to see your lights were on."

Arabella put up a hand to stop Brian as he began to unbutton his coat. "We're all going to my house for some pie and coffee."

"You don't have to ask me twice." Brian let his hand drop to his side. "I'll drive you." He looked at Emma. "As long as you don't mind the pickup truck."

"Not a bit."

Emma clipped on Bette's leash as Arabella, Brian and Francis went around turning out lights and checking that the front door was locked and the sign flipped to *closed*.

Bette had worn herself out playing, and fell asleep curled in Emma's lap before they even pulled out of the parking lot. Emma stole a glance at Brian's strong profile as they passed under a street lamp. His brown hair was neat but still slightly boyish-looking, with a lock that kept falling onto his forehead. Emma longed to reach out and brush it back. Brian had returned to Paris to help run his father's hardware store while also getting his own home renovation business going. Like Emma, he was recovering from having his heart broken—in his case by a career-minded lawyer in Nashville who hadn't wanted to move to what she referred to as "the sticks." Her loss was Emma's gain. She and Brian were now in a serious relationship.

"Here we are." Brian pulled into the driveway of Arabella's house with its huge, wraparound porch, where Emma had spent many hours as a child sitting on the swing, sipping endless glasses of sweet tea and listening to her aunt's stories of her travels to exotic places around the globe.

Arabella and Francis already had their coats off and hung up, and Arabella was pouring water into the coffeemaker when Brian and Emma walked in. Bette, revived by her short nap, began running in circles, her nose to the ground, sniffing furiously, while Pierre watched disdainfully from the comfort of his dog bed.

Brian and Emma perched on stools around the center island of Arabella's huge, old-fashioned kitchen. Emma found it hard to believe that a few short months ago, Arabella's kitchen had been nothing but blackened timbers and twisted pieces of metal. Brian had masterminded the renovation and had done a wonderful job. Arabella had been devastated by the fire but extremely grateful that the rest of the house had been spared. Along with the kitchen renovation, some new wallpaper in the hallway and some fresh paint in the living room had returned things to normal, much to everyone's relief.

Francis organized cups and saucers and poured coffee while Arabella cut slices of pecan pie. She slid an extra-large piece in front of Brian.

"I must look hungry," he joked, the tips of his ears turning pink.

"I know you do like your pie," Arabella responded.

"How did your sale go this evening?" Francis asked as he slid onto one of the stools.

"I think we did very well. We even sold that hideously expensive Lucie Ann ensemble I picked up at the Porter estate sale." Arabella shivered. "Good riddance to it, if you ask me."

Brian and Emma looked at each other. They could easily guess why Arabella felt that way.

Emma locked gazes with her aunt. "Now will you tell me who that man was?"

"What man?" Francis said with his fork halfway to his mouth. "Not going around behind my back, are you, girl?" He reached over and gave Arabella's hand a quick squeeze.

She made a face at him. "Hardly. Hugh is ancient history."

"Well, tell us about it; don't keep us in the dark." Francis said encouragingly, helping himself to another cup of coffee.

"I'm not sure I know where to begin. For years I refused to talk about it, and now it really *is* ancient history." Arabella turned thoughtful. "I met Hugh here in Paris. His family owned . . . owns . . . a big horse farm not far from here. But their real money came from a quarry at Crab Orchard Mountains on the Cumberland Plateau, not far from Knoxville. Crab Orchard stone, a rare type of sandstone, was used to build a lot of municipal buildings during the Depression. It made them very rich." She paused and poked at the wedge of pecan pie on her plate. "Hugh's first love had always been art. He studied business in college to please his father, but took every art history course he could squeeze in. After graduation, he enlisted in the air force and entered Officer Candidate School. You have to remember that the Vietnam War was in full swing at the time, and becoming an officer was a lot safer than waiting to be drafted and ending up as a GI in the trenches. He wasn't the only young man to take that route at the time." She took a sip of her coffee. "As it turned out, he wasn't sent to the Far East but rather to an air force base in Germany. Thanks to his knowledge of art, he was assigned to the Air Police detachment to conduct an investigation into art stolen by the Nazis during the war." Arabella absentmindedly forked up a piece of pie. "Eventually he returned to Paris to start his own art business. That's when we started to go out." Arabella stared into her coffee cup. "He was quite keen on me."

"Were you keen on him?" Emma scraped the last bit of pie off her plate.

"I guess you could say I was," Arabella admitted. "He was very handsome and very worldly. His business took him all over Europe and Asia, buying and selling paintings and sculpture worth millions of dollars. It also made him very rich in his own right." A dreamy look settled on Arabella's face. "I was traveling around Europe at the time myself, thanks to a small trust fund from my grandfather Parker, and he would catch up with me whenever he could. I remember our being at Wimbledon when Billie Jean King and Rosemary Casals won the women's doubles title. Hugh flew over on Pan Am's Boeing 747 maiden flight from New York to Heathrow."

"What happened?" Emma asked. "Did you argue or did you eventually lose touch?"

"Neither, really." Arabella looked down at the barely touched piece of pie on her plate. "We continued to see each other for several years . . . in Paris, Rome, once even in India. He pledged his undying love to me in front of the Taj Mahal." Arabella gave a bitter smile.

"How romantic," Emma breathed.

"I certainly thought so," Arabella quipped. She rolled her eyes. "I continued to travel, and he continued to follow me whenever he could. Finally, he convinced me to come back to Paris and marry him."

Emma gasped. "What happened?"

"I didn't decide right away. I saw Hugh off on the SS *France* in Le Havre on his way back to New York. On board he met someone named Elizabeth. By the time I'd made my decision and had flown home a couple of months later, Hugh was married, and they were expecting a baby. Back in those days, people *had* to get married. Not like today."

"How horrible for you."

Arabella gave a sad smile. "I put all my energy, time and money into Sweet Nothings. I'd lost my desire to travel—all my memories were too wrapped up with Hugh."

"What did he say when—"

Arabella laughed. "Oh, he tried to put the blame on me. I'd taken too long to make up my mind. I'd made him chase me for years when all he wanted to do was settle down. I didn't believe a word of it. Fortunately, until tonight, our paths rarely crossed. Although he still owns the family horse farm here in Tennessee, he spent most of his time in New York or traveling through Europe buying and selling art. He must have come back for some reason. Perhaps he's tired and has decided it's time to settle down."

Francis was looking thoughtful. "What is this fellow's name again?"

"Hugh. Hugh Granger."

"He invited us to a dinner dance at the Beau on Saturday night"—Emma glanced at Brian—"but Arabella turned him down."

"I don't really mind if you go," Arabella said, "although I'd rather you didn't. But still, a big party at the Beau is bound to be spectacular."

"I'd like to go," Francis said suddenly.

"You've got to be kidding." Arabella pulled away and looked at him sternly.

He nodded. "Yes, if you think you can bear it. The Tennessee Bureau of Investigation has been looking into Hugh Granger for years. There have been whispers about some of his dealings. We'd love the opportunity to get closer to his operation. This is a chance to at least enter his orbit, rarified though it is."

Arabella heaved a sigh. "If you really think it important."

Francis gave her his most winning smile.

"Oh, all right. I'll call him tomorrow and tell him we've changed our minds, and we'll be attending his big, fancy party. Are you satisfied now?"

Chapter 3

EMMA was on pins and needles until Saturday night finally arrived. Brian had once taken her to a friend's wedding at the Beauchamp Hotel and Spa, or the "Beau" as the locals called it, and it had been a spectacular event with elegant décor and delicious food.

The question of what to wear immediately reared its head. As a stylist in New York Emma had amassed a decent wardrobe, although here in Paris she found herself reaching for the same basic garments over and over again. The back of her closet had become unexplored territory. Emma plunged into the mass of skirts, dresses, pants and blouses and managed to unearth a dress she'd once worn to a charity ball in New York with her then-boyfriend, photographer Guy

Richard. She'd scored it at a sample sale, and it hadn't been out of her closet since.

It was no longer the height of fashion but considering that she was in Tennessee and not New York, she was certain it would do. Besides, Arabella had loaned her some magnificent jewelry to go with it.

Emma stood in front of her bathroom mirror and fastened the clasp on the exquisite ruby-and-diamond necklace. It felt heavy and cold against her bare skin. She slipped on the matching chandelier earrings and turned this way and that, admiring the sparkle of the gems in the overhead light. Had the set been a gift from Hugh Granger, she wondered? Or had there been someone else as well, and Arabella was keeping more than one secret from them?

Brian's eyes lit up when he arrived an hour and a half later to pick Emma up. He looked her up and down and gave a long, low whistle. "Wow, am I going to have to hire a Brinks guard to protect you?" he said, indicating her necklace and matching earrings.

"I'm sure I'm not going to be the only one at the party resplendent in fine jewels. From what Arabella has said, this Hugh runs with a pretty rich crowd."

"I'm certain that no one there will be wearing them nearly as well as you do." Brian took Emma in his arms and kissed her in a way that left her breathless and nearly made her toes curl up. "Do we really have to go to this party tonight?" he asked, his voice husky in her ear.

Emma laughed and pulled away. "We promised Aunt Arabella, remember?"

Brian made a comically sad face, and Emma laughed.

She had never seen him in dinner clothes before. Jeans

and work shirts were more his usual attire. He managed to look as if he wore black tie every day. He'd slicked his hair down just a bit, and Emma caught the faintest whiff of cologne.

"Shall we go?" he asked.

Emma picked up her gown with both hands to keep it from trailing on the stairs as they headed to the ground floor. She glanced at the dust in the corners and made a mental note to sweep the very next day.

"The way you look tonight, I feel like you deserve a limousine and not my sister's station wagon," Brian said indicating the car parked outside the back door to Emma's apartment.

"At least it's not a pumpkin."

Brian laughed as he slid behind the wheel. "Yes, and let's hope it doesn't turn into one at midnight, or we'll be riding brooms back to your place." He laughed again. "I think I'm mixing up my fairy tales."

The Beau was located about fifteen minutes out of town, and the drive went quickly. They passed miles of dark and shadowy open fields, prickly with matted, frozen vegetation. Suddenly they rounded the corner and Emma gasped as the Beau came into view. It glowed from stem to stern, like a great ship ablaze against the inky darkness of the night. Several sleek, black cars were pulled up to the entrance where white-jacketed valets quickly whisked them away. Men in dinner jackets and women in fur coats and elegant gowns mingled around the entrance.

Emma felt the stirrings of excitement. This was going to be a very glamorous evening indeed.

Brian pulled up to the curb with a flourish, put the car in park and went around to help Emma out. She made what she hoped was a reasonably graceful exit considering the width of her skirt. Arabella and Francis were already waiting for them by the door. Arabella was resplendent in a midnight blue, long-sleeved gown that set off her white hair, and Francis looked just as distinguished in his evening wear.

Hugh Granger greeted them as soon as they entered. "I'm so glad you changed your mind." His practiced smile was aimed at Arabella.

She nodded stiffly and gave a brief smile.

"This is my wife, Mariel." Hugh gestured to the woman standing next to him, her lips set in a thin line.

She was considerably younger than Hugh—around fifty—and what Emma supposed would be called handsome rather than pretty. She was tall and trim but with broad shoulders and large, capable-looking hands. Her thick, dark blond hair was swept back off her forehead, the ashy color hiding a sprinkling of gray. She greeted them somewhat disinterestedly and immediately turned to talk to an older couple who had come in after Emma and Brian.

"Well! Looks like he's on wife number two," Arabella said sharply as they moved away. "Or, number three or four, who knows? I only know that the first was called Elizabeth."

Francis forged a path through the throng of guests, and the rest of them followed, Brian's hand on Emma's elbow gently steering her past the knots of people milling around the reception area. Their chatter drowned out the trickle of a waterfall and the soothing, Zenlike music in the background.

The ballroom was down a corridor lined with windows on one side. The glass reflected Emma's image back at her, but she could just barely discern a courtyard beyond the mirrorlike windows.

"This is some place," Emma heard Francis whisper to Arabella.

Double doors led into a magnificent ballroom. It was white and trimmed lavishly with gilt. A small balcony ran along the upper level. Two enormous chandeliers dripping with crystals were suspended over the tables below, covered tonight in white cloths with deep blue overlays. The tables were set with glittering silverware and crystal and white plates with a dark blue and gold rim.

Brian ran a finger around his collar. "This is quite the setup."

"It sure is." Emma looked around her, not even trying to pretend she was too sophisticated to be impressed.

Waiters in black tie and tails and white gloves carrying trays laden with flutes of champagne and elegant hors d'oeuvres made their way through the crowd. A waiter suddenly appeared at Emma's elbow offering champagne.

"Thank you." Emma selected a glass. She was tilting it toward her mouth when someone jostled her arm.

Emma whirled around to see a woman standing by her side.

"I'm so sorry," she said. "My leg makes me clumsy. Let me call for a waiter to get you a cloth."

The woman wore a long dress, but judging by the slant of her hips, Emma suspected that her left leg was shorter than her right. And the shoes peeking out from under the swath of burgundy satin that made up the skirt of her gown were stout-looking ones with the sole built up on the left one. She was quite plain with pale skin, a sprinkle of freckles and only a dash of pink lipstick for makeup. Emma thought her to be in her late thirties or possibly early forties.

Emma glanced at her dress. "Oh, please don't bother. It's fine. It didn't spill."

"Are you sure?"

"Yes."

"I'm Joy Granger, Hugh's daughter." She put a hand out, steadying herself by clutching the back of a chair with the other.

Emma took her hand. "What a lovely name."

"Rather ironic, actually." Joy gave a bitter smile. "Are you sure about your dress? I can easily have the waiter bring you a damp cloth."

"Really, it's fine."

"In that case, I hope you enjoy the dog and pony show." She moved away awkwardly.

"What an odd woman," Francis said after Joy had disappeared into the milling crowd. "And that remark about her name was rather strange, don't you think?"

"She might have been referring to the fact that her arrival hadn't been particularly joyful—in which case, it would certainly be an odd choice for a name," Arabella said.

Francis nodded his head. "You're probably right."

Arabella turned to Brian and Emma. "Did you get our place cards?"

Brian held up four folded pieces of heavy card stock with names handwritten on them in fancy script. He glanced at one of them. "We're at table 14."

"I don't suppose we shall know the rest of our dinner partners," Arabella said, adjusting the light shawl draped over her shoulders. "No matter. I'm sure we'll get along." Arabella plucked an hors d'oeuvre from the tray of a circulating waiter. "Mmmm, caviar." She tapped the waiter on the arm and he spun around. "You must try one," she said to Emma, Brian and Francis. "It's divine. Osetra, if I'm not mistaken."

"What on earth is Osetra?" Francis raised an eyebrow as he reached for the tray.

"Very, very expensive caviar," Arabella said, taking his arm. "Savor it," she cautioned. "Burst the delicious, little bubbles with your tongue and cherish the flavor."

Francis raised both eyebrows. "I'm a country boy, Arabella. My pleasures are simple ones. Some good barbecue and a pitcher of Tennessee tea, and I'm a happy man."

"Nonsense." Arabella slapped him on the arm playfully. "Everyone loves caviar."

Emma turned to Brian who was trying, as discretely as possible, to spit the hors d'oeuvre into his cocktail napkin. He laughed when he noticed Emma watching. "Sorry, I'm just not as sophisticated as you are."

Emma squeezed his arm. "It's all a matter of taste. I knew some very sophisticated people who *hated* caviar."

Brian took Emma's hand as they wound their way among the tables, looking for number 14.

Suddenly Hugh's amplified voice came from the front of the room.

"I want to welcome you all here tonight and thank you for coming. My dear wife, Mariel, arranged this lovely get-together to celebrate not only my upcoming birthday, but also the fact that we have moved back to Paris to stay. I've spent most of my life traveling the globe, truly the peripatetic traveler, but now at my age"—he paused and there was polite laughter from the audience—"I'm ready to settle down. If you will find your tables, please, Mariel has a spectacular dinner and evening planned for you all."

A smattering of applause came from the audience, quickly dying away as people moved toward their seats, the ladies' gowns rustling as they moved.

Brian found their table easily enough and held out one of the gilt chairs for Emma while Francis did the same for Arabella. The centerpieces dripped with luscious pink and blue hydrangeas, and a dozen tea lights glittered among the crystal, china and silver. The beauty of it all—the elegant ballroom, the twinkling lights, the flowers, the caviar . . . everything . . . nearly took Emma's breath away.

"I think this is our table," Emma heard someone say behind her. She twisted around in her seat. "Oh."

Brian, meanwhile, had jumped to his feet. "John!" He pumped the other man's hand enthusiastically. He turned to Emma. "Emma, you remember the Jaspers, don't you? John and Lara?"

"Yes, certainly." Brian and Emma had run into them one night while dining at L'Etoile, Paris's most elegant restaurant. They were clients of Brian's, having employed him to completely renovate the mid-century modern house they had recently purchased.

"I think we're at your table." John gave a big smile, his round face flushed from champagne and the warmth of the room.

Brian introduced Arabella and Francis as John pulled out a chair, and Lara slipped into it.

"My wife, Lara," John said with a look of pride.

She was a beautiful young woman in her late twenties with long, golden brown hair and green eyes. Her low-cut, backless, sequined fishtail gown made the most of her figure, and Emma suspected it wasn't something she had picked up at the local mall. Fortunately, Lara was warm and gracious, and Emma had really liked her the last time they met.

"So how do you know Hugh Granger?" John settled in his seat, tilting the chair slightly backward on two legs.

"He's an old friend," Arabella said succinctly. "And you?"

"He's been my art dealer for a couple of years." John looked at Lara as if for confirmation. "We collect art—although it's not much of a collection yet." He gave a self-deprecating laugh. "Just the odd piece here and there."

Lara was turning her knife over and over. She smiled at her husband.

"It started with this piece a young art student had done of Lara in Sao Paulo. She used to model for the class." John glanced at his wife with a proprietary air. "It was a triptych—three panels—that was in the style of the portraits Andy Warhol used to do. Warhol did a lot of famous people—even Jackie Onassis and Marilyn Monroe. Lara showed me a picture of the student's work, and I decided I had to have it. It took me three years to track him down and buy the piece." John took a gulp of water from the glass next to his plate. "I guess I caught the collecting bug. Hugh has been helping us build our collection, as pitiful as it is."

Waiters had begun circulating among the tables, and one of them slid bowls of lobster bisque in front of them.

"Looks like we're in for some pretty impressive chow." John chuckled.

"So you've been a client of Granger's for a while," Francis said as he unfurled his napkin and placed it in his lap.

John nodded. "He's found some great pieces for us. Our

latest acquisition"—he spooned up some soup—"is a Rothko painting. Although actually, it was Hugh's son, Jackson, who found the painting for us. Gave us a wonderful price on it, too. It's definitely the star of our collection."

Waiters cleared away their soup plates and came back with dishes of rack of lamb, potatoes Dauphinoise and asparagus with sauce Maltese.

"Heavenly, don't you think?" Arabella said as she studied her artfully arranged plate.

A small orchestra had assembled on a platform at the front of the room and began playing, drowning out the sounds of silverware clinking against china and the low murmur of conversation. Emma recognized several tunes from Broadway shows she had seen while living in New York. They were finishing up the last bites of their meal when Hugh's voice came over the audio system again.

"Before dancing, and dessert, which I assure you will be spectacular, Mariel has organized a special treat." Hugh paused. "Fireworks," he said dramatically sweeping a hand toward the French doors that lined one wall of the ballroom. "On the lawn. The hotel staff has put heaters out on the patio. It's a beautiful night; I suggest you go outside and enjoy them."

A phalanx of waiters headed toward the French doors, opening them with a grand flourish.

A low murmur of excited voices floated up as soon as Hugh was finished speaking.

"The chap's gone all out, I'll say," John said pushing his chair back. "Are you game?" he asked Lara.

She nodded and picked up the beaded evening bag she had slung from her chair.

"How about you?" Brian looked at Emma. "Want to go outside? I can loan you my jacket if you get too chilly."

Emma pushed back her chair. "I wouldn't miss it."

Arabella and Francis were also getting to their feet. By the time they made their way to the doors leading to the patio, the first fireworks were lighting the sky with brilliant colors. The accompanying thunderous boom rattled the crystal and silverware on the tables.

A large outdoor fireplace stood in the middle of the patio and had been stoked with fragrant-smelling wood. Smaller heaters were placed strategically around the perimeter along with tall, flaming torches.

Emma and Brian secured a place close to the fire, and, with Brian's arms around her, Emma didn't mind the cold. The fireworks display was magnificent—splayed against the black, star-studded sky. She leaned against Brian's broad chest and watched as the colored lights streaked by overhead. They could hear the band playing in the background, and Emma thought it was one of the most enchanting evenings she could remember.

She glanced over toward Arabella, but her aunt wasn't there. Emma raised a questioning brow at Francis, but he just shrugged and gestured toward the ballroom. Emma supposed Arabella had become cold or had taken the opportunity to powder her nose. She imagined that Arabella had already seen any number of incredible things in her life, and she wasn't averse to missing a few fireworks.

Emma noticed a woman who had been sitting at Hugh's table make her way through the crowd, back to the ballroom, her orange dress bright against the black of the men's evening wear.

The finale had the crowd oohing and aahing, their heads tilted back, necks stretched, as they watched the brilliant lights illuminating the sky. Finally, the last rocket streaked silver and gold plumes, lighting up the darkness, the final boom sounded, and the crowd began to drift back toward the open doors to the ballroom.

Emma and Brian followed suit, Brian's arm lingering around Emma's bare shoulders. They were just stepping through the French doors into the candlelit ballroom when a woman's high-pitched scream sounded above the low murmur of voices. It rose to a crescendo, trailed away and was replaced by abrupt silence that seemed to pulse in the room like a living thing.

Emma and Brian froze, glancing at each other in horror.

"Something's happened." Brian tightened his arm around Emma.

"What the—" Francis, who was behind them, muttered. "Excuse me, perhaps I'd better see to this." He rushed past Emma and Brian and strode toward the point from which the scream had emanated.

Emma grabbed Brian by the hand. "Should we go see what's going on?"

"I don't—" Brian began, but Emma tugged him inside the room. The crowd was rushing toward the far corner of the ballroom, and Emma followed suit, Brian in tow.

Several women in the crowd screamed, some of the men groaned and the people at the back of the crowd jostled each other to see what was going on.

Emma managed to wiggle her way through the crowd to the front. "Oh," was all she could say when she got there. She put a hand to her mouth to stifle the scream that threatened to erupt. She heard Brian's sharp intake of breath behind her.

Hugh Granger's lifeless body lay sprawled on the floor at the foot of the balcony that encircled the room, his elegant dinner jacket barely ruffled, his starched shirt as pristine as ever. His blue eyes were open but sightless, his body motionless on the polished parquet floor.

Francis had already made his way through the crowd, which fell back slightly in response to his air of authority. He knelt and felt Hugh's neck with one hand while he dug his phone from his pocket with the other. He shook his head. "No pulse, I'm afraid." He quickly punched in 9-1-1 on his cell.

Emma stepped forward and touched Francis on the arm. "He fell?" She asked looking up at the narrow balcony that encircled the room.

Francis shrugged. "I don't know. He must have."

Chapter 4

"EVERYONE, go back to your seats," Francis commanded the crowd that had gathered around the body. He stuffed his cell phone back in his pocket. "An ambulance is on the way."

A fussy-looking man in a dark suit and shiny black hair in a comb-over hastened to where Francis was standing.

"Must be the hotel manager," Brian said, as he put his arm around Emma's waist and began to steer her away from the scene. "I imagine he'll know what to do."

People continued to mill around, the men shaking their heads, the women uttering small cries of dismay, until several waiters bustled over and formed a ring around Hugh's fallen body. Discouraged, the guests drifted back toward their tables. Emma heard a stout woman in an emerald gown ask her companion whether or not he thought they would still be served dessert.

It was surely not the finale poor Hugh had been anticipating. Emma shivered, and Brian tightened his arm around her.

Their table had been cleared of the dirty plates and used silverware and set with cups and saucers and dessert forks and spoons. Emma and Brian slid into their seats. The Jaspers were still milling in the crowd somewhere.

"Where is Arabella?" Emma looked at her aunt's empty seat.

Brian shrugged. "I saw her leave during the fireworks, but that was quite a while ago. I imagine she's gone to the restroom. You ladies always take so long in there." He grinned at Emma.

Emma gave the ghost of a smile before turning serious again. "Do you think I should go look for her? Perhaps she's been taken ill or something."

"I'm sure she'll be along any minute, but if it would make you feel better . . . "

Emma was about to get up when she noticed Arabella crossing the ballroom toward them. She sat back down with a feeling of relief.

"Arabella," Emma said as soon as her aunt reached their table, "we were worried about you."

"I'm sorry, dear. I didn't mean to alarm you."

"Where were you?"

"Where was I?" Arabella looked flustered. Her hands fluttered around her face, which, Emma noticed, was suddenly drained of color.

Just then the Jaspers returned to their seats.

"This is horrible," John said as he collapsed into his chair. "We were just getting to know Hugh—had dinner with him and Mariel only last week. It's hard to believe."

Lara nodded her head in confirmation, and put her hand over her husband's.

"Poor Mariel must be devastated." He shuddered. "And the kids. I hope they didn't have to see their father . . . just lying there like that."

"Children?" Arabella said. "We met the one daughter, Joy."

"Yes." John shook his head vigorously. "There's Joy, of course. Her mother died in the accident that . . . that . . . left her crippled."

"Was that Elizabeth?" Arabella asked.

John shrugged and wiped a hand across his brow. Emma noticed Lara's hand tighten on his. "I don't know. He didn't mention her name. There's also the boy, of course—Jackson. Although I don't suppose I can call him a boy." He gave a loud guffaw. "Shows how old I'm getting." He glanced at Lara and she gave him a tolerant-looking smile. "He's already twenty-five, following in his father's footsteps in the business. He played an aggressive game of lacrosse for UT for a bit, but college wasn't for him. It doesn't suit everyone." He glanced around the table as if seeking confirmation. "He's working hand in hand with his father. He's got quite an eye, too. I wonder what will happen now . . ." he trailed off.

A waiter appeared at their table with a tray of plated desserts. He slid a piece of chocolate volcano cake in front of each of them while another waiter circled the table pouring steaming-hot coffee into their cups.

John gave a nervous laugh and gestured at his dessert. "The show must go on, eh?" He picked up his fork.

Emma pushed her plate away. The cake looked delicious, but she had lost her appetite. She noticed that Arabella left hers untouched as well. She turned to her aunt.

"Arabella, would you like us to take you home? You're looking rather . . . tired." Emma chose her words with care. Her aunt didn't like to be reminded of her age.

"That would be lovely, dear, but do you suppose they will let us go?"

"I don't see why not." Brian took the last bite of his cake. "It was just a terrible accident."

Emma nodded. "And we didn't see anything, so there isn't much we can tell anyone."

They heard the shrill sound of sirens in the distance. The wail got louder and louder until it ended abruptly in a whimper.

"Sounds like the ambulance is here," Brian said, turning toward the entrance.

Several minutes later, a man and a woman in black pants and crisp, short-sleeved white shirts rushed in carrying red emergency kits. Emma couldn't see what they were doing, and she was grateful. She tried to keep the conversation going, to help take Arabella's mind off of what was happening, but Brian and John answered every gambit with monosyllables, and Lara didn't contribute a word.

A waiter was pouring second cups of coffee when several more sirens could be heard approaching the front entrance of the hotel.

"Hopefully, we'll be able to go home soon," Brian whispered to Emma. He yawned. "Sorry, but it's been a long day.

I was on a job early this morning. The owners want the place done ASAP, so we're working six days a week."

"I wonder where Francis is?" Arabella fiddled with the napkin in her lap. She stood up suddenly and looked around. "I do wish he would come back."

"Can you see him?" Emma got to her feet as well.

Arabella shook her head. "Unfortunately not. There's still a crowd gathered around the—around Hugh."

Emma glanced in the direction of the balcony. The emergency medical technicians had been joined by several uniformed policemen. She thought she caught a glimpse of Francis's dark hair among them, but she wasn't sure.

Emma sat down and was finishing her second cup of tea when she looked up to see Francis striding toward their table.

"I'm so sorry," he said, kissing Arabella on the check. "The hotel manager proved useless in handling the situation so I felt I needed to stick around and get things under control. The local team is finally here. I don't want to appear to be stepping on their toes."

"Does that mean we can go?" Arabella asked hopefully, gathering up her purse and shawl.

"I'm afraid not. The police will want to question us. Or at least take our names and contact information."

"But why?" Arabella said somewhat petulantly. "It was just a terrible accident. We can't tell them anything."

Emma noticed that Arabella's hands were shaking. Her face was really white now, and she seemed smaller, as if she had shrunk.

"Surely, you can convince them to let Arabella go,"

Emma said to Francis. "This has obviously been very difficult for her."

"I know." Francis took one of Arabella's hands in his. "You're freezing," he said, his black brows drawn together in concern. He took both her hands in his and began to rub them.

"But if it's an accident, I don't see why they need to talk to us," Brian said.

"It's still a sudden death," Francis explained. "We don't know that he wasn't pushed."

Arabella gasped. "But surely you don't mean that. Who would do such a thing?"

"I'm not saying that someone did." Francis put an arm around Arabella, who had started to shake. "But there will have to be an investigation. It's just routine when there's an accidental death like this."

"I do hope they hurry up." Arabella's lower lip quivered.

Just then, a uniformed policeman approached their table. "If I could get your names and contact information," he asked politely, his pen poised above a pad of paper.

"Finally!" Arabella exclaimed.

EMMA slept late on Sunday. It had been after midnight by the time they'd left the Beau, and, as tired as she had been, she hadn't been able to fall asleep right away—especially not after a brisk walk in the chilly night air with Bette, who had been waiting not so patiently for Emma's return. In the end, she had stayed up watching reruns of *Friends* until two o'clock in the morning.

Bette was exceptionally playful on her morning walk although Emma wasn't so sure who was walking whom as Bette dragged Emma down Washington Street past all the darkened and shuttered shops. She spent a good five minutes sniffing a trash container before Emma urged her along.

As soon as she got back to her apartment above Sweet Nothings, Emma reached for her phone to call Arabella, but then just as quickly put it down again. Her aunt would insist she was fine no matter what. Emma would drive over to Arabella's instead and see for herself.

Emma bustled Bette into the car and headed out. Fortunately, Bette loved car rides and was always eager to tag along.

There were dark circles under Arabella's eyes when she answered the front door, and her normally fastidious white hair was stuck on top of her head in a haphazard bun.

"Who's that, dear?" Emma heard Francis call from the back of the house.

"It's me," Emma said as she followed Arabella out to the kitchen. She dumped her purse on one of the kitchen chairs and slipped off her coat, watching in amusement as Bette tried to cajole Pierre into playing. Woken from a nap lying in the warmth of the air blowing from the heating vent, Pierre was not amused.

"I've got some of that green tea you like." Arabella rummaged in the pantry and came out holding an unopened box. The maneuver had unmoored her bun further, sending it slipping to just above her right ear. "If you'll put the kettle on."

Emma turned on the tap and swung the red enamel teakettle under the faucet and filled it.

"I picked up some croissants from Kroger's." Francis indicated a plate on the table. "And there's some honey we bought at a local farm."

"You have to try the honey," Arabella said as she wrestled with the plastic wrapping on the box of tea. "You can actually taste the flowers and clover in it."

Francis had the Sunday *Post-Intelligencer* spread open on the table, and his nearly empty coffee cup sat companionably next to Arabella's. Emma suddenly felt as if she was intruding. She should have realized that Francis would have headed to her aunt's first thing in the morning to check on her.

The kettle whistled, and Emma poured the hot water into the mug Arabella handed her. She added a tea bag from the box Arabella had finally managed to open and dunked it several times, sliding into a seat opposite Arabella and Francis.

"Last night certainly didn't turn out as we expected, did it?" Arabella said, buttering a piece of her croissant. "I imagine with Hugh dead, there won't be much of anything left for the TBI to investigate." She turned toward Francis.

"Not necessarily. We know he has a partner, Tom Roberts, who will probably take over."

"Did we meet this Mr. Roberts last night?" Arabella paused with a spoon of honey over her croissant.

Francis shook his head. "No. You might have noticed his wife though. A very beautiful woman, rather exotic, with dark hair. She was wearing an orange dress."

"Tangerine," Arabella corrected him. "Isn't that what you'd call it?" she asked Emma.

"Yes. It sounds better than orange."

"Looks the same to me," Francis grumbled as he turned the page in his newspaper.

"I think I remember seeing her. You're right. She is very beautiful. And she was the only woman there wearing that color." Emma blew on her hot tea.

"Yes, I think I remember her, too," Arabella nibbled on the end of her croissant. "Do you suppose the son knows what his father was up to? John said he had gone into the art business with Hugh."

"Probably," Francis said, taking the last sip of his coffee. He reached for the pot and helped himself to another cup. "But I doubt he'll tell us." He smiled.

"I should imagine you're right."

Emma was reaching for a croissant when the doorbell rang. This time Pierre and Bette were in tandem as they began a fit of barking and headed immediately toward the front door.

"Who on earth could that be?" Arabella wrinkled her brow. She wiped her hands on her napkin and pushed back her chair.

Francis raised an eyebrow. "Do you want me to get it?"

"Perhaps you'd better." Arabella sat down again.

Emma and Arabella listened as Francis made his way down the hall. "Quiet, you two," they heard him call to the dogs. Then there was the sound of the front door opening.

Voices drifted toward the kitchen.

"Can you hear who it is?" Arabella kneaded the napkin in her lap.

"No. I think it's a man." Emma closed her eyes trying to make out the words coming from the hallway.

They heard footsteps heading toward the kitchen, and Arabella sat up straighter, putting a hand up to tidy her bun. "I must look a wreck," she murmured as she struggled with a hairpin. "I can't imagine who it is at this time of day. Everyone in town is probably in church."

They looked up to see a man silhouetted in the door to the kitchen. Emma recognized him right away as Detective Bradley Walker of the Paris, Tennessee, police department.

Arabella got to her feet. "What can I do for you?" Her voice quavered slightly on the last words, and Emma looked at her in alarm.

"Ms. Arabella Andrews?" Walker asked.

"Yes." Arabella put a hand to her throat and fiddled with the collar of her blouse.

"I'd like to ask you a few questions, if you don't mind."

"Of course. Please come in and sit down. Would you like some coffee?"

She gestured toward the pot sitting on the table.

"That's very kind of you, but no, thank you." Walker's eyes met Emma's, and he smiled.

Walker was all Southern gentleman with dark hair and dark eyes. Emma had met him before, and he had made it quite plain he found her attractive. The look in his eyes said he still did.

Francis went to stand behind Arabella, his hands on her shoulders. She glanced up at him, a frightened look in her eyes. Walker perched on the edge of one of the kitchen chairs, a spiral-bound notebook balanced on his knee.

"I understand you were at the party last night given by Mr. Hugh Granger."

Arabella nodded curtly.

"I also understand"—he consulted his notes—"that you are an old friend of Mr. Granger's."

Arabella nodded again. "That's true. Although we haven't been in communication for years," she clarified. "There were plenty of people at the party who knew him much better than I."

Walker nodded and jotted something in his notebook.

"But you were invited to the party." It was a statement not a question.

"Hugh and I did an admirable job of avoiding each other for close to forty years," Arabella said somewhat sharply, "when he suddenly appeared at my lingerie shop the other night."

Walker raised a thick dark brow. "Avoiding each other? Why?"

Arabella took a deep breath. "If you must know, in our youth we had a romantic liaison that ended badly." She clamped her lips together.

"I'm sorry, Detective, but why all these questions?" Francis interjected in his most authoritative voice. "The man fell from the balcony. It was an unfortunate accident."

Walker looked up slowly. "It wasn't an accident. When we turned the body over, we discovered a bullet wound. He had been shot."

"What!" Arabella's hand flew to her mouth.

Walker nodded. "It was murder."

Chapter 5

EMMA, Arabella and Francis sat in stunned silence.

"What do you mean he was shot?" Arabella asked.

Walker looked up from his notebook again. He ignored Arabella's question. "Do you own a gun, ma'am?"

"A gun? Me? Absolutely not. What on earth would I do with a gun?"

"It appears that Mr. Granger was shot during the fireworks. That would explain why no one heard the report from the revolver. Can you tell me where you were during that time?"

Two bright spots of color had appeared on Arabella's cheeks. She raised her chin, and her precariously seated bun wobbled threateningly. "I was outside with Francis and Emma and Emma's friend Brian," she said with a defensive edge to her voice. "I've seen plenty of fireworks in my day. Once even in Paris, France, over the Eiffel Tower with Hugh . . ." A faraway look crossed Arabella's face, and she shook herself abruptly. "All that to say, that I decided not to stay and watch but to go inside to . . . to powder my nose."

"Did you see anyone? Did anyone see you?" Walker didn't look up this time, all his concentration on his notebook.

"Well I suppose I saw lots of people, but I didn't know anyone else at the party so I can hardly give you their names."

"How about in the ladies' room? Was there anyone in there with you? Can you describe them?"

Arabella gave a hiss of impatience. "I was alone. Everyone was on the patio or by the French doors watching the fireworks."

Walker slapped his notebook shut. "Thank you for your time, Ms. Andrews. I'm sorry to have disturbed your Sunday morning." He gestured toward the coffee and croissants on the table.

Francis dropped his hands from Arabella's shoulders. "I'll see you out."

Pierre and Bette scrambled to their feet and followed the men out of the kitchen and down the hallway.

Emma and Arabella were quiet while they waited for Francis to return.

"He almost sounded as if he suspected me," Arabella said as soon as Francis had taken his seat again.

"I'm sure it's just routine," Francis said, but Emma thought the look on his face said something quite different.

"It's very upsetting." Arabella put her head in her hands.

"I'm sure we won't hear another thing about it," Francis said reassuringly as he put his arms around her.

WHEN Emma got back to her apartment, she noticed that she had missed three calls on her cell phone. One was from her mother. Emma's parents had retired to Pensacola, Florida, where her father was perfecting his golf game, and her mother, Arabella's younger sister, was devoting much of her time to her ceramics, a hobby she had dabbled in before leaving Paris, but as the hospital administrator of the Henry County Medical Center, hadn't had much time for.

She dialed her parents' number in Florida but got their voice mail so she left a message.

The second call was from Brian checking up on her and making sure she was okay. Emma smiled as she listened to the message.

The third call was from Liz, who was home when Emma dialed her. Liz was Emma's oldest friend and Brian's younger sister.

Liz sounded happy to hear from her. "I can't wait to get the lowdown on your big night at the dinner dance. Did I tell you, I'm doing some work for Hugh Granger?"

"No," Emma answered warily. She doubted Liz had heard the news of Hugh's death yet. It obviously hadn't made the Sunday papers.

"He's hired me to create a web site for his art business. I can't believe he's been operating without one this long. I gather his son—what's his name?—Jackson, I think, convinced him that it was time to enter the twenty-first century.

Plus I'll be taking pictures of a lot of the works so we can have them on the web." Liz took a breath. "But I'm rambling on when I want to hear all about your evening."

Emma didn't know where to begin. The end seemed the logical place. "It would have been wonderful, but there was a terrible accident." Even as she said the word *accident*, she realized it was the wrong word. Detective Walker had called it "murder."

"Oh no, what happened? Is everyone okay? Arabella?"

"Arabella is fine." But even as she said it, Emma wondered if that was really true. "We had dinner and then afterward there were fireworks. When we came back in from the patio we found Hugh's . . . body . . . on the floor. It appeared he'd fallen from the balcony that encircles the ballroom."

Liz gasped. "But that's terrible. Was he—"

"Yes," Emma said. "But that's not the worst of it. Detective Walker stopped by Aunt Arabella's house this morning and said that before he fell he'd been . . . shot."

Stunned silence came over the line.

"And worse than that"—Emma swallowed hard and cleared her throat—"he seemed to insinuate that he thought Arabella had had something to do with it."

"Arabella? Why on earth would he think that?"

Emma hesitated. She wasn't sure Arabella wanted the world to know about her romance with Hugh. But Liz was Liz. Surely Arabella wouldn't mind. She explained as succinctly as possible about Arabella and Hugh's relationship and how he'd practically left her at the altar.

"The cad!" Liz exclaimed. "I wouldn't blame Arabella one bit. Not that I think she had anything whatsoever to do with it."

"I know." Emma paced up and down her small living room. "I just hope Detective Walker will believe that."

ARABELLA was still pale when she arrived at Sweet Nothings on Monday morning.

"You look like you've seen a ghost," Sylvia said when Arabella walked in a little later than usual.

"Yes, you do." Emma said, biting her lower lip. She was becoming more and more concerned about her aunt. This kind of stress couldn't be good for her.

Arabella pinched both her cheeks with her fingers, turning them pink. "There, does that satisfy the two of you?"

They laughed. Pierre scampered off to his dog bed for the first of many naps. Emma had arrived at the shop early, and Bette had had her fill of exploring and was already asleep in her crate.

"You'll never guess who called me last night." Arabella looked at Emma.

"Who?" Emma was straightening the contents of one of the armoires.

"Your mother."

Her tone of voice made Emma spin around.

"She's coming for a visit," Arabella announced.

"When?" Emma asked, realizing that her mother hadn't called her back the previous evening.

Arabella glanced at her watch. "In about eight hours. She ought to arrive around six o'clock. She said she was getting an early start, but what with stopping and traffic, it will probably take longer than the nine hours' travel time she's anticipating."

"Tonight?" Emma squeaked.

"Yes."

"But why . . . she didn't say anything about—"

"Apparently, she's worried about me." Arabella's voice broke.

Sylvia looked up sharply. "Is something wrong? Is there something you haven't told me?"

Just then the bell over the front door jingled, and they all snapped to attention as a well-preserved blonde on the wrong side of forty walked into the shop. She sported a pair of diamond stud earrings the size of headlights; it was obvious she had money to spend.

"Can I help you?" Arabella gave the woman her most professional smile, her head tilted slightly to one said, her whole countenance inviting the woman to spill her innermost secrets.

The woman batted her enormous fake eyelashes at Arabella. "I need a little something that will get my husband"—she lowered her lashes shyly—"you know . . . going again?"

Arabella patted the woman's arm comfortingly. "Now, now," she said as she led her to one of the cupboards. "I'm sure we have just the thing to put the, er, fire back in your relationship." She smiled at their new customer. "You're a very beautiful woman, you know. You have a splendid figure. Just a little icing on the cake is all you need."

The woman threw back her shoulders and preened like a peacock.

Arabella opened the cupboard and began clicking through the hangers. She pulled out a garment and hung it from a hook on the door.

"The baby doll nightgown has been the staple of the seductive woman's wardrobe for decades." Arabella waved a hand in front of the negligee, a chiffon peach confection with chocolate lace trim. "This is from the late 1950s, and was made by Glyndons of Hollywood. It is unusual in that it comes with a matching peignoir." Arabella waved another garment in front of the woman like a conjurer performing a magic trick.

Even from across the room, Emma could see the woman's eyes light up. It looked as if the sale was in the bag.

Sylvia sidled up next to Emma and whispered to her. "So what's up with your aunt?"

Emma explained about the dinner dance, Hugh's death and the visit from Detective Walker. Sylvia's mouth set more firmly with each word Emma spoke.

"There's no way anyone is hanging this on your aunt. No way." Her voice rose, and Arabella shot her a warning look. "No way," Sylvia whispered a final time for emphasis.

Emma picked at a piece of loose cuticle. "I'm a little worried though. Arabella seemed . . . confused . . . about where she'd been at the time of the murder. She said she went to the ladies' room, but claims she was alone. Something about it just didn't ring true."

"Seriously?" Sylvia frowned. She pulled a tissue from her pocket and rubbed at a smudge on the glass case.

"Don't get me wrong. I know my aunt had nothing to do with Hugh's death. But I do think she's hiding something." Emma sighed. "I just don't know what it is."

"Maybe she'll spill the beans to her sister while she's here."

Emma pursed her lips. "I don't know. Arabella and Priscilla don't always see eye to eye. Mother has never really approved of Arabella."

"Why on earth not? Your aunt is a marvelous woman."

"Mother is just very . . . different. While Arabella was traveling around the world, my mother spent her trust fund on college. She had her whole life mapped out from the time she was twenty—she graduated from UT a year early, married my father, had me—more than one child might have interfered with her work. So far, everything has gone according to her plan. Her career goals were met right on schedule, she retired at sixty as she had intended and now she's concentrating on her other passion, ceramics."

"But you know what they say: blood is thicker than water."

"Oh, you're absolutely right. Arabella and Mother may not be close, but they are sisters. That doesn't mean, however, that there aren't going to be fireworks of a very different sort when she gets here."

Chapter 6

PROMPTLY at five o'clock, Emma closed the door to Sweet Nothings behind their last customer and flipped the *open* sign to *closed*. Her mother was due to arrive in Paris shortly. She was heading straight to Arabella's house, where she would be staying in the guest room.

Emma slipped on her coat and took Bette for a quick sprint around the block, then they both dashed up the stairs to Emma's apartment. She wanted to wash her face and hands and run a comb through her hair before going to Arabella's. She hadn't seen either of her parents in over a year. She was sorry her father had decided not to come along, but apparently he was playing in a golf tournament he didn't want to miss.

The last time Emma had seen her parents had been in

New York, when they visited her there. Her mother had complained about the dirt, the noise and the cost of their hotel, but they had enjoyed the restaurants and several Broadway shows.

Emma tipped some food into Bette's bowl and refreshed her water. Bette gobbled down her dinner, and by the time Emma had turned on the tap in the bathroom, was sound asleep on the fluffy throw rug in front of the bathtub.

Emma freshened her makeup, ran some product through her hair to revive it and changed her black pants for a pair of skinny jeans and her leather boots for some ballet flats.

"Come on, Bette, we're going to Pierre's house."

In one swift movement, Bette rolled from her back to her feet and galloped toward the front door as if she hadn't just been sound asleep. Emma wished she could wake up that quickly—instead it took her fifteen minutes of yoga stretches, a hot shower and at least one cup of green tea to join the living every morning.

Emma clipped on Bette's leash, and they bounded downstairs to her VW Beetle.

Arabella's driveway was empty when Emma got there. Emma was relieved that her mother hadn't yet arrived; she wanted to be there to greet her. Pierre was already by the front door barking when Emma mounted the front steps. The front door was open, as usual. No amount of warnings was able to persuade Arabella that times had changed and she ought to keep the house locked up.

Her aunt was nowhere to be seen when Emma entered, but familiar noises were coming from the kitchen. "I'm here," she called out, bending down to unsnap Bette's leash. Untethered, Bette made a beeline for the kitchen, rounding the corner on her two left paws. Emma followed at a more sedate pace.

Arabella was at the kitchen counter. She had a platter of cut-up chicken pieces in front of her and a paper bag that Emma knew was filled with flour and the spices that Arabella put into her fried chicken. Arabella was as secretive as the Colonel about what went into her special recipe. According to her, it had been handed down verbally from generation to generation. It would be passed to Emma when she married.

Emma kissed her aunt on the cheek and opened the refrigerator, where she knew a pitcher of sweet tea would be waiting.

"Oooh, you've made your chess pie," she said, closing the door and opening the cupboard where the glasses were kept.

"It's not every day my younger sister comes to visit." Arabella dropped a chicken leg into the paper bag and began to shake it. "Although what all the fuss is about, I don't know. I'm perfectly all right."

"You know how Mom is when she gets a bee in her bonnet."

"Do I ever," Arabella exclaimed. "Sometimes I think she ought to have been the older sibling, not me."

Emma thought Arabella was looking considerably better—she was less pale and the sparkle had returned to her blue eyes.

Emma was setting the table when the doorbell rang. Pierre and Bette launched themselves onto their feet and skidded together down the long front hall. Arabella dried her hands on her apron and scurried after them.

"Priscilla," Emma heard her aunt say as Emma rounded the corner to the front hall.

Despite more than eight hours of car travel, Emma's mother's blond hair looked as if she had just left the salon, her makeup was perfect and her clothes were as fresh as they had no doubt been when she'd left that morning. Emma thought of all the car trips she'd taken where they were barely out of the state before she'd dribbled a blob of ketchup from a fast food hamburger on her top or had a grease stain on her pants from a dropped French fry. Her mother was as slim as ever in a pair of perfectly creased khakis, white blouse and brown leather driving shoes.

"Emma," Priscilla called, holding her arms out.

Emma hugged her mother while Priscilla offered her cheek for a kiss.

"So good to see you, darling. It's been too long." She stood back and held Emma at arm's length. "Are you going to leave your hair like that? Men don't like women with such short hair, you know."

"I think she looks adorable," Arabella said, rolling her eyes behind her sister's back.

"How was your trip?" Emma asked, anxious to change the subject.

"Rather tedious, I'm afraid. I hit a patch of bad weather outside of Birmingham, which slowed me down. Very annoying."

"I imagine you'd like to freshen up before dinner. I've put you in the guest room at the back of the second floor."

"Wonderful," Priscilla cooed. "Last time you had me in the front and the traffic kept me up nearly all night."

Emma and Arabella looked at each other. The only

sounds Emma had ever heard at Arabella's at night were the chirping of crickets and the sighing of the wind in the tree branches.

Priscilla grasped her rolling bag by the handle and headed toward the stairs.

"Do you want me to help you with that?" Emma asked.

"Of course not. I can manage."

Emma and Arabella retreated to the kitchen where they could hear the thump of the wheels as Priscilla bumped the suitcase up the stairs.

"Some things never change," Arabella said as she placed the last of the chicken pieces in the bag and shook it.

Emma laughed. Arabella was right.

Arabella poured oil into a pan on the stove and hesitated, her hand on the burner. She looked over her shoulder at Emma. "This is the part I hate."

Emma knew exactly what she meant. It had been a pan of oil that had started the fire that had nearly destroyed Arabella's kitchen.

Arabella finally turned the burner, and the flame sprang to life. A few minutes later, she began adding the chicken pieces, one by one, to the pan.

Light footsteps sounded down the hall, and Priscilla reappeared with Pierre and Bette right on her heels. She'd exchanged her blouse for a cream-colored sweater.

Priscilla bent and scratched Pierre behind the ear. "You've put on some weight haven't you, darling."

Emma noticed Arabella bristle slightly.

"And who is this?" Priscilla held out a hand toward Bette, who approached her with unusual caution.

"That's Bette. She's Pierre's puppy."

Priscilla studied Bette, her head tilted to one side. "I see elements of Pierre—certainly the ears—but she's obviously not a French bulldog."

"Pierre had a"—Arabella cleared her throat—"liaison with a dachshund."

"Pierre, you scamp. I'm surprised you allowed it, Arabella."

"I didn't," Arabella said, frowning.

Again, Emma thought it might be best if she changed the subject. She glanced at her mother. "I thought you would be tanner."

"You should see your father! I keep telling him sunscreen, sunscreen, but he doesn't listen. And he's out on that golf course all day. Well, no matter. It gives me time for my ceramics."

Emma noticed a strange look cross her mother's face.

"How is that going?" Arabella turned away from the stove briefly.

"Very well. I couldn't be more pleased. I'm having a showing at the Belmont Arts and Cultural Center in May."

"That's wonderful. You'll have to send me some pictures," Emma said.

"There's a small arts and crafts store over on Market Street," Arabella said, swiping at her nose and leaving it dusted with flour. "You might put some of your pieces up for consignment."

"I hardly think of my work as *arts and crafts*." Priscilla walked over to the stove, where the chicken was now spitting and crackling in the pan. She clapped her hands together. "Oh, this will be a treat. I love your fried chicken, Arabella. Mine never comes out quite as flavorful and crisp as yours."

Arabella's face glowed with pleasure. She removed the chicken pieces from the pot and placed them on a white platter.

"Emma, if you could put this on the table . . ." She handed Emma the dish, then opened the oven and took out a cast iron pan of cornbread and a green bean casserole.

Finally, everything was on the table, and they were all seated around it.

Emma looked from her mother to her aunt and back again. There was a slight resemblance—the vivid blue eyes and the shape of the nose—but otherwise they were as unalike as two sisters could be.

"So tell me about this murder of yours, Arabella. You two have been getting up to some awfully unsavory things."

Arabella bristled again. "What on earth do you mean by that?" Arabella said.

"You told me that you actually had a detective here, questioning you. I've never heard of such a thing." Priscilla took a bite of her chicken. "Mmm, you do make the most divine fried chicken." She dabbed at her lips with her napkin. "But I don't understand why the police questioned *you*, Arabella. The wife is always the logical suspect, isn't she?"

Emma stopped with her fork halfway to her mouth. "She certainly is, in books and the movies."

"Actually, it's a fact." Priscilla put down her fork and swiveled in her chair to face Emma. "I've read studies that show the spouse is usually the culprit when someone has been murdered." She waved a hand. "I forget the percentage but it's quite high." She picked up her fork again and pointed it at Emma and then at Arabella. "So what do you know about the wife of this Hugh Granger?"

Emma and Arabella shrugged in unison.

"Almost nothing," Emma answered.

"Very little," Arabella said at almost the same time.

"Her name is Mariel," Arabella said. "She looks to be a good twenty years younger than Hugh. They've been married quite a while—their son, Jackson, is in his early twenties."

"Well," Priscilla said in a very chipper tone of voice. "We'll just have to get some more information on her then." She looked from Emma to Arabella and back again. "It will be fun."

Arabella rolled her eyes as she picked up the empty dishes and stacked them on the counter. "Why don't you two go on into the living room. We can have our pie and coffee in there."

Priscilla put her napkin on the table and stood up. Emma followed suit and walked with her mother down the hallway to the living room.

Priscilla settled herself in an armless chair, back straight, knees together and legs tucked to the side. Emma sat on the couch and tucked one leg underneath her, causing her mother's eyebrows to draw together slightly and her lips to pucker almost imperceptibly.

"Now that I'm here," Priscilla said, "I'd love to know what your plans are."

"Plans?"

"Yes. For the future. You can't leave things to chance."

Emma stared at her mother blankly. "What do you mean?"

"Well, you can't stay here running Arabella's dusty old lingerie shop forever."

Emma's lips tightened. "It's not dusty. We've redone the whole shop. You'll see it tomorrow."

"But there's nothing *here* for you. I was lucky that my career allowed me to advance at the hospital, and of course your father had his law practice. But I can't imagine what kind of career you could forge in such a small town."

Emma thought of Brian but bit her lip.

Before Priscilla could say anything more, Arabella came back into the room with the chess pie and a stack of plates. Emma breathed a sigh of relief.

"Oh, chess pie," Priscilla exclaimed. "Arabella, you've outdone yourself."

Arabella looked slightly mollified as she passed around plates.

"You know," Emma said suddenly, "I talked to Liz." She turned to Priscilla, "You remember Liz O'Connell, don't you? She's Liz Banning now."

Priscilla nodded. "You two were inseparable. How is Liz?"

"She's fine. She has a boy and a girl—Alice and Ben."

"Yes, I remember you were asked to be the little girl's godmother, weren't you?"

"Yes," Emma said. "But get this, before he died, Hugh Granger hired her to design a web site for his art business."

"That's wonderful," Priscilla declared. "You'll have someone right on the spot, so to speak."

"She's not sure what the status of the project is now that he's dead. We're hoping the son will want to continue with the web site."

"Let's hope he does. It will give Liz a chance to keep her

ear to the ground." Priscilla rubbed her hands together. "We can't let that detective continue thinking that your aunt is a murderess."

EMMA lay in bed, staring at the ceiling, unable to sleep. Her mother's words echoed nonstop in her head. What did the future hold for her? She'd abruptly left her big-city, New York life behind when she found out her boyfriend was cheating on her. It seemed perfect that Arabella needed help renovating Sweet Nothings. The shop had been dying . . . now it was thriving. And Emma's broken heart had not only healed, but she'd found a new love in Brian.

But how long would she be content behind the counter of Sweet Nothings selling vintage lingerie? She flung herself onto her left side. Bette grunted and moved down toward the end of the bed. Emma didn't know the answer to that. Right now her life seemed perfect, but would it pale in another year or two?

And if she married Brian—the thought brought a rush of pleasure—would she eventually long for something more challenging than running Sweet Nothings? And would she be able to find it in her small hometown?

Emma did eventually fall asleep, but she woke up the next morning without any of the answers having magically revealed themselves to her. She was brushing her teeth and thinking about her previous night's conversation with her mother when she remembered she wanted to call Liz. Perhaps Liz had had word as to whether or not the web site project for Hugh Granger's business was still on. Emma dried her hands and went out to the kitchen to get her phone.

She took it over to the window seat, where she had a wonderful view of Washington Street. She noticed Mr. Zimmerman walking past on the other side of the street with Bertha, his dachshund, and Fritz, one of Bette's siblings. Bette jumped onto the window seat and began barking furiously, her breath fogging the glass.

Emma waited until Mr. Zimmerman had passed and Bette had calmed down before punching in Liz's number. Liz answered on the third ring. Emma could hear the sounds of children squabbling in the background.

"Hello," Liz said, then, "Ben, leave your sister alone, and both of you go brush your teeth. You're going to be late. Sorry about that," she said to Emma.

"No, I'm sorry. I'm obviously calling at a bad time— you're trying to get the kids off to school. I just wondered if you'd heard from Jackson about the web site."

"Yes, and he's going ahead with the project. He said you can hardly do business in this century without a web site. And get this," Liz said, her voice bubbling with excitement. "He told me they need someone to work for them part-time taking an inventory of the works in their collection. They'll need it for the IRS and to settle the estate. I could mention your name to him. It would give you the chance to do some snooping."

Emma felt a burst of excitement, but then she thought of Arabella, and it fizzled like a wet firecracker. What would her aunt do without her?

Emma chewed on the thought as she got dressed. It would be a shame not to take advantage of such a perfect opportunity. Perhaps she could enlist Francis's support? He had mentioned wanting to get close to Hugh Granger and his operations. This would put someone on the inside.

Emma clipped on Bette's leash, and they hurried down to Sweet Nothings. Sylvia and Arabella arrived just as Emma was starting a pot of coffee. Emma was too excited to wait, and the words tumbled out before Arabella had even gotten her coat off.

"Liz says there's a part-time job available with the Grangers—cataloging their collection. If I took it, it would put me on the spot. And it's only part-time. If you think you could manage . . ."

"You should definitely take the job," Arabella said. "Detective Walker came by with some more questions this morning. I'm beginning to feel the noose tightening." She tugged at the black-and-white print scarf tied around her neck.

"We can ask Eloise Montgomery to come back and help," Sylvia said from her post behind the counter.

Eloise was a fellow resident of Sunny Days, the retirement community where Sylvia lived. She had helped out in the shop when Arabella had been recovering after her house fire.

"Do you think she would do it?" Emma looked up from measuring water into the coffeepot.

Sylvia nodded her head vigorously, and her gold chandelier earrings spun to and fro. "Yeah, she said she loved working here and to call her anytime. I know I'm grateful I've got somewhere to go besides bingo and the movies at old Sunny Days."

Emma grinned. "Sounds like a plan, then. I'll tell Liz to throw my hat into the ring."

As Emma went about her day at Sweet Nothings, a thought occurred to her—one that left her feeling decidedly unsettled. Was she anxious to get close to the Grangers and possibly pick up some clues, or was she in reality dissatisfied with her current life, as her mother had suggested?

LATER that afternoon, the door to Sweet Nothings opened and Priscilla stood on their doorstep. "I've come to see what you've done with the shop."

Emma was surprised to find herself feeling nervous. She very much wanted her mother to like what they'd accomplished with the store.

Arabella bustled over to Priscilla and took her by the arm. "Come on in and look around. What do you think?" She waved a hand around the interior. "Quite a change, isn't it?"

Priscilla walked over to the wall of cabinets and ran her hand down the glossy white finish. "These are beautiful." She opened one of the doors. "And so clever. You can hang the longer gowns, and they won't wrinkle." She turned to Emma. "Was this your idea?"

Emma nodded.

"Brilliant."

Emma felt a sense of warmth wash over her.

Priscilla trailed her fingers along the row of colored silk and satin gowns. "Such beautiful things." She gave a smile that Emma thought was almost impish. "I might have to do some shopping while I'm here."

She closed the cabinet door and went over to one of the two distressed shabby chic armoires Emma had ordered. "These, too, are terribly clever. They're perfect for the space." She looked around. "And the lovely pink paint makes me feel as if I'm on the inside of a fancy chocolate box." She turned to Arabella. "Was it hard to let go of the old things?"

"No, not once Emma described her plans to me. I was ridiculously sentimental about the décor for way too long as it was. That pea green shag rug . . ." She shuddered. "And Emma encouraged me to include the vintage items I'd been collecting along with some new stock."

"It gives a unique twist to the shop," Priscilla said approvingly. "Something the chain stores don't have." She glanced around again. "It's lovely. Just lovely. Hard to believe it's the same place. You did a wonderful job." She smiled at Emma.

"Brian helped," Emma said. "He did all the carpentry and painting."

"He's a very talented young man."

Emma felt a frisson of pride.

"It's just too bad," Priscilla added, "that he's wasting his time in this tiny little town."

Arabella rolled her eyes behind Priscilla's back.

"I'll be off then." Priscilla waved good-bye as she headed out the door. "Lucy invited me to her shop for a cup of coffee and some pastries."

It was later that same afternoon when Liz called. Emma could tell by the excitement in her voice that she had good news.

"I talked to Jackson Granger, and Hugh's partner, Tom Roberts. They'd love to chat with you about the part-time position. They seemed quite keen. Relieved, actually."

"That's wonderful." Emma sank into Arabella's desk chair in the stockroom and eased off her shoes. They'd been run off their feet all morning—a group of women from the local Newcomer's Club in Memphis had made a special trip to the store, and the ladies had been enchanted with Sweet Nothings. The cash register had been ringing all morning, and the group had departed with plenty of black-and-white Sweet Nothings bags swinging from their arms.

"They wondered if you could stop by around five o'clock tonight for an interview? I know it's short notice, but I think it's just a formality."

Emma glanced at her watch. It was almost four o'clock. Things in the shop had died down, and she ought to be able to sneak upstairs to freshen up. She was quite sure Arabella would watch Bette while she was gone.

"Tell them I'll be there," Emma said. "And thanks, Liz. This is a wonderful opportunity."

"It will be fun working together." Liz giggled and suddenly Emma felt as if they were back in middle school, heads bent over some romance novel that was sending them into fits of laughter.

Emma clicked off the call, slipped her shoes back on and went out to the shop to talk to Arabella.

"Good news," she announced. "I have an interview with Jackson Granger and Hugh's partner at five o'clock."

Arabella's face lit up. "Wonderful!"

"Good work," Sylvia said gruffly.

Just then the front door to Sweet Nothings opened, and Francis stepped in. "Hope I'm not disturbing you ladies. I was just over at the Meat Mart picking up some lamb chops for our dinner." He nodded at Arabella. "My night to cook."

"I told you that I could make dinner," Arabella protested.

Francis shook his head. "No, no; fair is fair. It's time I

took a turn. You've been feeding me very well"—he patted his stomach, which was still as flat as a teen's—"and now it's up to me to return the favor. I do a mean grilled lamb chop, and I think I'm capable of tackling some baked potatoes and a green salad."

Arabella smiled. "You are a dear. As it is, we've been terribly busy, and I'll definitely relish the chance to put my feet up and be catered to."

Sylvia cleared her throat. "Aren't you going to tell him your news, kid?" She gestured toward Emma encouragingly.

"Liz told me that Hugh Granger's son and his partner are looking for someone to help catalogue their collection. I've got an interview with them in an hour."

"Oh," Francis said quietly.

"I thought you would be pleased," Arabella said. "Emma will be on the spot and can glean all sorts of information."

Francis took a deep breath and let it storm out his nose. "I don't know how I feel about that." He looked at Emma. "It could be dangerous. If they *are* hiding something, they're not going to appreciate having someone poking around in their affairs."

"I'll be careful," Emma reassured him. "Honest."

Francis made a sound like a grunt. "All right. But if you sense anything going wrong, get out of there immediately, okay?"

"Okay," Emma agreed.

A half hour later, Emma pulled onto the hard dirt road leading to the Grangers' house. Pastures, no longer green but shriveled and brown, sloped down on either side of the road. They were bordered by at least a mile of white picket fence—the kind that was synonymous with horse country. The house, when it came into view, was surprisingly modest—long and low with white clapboard siding and green shutters. Doric columns flanked the front door, and the large porch had two rockers set off to one side. Emma imagined it would be beautiful to sit in those chairs in the summer and enjoy the scents of just-mown grass and fresh hay wafting on the breeze.

A gravel drive wound around in a semicircle in front of the house. Emma pulled up just beyond the house, parked and got out of the car. She stood for a moment looking at the house and the field beyond then started up the broad steps leading to the porch. Warm, yellow light spilled from the narrow windows on either side of the front door.

Emma hesitated, rang the bell and waited, her heart thumping slightly. A very tiny older woman answered the door almost immediately. She had a white apron around her waist, and her steel gray hair was pulled back into a bun. Her weather-beaten face was crisscrossed with deep wrinkles, and she looked like something out of an illustration for Grimm's Fairy Tales. Emma half expected her to produce a wand and turn them both into pumpkins.

"Well don't just be standing there," she said with an Irish lilt to her voice, "come on in out of the cold." She led Emma into the foyer—a large, open space with polished wood floors dotted with worn Oriental rugs. Emma caught a glimpse of a comfortable-looking living room off to one side. Bookshelves lined one wall and a huge, stone fireplace filled the other. A colorful, modern painting hung over the mantel.

"I imagine you've come about the job. Mr. Jackson tried to get Miss Joy to take it, but she wanted no part of it." She shook a finger at Emma. "Spent her whole life trying to win her father's approval. I imagine now that he's gone, she can't be bothered. Spends most of her time out with those horses." She paused to take a breath. "Now, if you'll just wait here."

She disappeared down the hallway, her slippered feet making a soft shuffling sound. Moments later, Emma heard footsteps striking the polished wood floors, and a young man appeared around the corner. He had dark hair that flopped onto his forehead, and, despite his strong brows and a chiseled nose, overall he had a slightly soft appearance. Emma thought perhaps it was the slackness of his jaw line combined with a rather weak chin. His appearance was at odds with John Jasper's description of him as an aggressive lacrosse player.

He held out his hand to Emma. "I'm Jackson Granger. So glad you could come. Liz has told us about you, and we hope you'll be able to find the time to take on our little project."

His handshake was firm enough. Emma wondered if she ought to offer her condolences on the death of his father, but Jackson had already turned around and obviously expected Emma to follow him. They went down a short hall and into a room that had been turned into an office. Two partner's desks faced each other across a softly worn Oriental carpet and a wooden filing cabinet, disguised somewhat unsuc-cessfully as a piece of furniture, was pushed against one wall.

Jackson flung himself into the cracked-leather swivel chair behind one of the desks, and indicated that Emma should take the armless one placed strategically in front of it.

"I imagine you've heard about my father's death," Jackson began. "I understand you were there."

Emma nodded. "I'm terribly sorry—" she began.

"That's very kind of you," Jackson interrupted.

Emma could see his eyes were red-rimmed, and his hand shook a little as he played with the glass paperweight on the desk, turning it over and over again. He immediately dispensed with small talk and began to explain what the project entailed—basically taking an inventory of the works of art in their collection.

"There might be a little research involved as well," he said, swiveling back and forth in the chair. "Looking up the provenance, or the history, of certain paintings. Things like that. Nothing we couldn't show you how to do."

"It certainly sounds very interesting."

"Could you start tomorrow?" Jackson said suddenly, plunking down the paperweight he'd been toying with.

Emma hesitated. She had been expecting more questions and had even brought along her resume. She still had to talk to Eloise about taking her place at Sweet Nothings, but she didn't want to lose this opportunity. "Certainly."

"Great." A brief smile whispered across Jackson's face. "Would one o'clock work for you? Liz did tell you it was part-time?" he said with a sudden frown.

"Yes, she did. And that's fine."

As if by magic, the wizened old woman in the apron appeared in the doorway. Jackson turned toward her.

"If you will please see Miss Taylor out."

She nodded and waited silently while Emma shook hands with Jackson and collected her coat and purse.

Emma followed the woman back down the hall. She looked about her as they walked. The house wasn't particularly grand—at least not in the way that she expected. It was more comfortable than pretentious, but the walls were lined with artwork worthy of a museum. Emma glimpsed a few pieces she recognized as they went past—a Giacometti drawing, a sketch she thought was a Lucien Freud and a fanciful Chagall watercolor. She was looking forward to having a better look when she came back.

They had almost reached the foyer when Emma heard a strange thumping sound coming from behind. She turned around to see Hugh's daughter, Joy, walking toward them surprisingly quickly despite her crippled leg. She nodded at Emma, but Emma got the impression Joy didn't remember her from the dinner dance.

They were all standing in the foyer when the front door swung open, and a woman strode in. Emma recognized her as Hugh Granger's widow, Mariel. She was wearing leather chaps over a pair of jeans, black riding boots and a quilted barn jacket. She slapped a pair of leather gloves down on the foyer table and plunked her riding hat on top of them.

"Molly," she said to the old woman in the apron, "can you please put these things away for me?"

Joy continued moving forward awkwardly, her hips going up and down like a piston, until she came face-to-face with Mariel. Mariel stared at her coldly for a moment before sweeping past and continuing down the hall.

Emma was startled. What on earth was that all about? She was now more eager than ever to start her part-time job. She had a feeling there were a lot of secrets to be uncovered. Hopefully one of them would lead to the murderer.

Chapter 7

EMMA checked her cell phone when she got back to her car and discovered a text message from Arabella. Francis had purchased enough lamb chops to feed an army—just like a man—and would Emma like to come to dinner? Brian had already accepted Arabella's invitation.

Emma smiled as she put her car in gear and headed down the gravel drive. Brian was now universally accepted as her *plus one*. Emma had a sudden thought that nearly made her slam on the brakes. She hadn't told her mother that she and Brian were dating—what would she think?

Emma had another thought as she drove along through the deepening dusk—had Arabella told Priscilla about Francis, and what would Priscilla think about that?

There was only one way to find out. Emma put on her left blinker and headed toward Arabella's house.

A few minutes later, Emma pulled into Arabella's driveway. Brian's red pickup truck was already there, and she parked behind it. She flicked on the interior car lights and dug in her handbag for her compact and lipstick. Her nose powdered, lip color renewed and hair combed, she got out, beeped the doors to the VW closed and headed toward the front door.

It was open as usual so Emma called out a hello as she stepped into the foyer. She stopped to pet Bette and Pierre, who had both come racing down the hall to see who was at the door. Voices drifted toward Emma from the living room, and as soon as both dogs had finished their energetic greeting of much face-licking and tail-wagging, she headed in that direction.

Arabella's front parlor, as it would have been known in the days when the house was built, was a comfortable room with an elegant marble fireplace, a bay window and many souvenirs from her travels, including a stone Buddha on the mantel and several Oriental silkscreens adorning the walls.

Francis was seated in one of the armchairs, a tumbler of Pritchards, a fine Tennessee whiskey Arabella kept just for him, in his hand. Arabella was perched on the ottoman at his feet, one hand draped over Francis's knee. Priscilla had a straight-backed chair with wooden arms and needlepoint cushions. She was cradling a small cut crystal glass of sherry. Brian was on the sofa, legs stretched out, the picture of relaxation, a foaming glass of beer on the coffee table in front of him.

Everyone looked to be getting along, and Emma hoped that was the case. Priscilla could be quite prickly when she didn't like someone.

Francis and Brian got to their feet when Emma entered the room. Brian came over and gave Emma a quick kiss. He rested his hands on her shoulders proprietarily. Emma noticed her mother glancing at them, one eyebrow raised.

"Emma!" Arabella exclaimed. "How did it go?"

"First, you need a drink," Francis said, moving swiftly toward Arabella's drinks cabinet. He opened the double doors. "What's your pleasure? Whiskey? Scotch? A gin and tonic?"

"Just a glass of wine for me."

"There's a bottle of white in the refrigerator," Arabella said. "Brian, would you get Emma a glass? The glasses are in the cupboard next to the refrigerator," she called out as he headed toward the kitchen.

Emma took a seat on the sofa and put her hand on the cushion next to her. She could feel the warmth Brian had left behind. It was a comforting feeling.

Brian almost immediately returned with a glass of chilled chardonnay.

"Tell us how your afternoon went," Priscilla prompted. She was as pristine as ever in a pale pink blouse, black pants and black patent leather–tipped flats.

Emma told them about her meeting with Jackson and the rather strange run-in between Granger's daughter, Joy, and his wife.

"Sounds like there's no love lost between those two," Arabella said.

Emma sipped her wine. "I know."

"It's rather sad. She might have been a second mother to Joy, but it sounds as if that wasn't the case." Arabella reached for her glass of wine, which was on an occasional table alongside the armchair. "More like Cinderella's stepmother from your description."

Brian put a hand on Emma's knee. "Just be careful, okay?"

Emma looked up to find her mother watching her and Brian intently. Priscilla pursed her lips and then looked away. Her look plainly said *we'll talk about it later.*

Francis eased back in his seat and took a glug of his whiskey. He placed the tumbler on the table alongside Arabella's glass of wine. "I've been talking to the local boys. They've been really decent about keeping me in the loop even though this isn't my case. But they did tell me a couple of interesting things."

Everyone leaned forward in their seats.

Francis stretched his arms out in front of him, fingers interlaced, and cracked his knuckles. "As you know, they took down the names and contact information of everyone who was still in the ballroom after Hugh's fall. Unfortunately, the list is hardly conclusive. It wasn't possible to seal the scene immediately after Granger's body was discovered, so any number of people could have slipped out in the meantime."

"In other words"—Arabella had another sip of her wine—"the killer was probably gone by the time the police got there."

Francis nodded. "I took a drive over to the hotel and checked out that balcony. There's a spiral staircase leading up to it in the east corner of the ballroom. But it's easily reached from the second floor as well—there are double doors on two sides that open to the balcony. It wouldn't have taken the killer any time at all to make her exit through those doors, and catch an elevator down to the first floor. That would leave her in the lobby, a stone's throw from the front entrance."

"And her escape route," Arabella said, and Francis nodded.

Francis picked up his glass and regarded the amber liquid for a moment. "What's really interesting," he said so softly that everyone leaned in even closer, "is who *isn't* on the police list of names and contacts."

"And who would that be?" Arabella asked, pulling her cardigan around her shoulders.

"First off, Mariel Granger." Francis took another sip of his drink and put it down on the table. "Don't you think that's a bit odd? You would hardly expect her to leave her own husband's birthday party early—a party she herself had planned. Especially before the big finale."

"That is odd," Arabella said. "You would have thought she'd have been eager to bask in the glow of an eminently successful party."

"Didn't I tell you that the wife is the most logical suspect?" Priscilla piped up. She put her glass of sherry to her lips but appeared to merely wet them.

Francis held up a hand. "But she's not the only one who is missing from the list. Jackson, their son, is as well."

"That doesn't surprise me. I can see a young man wanting

to scamper from a party filled with a bunch of old goats," Arabella said and laughed. She glanced at Emma and Brian. "Present company excepted, of course," she added quickly.

"I agree," Francis said. "It doesn't necessarily mean anything in and of itself. But it is interesting." He started to get up from his chair. "The killer might also have calmly walked back down the stairs to the ballroom and mingled with the crowd, waiting for Granger's body to be found. Almost everyone was still outside. There was every chance he would go unnoticed." He rubbed his hands together. "And now I'd better see to those lamb chops, since I'm in charge of dinner tonight." He winked at Arabella.

"Let me help you." Arabella pushed off from her seat. She turned to Brian. "Brian, I left a case of ginger ale out in the garage. Would you mind bringing it in for me?"

"It would be my pleasure." Brian patted Emma's knee and got up.

"Do you need any help?" Emma half rose from the sofa. She didn't want to be left alone with her mother and the questions Emma could already read in Priscilla's eyes.

Both Arabella and Francis shook their heads no.

Emma reluctantly sank back down into her seat. She and Priscilla stared at each other for a moment. Priscilla wet her lips with the sherry again.

"Arabella seems to be doing just fine," Priscilla said rather huffily. "That's not the impression I got when I last talked to her."

"Yes, of course," was all Emma could think to say.

"I do wish someone had told me about this Francis." The way Priscilla said his name you would have thought Arabella had dragged him in off the street. "If I'd known I might not have come rushing up here from Florida." She fixed Emma with a stare, her blue eyes sharp and piercing. "It was a very tiresome drive, especially when you are by yourself." A strange look crossed her face, and she threw her head back. "I'm not getting any younger, you know."

Emma went to protest, but Priscilla waved away the words before they left Emma's lips.

"This Francis seems to be taking care of Arabella just fine. Not that I'm not grateful; don't get me wrong. Arabella has always needed someone to look after her."

"I don't think that's true," Emma rose to Arabella's defense. Her aunt was one of the most independent women Emma knew.

Priscilla waved away Emma's objection. "So," she said changing the subject with relish. "I gather that young man is the reason you're so keen to stay in Paris," she said smugly, as if she had ferreted out a top national secret.

Emma was flustered. She didn't know what to say that wouldn't make her sound defensive. She settled for a simple "Yes," but then quickly added, "and Aunt Arabella, of course."

"He seems like a nice enough young man. He's Liz O'Connell's brother, right?"

Emma nodded warily.

"What are his plans?"

"Plans?" Emma repeated, much as she had earlier when she and her mother had had this conversation about her.

"Yes. What does he plan to do with his future?"

"He's helping to run the family hardware store, O'Connell's. It's across the street from Sweet Nothings."

"I remember it. Your father often went there for things

he needed to fix stuff around the house. Although in the end I usually had to call in a professional."

The mention of her father suddenly made Emma wish he was there. He would like Brian. She was sure of it.

"And he's started his own renovation company. He's an architect," Emma added rather proudly.

Her mother's eyebrows shot up at that, and a gleam lit her eyes. "Oh, an architect. But why is he wasting his time in this town when he could go to Nashville or Memphis or . . . or anywhere and make buckets more money?"

"Making buckets of money isn't that important to Brian." Emma raised her chin. "He's more interested in doing what's right. And right now that's helping his father because his father can no longer run the business himself. It's been in the family for years—Brian doesn't want to have to close the doors or sell to someone else."

"Pity." Priscilla picked up her glass. She studied it for a moment before taking an actual sip. She had opened her mouth again when Brian came into the room. She shut it quickly and managed a tight smile, much to Emma's relief.

EMMA spent the morning at Sweet Nothings helping Arabella and Sylvia. A new shipment had come in from Monique Berthole in New York, and Emma was excited to display all of the pretty things. She thought back to several months earlier when she'd been afraid to order anything for fear of blowing the business's terribly meager budget, but sales had improved considerably. When Emma ran the numbers, they had turned from red to a good, solid black.

Sylvia had contacted Eloise Montgomery, and she was

absolutely thrilled to be asked to help out in the shop. She arrived at Sweet Nothings in a cloud of Evening in Paris perfume shortly before noon. Emma remembered her grandmother wearing that scent. Eloise's gray hair was perfectly coiffed—it had remained remarkably thick even though she was in her seventies—and she was resplendent in a purple pantsuit, pale gray shell and paisley shawl thrown over her shoulder like a matador's cape.

Emma left the shop somewhat reluctantly at eleven forty-five. Arabella, Sylvia and Eloise were having a wonderful time playing *remember when* and although she felt decidedly de trop, she wished she could have stayed and enjoyed the laughter and the fun.

But she had a more important mission. Emma consoled herself with that thought as she freshened up and got ready to head to the Grangers' horse farm. Fortunately Liz would also be there, meeting with Jackson about the creative direction for the firm's new web site.

Liz's station wagon was already parked in the gravel drive when Emma arrived. She pulled in behind it and was about to get out when she heard the pounding of hooves, and the Bug was enveloped in an enormous cloud of dust.

Mariel, dressed in jodhpurs, a black velvet jacket, expensive leather boots and a white stock tie blouse, blew past on a well-lathered horse, which kicked up a tsunami of dust and gravel in its wake. She pulled up short in front of the house and dismounted, throwing the reins to a young boy who had magically appeared at just the right moment.

She and Emma met on the broad steps leading to the porch.

Mariel smiled and put a hand to her back. "I've overdone it, I'm afraid. I'm going to feel this tomorrow."

"Maybe a hot bath?" Emma suggested.

"At the very least," Mariel replied. She pushed open the front door, and Emma followed her inside. Mariel sat down on a bench in the foyer and began pulling off her boots. "Dr. Sampson told me I needed to take it easy." She made a disgusted sound. "I'm not going to stop riding no matter what he says."

She winced as she pulled off her right boot.

Emma wondered if riding was such a good thing if it had put her in such pain.

Mariel started to get up when she put a hand to her back and sank down onto the bench again. She groaned.

Emma looked at her in alarm. "Is there something you can take for the pain?"

Mariel shook her head. Her face was getting paler and paler until it was the color of putty. "I refuse to become hooked on those dreadful painkillers. I know what happens to people who take them. Just pick up the newspaper, and you'll see all the stories. I told Dr. Sampson that I was having none of that." She took a deep shuddering breath and struggled to her feet.

"I don't want to end up like that talk show host . . . what was his name?" she threw over her shoulder as she made her way down the hall.

Chapter 8

EMMA stood in the foyer, undecided as to what to do or where to go, when Jackson came rushing in, sliding to a stop in front of her. He was wearing light-colored corduroy pants and a black turtleneck with the sleeves pushed up. Emma noticed he had a small tattoo on the underside of his wrist, but she wasn't close enough to see what it was.

"Sorry. I do hope you haven't been waiting long."

"Not at all."

Emma followed him back down the art-lined hall to the same office where he had interviewed her the day before. Liz was seated at the other partner's desk, her blond head bent over a laptop.

She looked up when Emma walked in, and her broad, freckled face broke into a grin.

"The two of you obviously already know each other." Jackson stood awkwardly, his hands dangling at his sides. Emma noticed how thin his wrists were. It gave him a very boyish appearance.

"Tom Roberts is here, too," Jackson said. "He is . . . was . . . my father's partner. He's working in the library, but he does want to meet you. He should be along in a bit."

Emma smiled encouragingly.

"Well." He stood for a moment, hovering between one foot and the other as if uncertain what ought to happen next. "I suppose I will have to show you what needs to be done."

"That would be helpful," Emma said with only a trace of sarcasm. She felt a little sorry for Jackson—he appeared to be adrift. His father's death had obviously had an unsettling effect on him.

"We have to create an inventory of all the works in my father's collection. The IRS wants it, and our lawyers will need it to settle my father's estate." He ran a hand over his face. "Unfortunately, Father was allergic to computers and absolutely refused to have one in the office." He gave a wry smile. "Our inventory, such as it is, is all handwritten."

He reached over to the bookcase and pulled a book from a row of similar ones. It was an ancient notebook covered in worn and faded red fabric. The pages had gilt edges, and the spine was broken and crumbling. Jackson flipped it open randomly, and a musty smell rose from the paper. He showed Emma a page. Small but neat handwriting followed the blue lines carefully. Some of the entries were crossed out.

"Father wrote all his purchases down in these." Jackson pointed to the half-dozen books behind him on the shelf. "Sometimes he remembered to cross out an entry when the work was sold and sometimes not. It's a positively antiquated way of doing things—plus the books are falling apart." He pointed to the broken binding. "There's no way the IRS is going to accept this as an accurate inventory of what comprises my father's estate. Unfortunately, it means more work for us, transferring all of this"—again he waved a hand toward the books—"onto a computer. We do have a customized database all set up, so it's a matter of getting the information from the paintings and sculpture and entering it." He looked down at his feet for a moment. "Always assuming the complete information is there. Father wasn't a stickler for details. For him, the thrill was in the buying, selling and negotiating. He wasn't concerned with keeping records. If you want to have a go at tracking down provenances or dates, please feel free, but don't feel obligated. The biggest task is going to be getting everything entered properly into the database." He scratched his leg idly. "I started entering some of the information myself—I bought the computer that's set up in the library the day after my father died—but I only got through the works that are hanging in the house and some of my most recent purchases. That's when I realized we were going to need help."

Emma nodded. She wondered where the artwork was kept and how much of it there was.

"I'll show you where the collection is housed," Jackson said as if reading her thoughts.

Liz and Emma smiled at each other as Jackson led Emma out of the room. *Talk to you later*, Liz mouthed.

"We had a special room built—temperature-controlled, fireproof, perfectly secure."

They went back out through the foyer and entered a back

hallway that, unlike the other, was bare of any decoration. At the end of it was a gray metal door. Jackson punched some numbers into the keypad affixed to the front and pulled it open.

The room they entered was fairly large, windowless, and lined with shelves designed to hold paintings and others created for housing sculpture. There were also three metal cabinets, each with a half-dozen shallow drawers. Jackson walked over to one of the cabinets and patted the top.

"These are for unframed drawings, prints and the like." He gestured toward the lock on the drawer handles. "You'll be given a key, of course."

A sturdy wooden table stood in the center of the room, and a comfortable-looking, padded desk chair was parked in front of it. On top of the table was a desktop computer.

"You'll be doing most of your work in here," Jackson said. "I hope it won't be too uncomfortable. It seemed to make the most sense. No point in copying down all the information then having to go back to the office to enter it. Of course, if you need to look something up, we have a fairly complete library. Would you like to see it?"

Emma nodded and again followed Jackson down the back hallway. They crossed the foyer, where Molly was dusting, passed the door to the office and entered another door just beyond it.

The room was lined with book-stuffed shelves, and there was a ladder that attached to the top shelf and could be slid along a rail to where it was needed. A wooden desk, smaller than the ones in the office, was placed to one side. A desktop computer and large monitor sat on top. A tufted leather sofa was opposite. A man was seated on the couch, his short, stout legs stretched out in front of him, a pair of half glasses perched on his nose. He was reading *Art International*.

He looked up when Jackson and Emma entered.

"Emma, this is Tom Roberts. Tom, this is Emma. She's going to be helping us out with the inventory."

Roberts scrambled to his feet, pulling his pinstriped vest down to cover his rotund belly. His gray hair had receded to the middle of his head, and he did his best to hide the fact by plastering long strands across the top of his skull. One had gone awry and hung down alongside his right ear.

He shook Emma's hand, holding it in his a moment longer than necessary. His was slightly damp. Emma had to restrain herself from wiping her palm along the leg of her slacks.

Tom put his thumb in the magazine he'd been reading to hold his place. "Have you seen Sabina?" he asked Jackson. He looked around as if she might be hiding somewhere in the library.

"I thought I saw her go out earlier. Perhaps she wanted a bit of air." Jackson danced impatiently from one foot to the other.

"Here I am," a voice from the door startled them all.

Emma swiveled around to face the beautiful woman she had seen at Hugh's dinner dance—the one in the tangerine-colored dress who had stood out from the crowd. She looked no less exotic in an everyday pair of black pants and a sapphire blue silk blouse. Her dark hair flowed around her shoulders and her emerald eyes, dotted with specks of hazel, reminded Emma of a cat's. She was clearly many years her husband's junior.

She extended her hand to Emma, and, unlike her husband's sweaty palm, hers was as cool as a sliver of ice. A large, square-cut diamond ring winked from her finger and was surrounded by bands of sapphires, more diamonds and rubies.

She had a lovely voice—deep and musical—with a slight accent Emma couldn't place. Russian? German?

"Lovely to meet you," Sabina said briskly. "Tom, I'm going now. I have a rehearsal this afternoon." She turned to Emma with a smile. "I play the violin with the Nashville Symphony."

Before Emma could reply, Sabina had exited the room, leaving behind nothing more than the scent of expensive face cream.

Tom smiled benignly at his departing spouse. "Sabina studied at the Nuremberg University of Music."

"She's German?" Emma asked. "I couldn't quite place her accent."

Tom shook his head. "Yes, her ancestors are from Berlin. They fled to London just before the war. They spent many years there, but when it was safe again, Sabina's grandfather decided to return to Germany. Sabina was born and educated there."

Jackson had begun to look impatient during this exchange, clearing his throat several times. Emma looked at him and smiled.

"Guess we'll move on then," he said scratching behind one ear. "I'll show you how things are done."

Emma spent the afternoon learning the computer database program and entering some sample information from the labels on the backs of the paintings—blue slips of paper with *hugh granger fine arts* written all in lowercase and with space to enter the title of the artwork, date of execution, measurements and a brief provenance.

As soon as Jackson felt Emma was comfortable with the process, he bolted from the room and rushed off to do something else. Emma worked diligently all afternoon—the job wasn't complicated and would have been dreadfully dull had it not been for the opportunity to see so many beautiful works of art. There was a particularly charming Matisse drawing Emma would have loved to own, but she was quite certain it wasn't in her price range. Her budget ran more toward framed posters than original artwork.

Emma was surprised when she looked at her watch and it was already a few minutes after five. She saved her work and powered off the computer. It felt good to stand up and stretch after sitting for so long. She was getting a cramp in her shoulder and her right foot had gone to sleep. She wondered if Liz was still working in the study or had already left to go home and get dinner for Matt and the kids.

As Emma turned out the lights and picked up her coat and purse, she realized she had become so engrossed in her task she had forgotten that her main purpose in being at the Grangers' was to snoop. She chewed her lower lip. She wasn't going to find out much of anything if she spent all her time alone in a windowless room. She would have to find excuses to poke around and talk to members of the family.

Emma let the door close behind her. According to Jackson, it would lock automatically, but just to be sure she checked the handle. It didn't turn. Emma headed down the hall, through the lobby and down the front hallway. She peeked into the office and was pleased to see that Liz was still there.

"Hey, how's it going?" Liz asked when she saw Emma

in the doorway. She stretched her arms over her head and yawned. She gestured toward her laptop. "I'm roughing out an idea for the web site. There's so much inspiration to be had in all the amazing artwork around here. Jackson is definitely trying to take the business in a whole new direction now that his father is gone."

Emma slipped into the seat opposite Liz's desk. "Could that be a good motive for murder?"

Liz frowned. "I don't know. Jackson seems genuinely distressed over his father's death, but"—she shrugged—"that might be a good act, who knows? I do know it took some convincing to get his father to even agree to having a presence on the web."

"Fortunately Aunt Arabella is more with it than some people half her age."

Emma glanced toward the window. The sky was darkening and was splashed with streaks of purple and pink in much the manner of some of the contemporary paintings she had been cataloging. Movement and a flash of white caught her eye.

She got up from her chair and walked closer to the window.

"What is it?" Liz asked, pushing a hand through her hair, leaving her dark blond locks disheveled.

"I think someone is out there." Emma peered out the window. "Probably just one of the staff . . ."

Liz jumped up and joined Emma, and they both looked out the window. A raised terrace extended out from the house and was surrounded by a low stone wall. Various pieces of outdoor furniture, shrouded in dark green canvas covers, were pushed to one side, and empty terra-cotta planters ringed the circular-patterned brickwork. A beech tree with spreading branches deepened the shadows on the right side.

Movement again caught Emma's eye. "It's only Mariel," she said.

Mariel was standing in the shadows of the beech, just beyond the circle of light cast from the back windows. She was wearing the same dark barn jacket Emma had seen her in earlier and had a white scarf tied around her throat.

"Isn't she cold?" Liz wrapped her arms around herself and shivered.

There was more movement and what looked like one shadow separated and became two.

"Who is that?" Liz hissed, pointing.

"It's a man," Emma said.

"I can see that," Liz grumped. "Do you know who it is?"

"No. But they must be very friendly. They were standing terribly close."

"Lovers, do you think?"

Emma shrugged. "I don't know. Possibly. They obviously don't want to be seen."

"Well, well, well. Maybe everything wasn't wine and roses between Hugh Granger and his wife after all." Liz turned to Emma. "We may very well have another suspect on our hands."

Chapter 9

ARABELLA and Sylvia greeted Emma the next morning
when she arrived at Sweet Nothings as if she'd been gone
for days. They were both eager for news of her time spent
at the Grangers'.

While Emma put tags on some new items that had come
in, she told her aunt and Sylvia about seeing Mariel Granger
outside with another man in what could practically be
termed a clutch.

"She is a lot younger than Hugh," Arabella said thoughtfully as she slipped a new gown over the head of one of the
mannequins. "I'm assuming this man was more her age?"
She raised an eyebrow at Emma.

Emma nodded. "Yes. Perhaps even a bit younger although
it was hard to tell—it was getting dark, and they were

standing in the shadows. He had brown, curly hair and, while he was taller than her, he didn't strike me as being particularly tall."

"Pardon me for playing devil's advocate," Sylvia said, "but could he be a relative? Perhaps she has a brother?"

"I don't know," Emma mused. "There was something furtive about their meeting. I can't describe it, but I got the distinct impression they didn't want to be seen. Besides"—she turned around to face Sylvia—"if it was completely innocent, why didn't she invite him inside? Why stand on the terrace in the cold?"

"But why worry now?" Sylvia asked, fiddling with the fringe on her scarf. "The husband's six feet under, after all, or about to be."

"This isn't New York," Arabella said, her lips slightly pursed. "This is a small town. It wouldn't be seemly for her to be seen with another man so soon. News would get around faster than ice melts on a hot day."

"Wish we could get a bead on who the guy is." Sylvia ignored the rebuke in Arabella's tone.

"Hopefully I'll pick up something eventually," Emma said. "There's a woman who works for them—Molly. I think she's a sort of cook and housekeeper. I'm hoping I can persuade her to talk. Jackson did tell me to help myself to coffee or tea or anything I wanted from the kitchen, so I'll have an excuse to be in that part of the house."

"Just be careful." Arabella lowered her brows. "Remember what Francis said."

"Ditto," Sylvia said.

Emma was about to reassure them when the door opened.

She spun around and was startled to see who their customer was.

"Good morning," Joy Granger said quietly. She was clutching a Sweet Nothings bag in one hand.

Emma tried not to wince as Joy made her way, slowly and painfully, to the counter. She was wearing the same lace-up shoes she'd had on the night of the dinner dance, with the sole of one shoe built up higher than the other. Her coat was a plain and serviceable black, and the beige, wool scarf tucked into the neck did little to liven it up. Joy's short, brown hair was parted in the middle and held off her face on either side with two tortoise-colored barrettes. Her cheeks were pink from the cold, but her lips were pale and colorless.

She put the bag on the counter and eased out the tissue-wrapped contents.

"My father," she stumbled slightly over the word, "bought this for my aunt Georgina." She opened the tissue paper and slid out a nylon, pale blue gown with Alencon lace trim.

"Ah, the Miss Elaine." Arabella bustled over and slid behind the counter. "I sold this to Mr. Granger the night of our Valentine's event. It's vintage nineteen-sixties," Arabella said, fingering the soft fabric. "He thought his sister would enjoy it." She looked up at Joy over the top of her half glasses. "Is there something wrong with it?"

"Oh no." Joy shook her head vigorously. "It's perfectly fine. It's just that it doesn't fit. Father didn't realize, but Aunt Georgina has"—she paused as if searching for a way to put it delicately—"put on a bit of weight."

Arabella made a *tsk*ing sound under her breath. "Men never do get sizes right, do they?" Arabella held the gown up and examined it. It flowed straight from the shoulders in a generous circle.

"I wouldn't know," Joy said with an edge of bitterness to her voice.

Arabella tilted her head to the side in a way that normally invited confidences, but Joy clamped her thin lips closed and didn't elaborate.

"Well," Arabella finally said, "if this gown doesn't fit, I'm not sure we have anything that will."

"That's all right," Joy said, folding up the Sweet Nothings bag. "Aunt Georgina is a little . . . dotty." She made small circles around the side of her head with her finger. "I'm surprised Father even bothered to buy her something. He rarely went to visit."

Joy's mouth turned down, and for a moment, Emma was afraid she was going to cry. "He doesn't like . . . broken things." She tucked the empty shopping bag under her arm.

"We can give you a credit or perhaps there's something you'd like," Arabella said, not being one to let a customer leave the shop empty-handed.

Joy gave a laugh that was halfway to a sob. "Me?" She pointed a finger at her own chest. "What would I do with"—she waved her hand around Sweet Nothings—"these things?" She handed Arabella the receipt for the gown.

Arabella punched some numbers into the credit card machine, which, after a brief pause, spit out a piece of paper. "If you wouldn't mind signing here." Arabella handed Joy a pen.

Joy signed her name and handed the pen back to Arabella. She glanced at the receipt. "Your things sure are expensive." She turned to head toward the door. "I'm saving every penny for something much more important."

"I wonder what on earth she's hoarding her money for," Arabella said as soon as the door had closed behind Joy.

"Not too bitter, is she?" Sylvia noted.

"Indeed," Arabella agreed. "I feel sorry for her. She seems so unhappy."

"I gather she was hurt in the accident that killed her mother. I suppose that might make anyone bitter." Emma went back to tagging a stack of pastel-colored panties. "What was that she said about her father? He doesn't like *broken things*?"

"That was peculiar, wasn't it?" Sylvia pulled open one of the drawers and began straightening the bras that were arranged in rows like muffins in a tin. "I wonder what she meant by that?"

"I think I know." Arabella put down the gown she'd been examining for any worn spots or small tears. "I suppose it was his art background, and his eye for color and symmetry, but Hugh really disliked things that weren't attractive. It was very hard on him when we were in India. So many beautiful things—if you've never seen the Taj Mahal, you really must, especially at sunset and sunrise—but so much ugliness, too . . . poverty and disease." She put down the gown she was examining, opened the cupboard behind her and pulled out her sewing kit. "Joy is not the most attractive young woman—she's not ugly, just plain—but she's also crippled. That would have been difficult for Hugh to accept. He would want his children to be beautiful and certainly unblemished." She unwound a piece of white thread, cut it and began attempting to thread a slim, silver needle. Finally she put it down in disgust.

"Emma, would you be a dear and thread this for me?" She handed the needle to Emma.

Emma slipped the thread through the tiny slit in the needle and handed it back to her aunt.

"Thank you, dear. I'm quite convinced they're making the slits in the needles smaller than they used to."

"I wonder what it is she's saving her money for," Sylvia said as she folded a bra and tucked it into a row alongside the others. "Whatever it is, it must be awfully expensive. I thought you said these Grangers were rolling in dough."

"They are," Arabella said simply. "I can't imagine what it is she wants. She's Hugh's daughter—she's bound to come into some sort of inheritance."

"Unless he's leaving it all to his wife, Mariel." Emma glanced at her watch quickly.

"Oh, I can't imagine Hugh would do that. And what about the son? I suppose he's making some money through Hugh's art business. But surely Hugh would have made sure to take care of both of them."

"We don't know, do we?" Emma said as she pulled her purse out from under the counter. "But I'm heading over there now, and maybe, just maybe, I'll find out."

Arabella's words, "Be careful, dear," echoed after Emma as she ran up to her apartment to get her coat.

EMMA stared out the car window at the empty fields rolling past. She thought about what Arabella had said as she drove toward the Grangers'—how everyone should see the Taj Mahal at some point in her life. And she thought of her conversations with her mother and whether or not she would be satisfied living her life out in her small hometown, when she'd always longed to see the world.

Emma sighed as she pulled up to the Grangers' house. Perhaps Brian was longing to see more of the world, too, and they could travel together. She would have to talk to him about it.

Emma was glad to see Liz's station wagon already parked in the driveway. She pulled up in back of it and got out, shivering as the sharp wind knifed through her jacket. She pulled her collar up around her neck, ducked her head against the wind and scurried toward the shelter of the house.

She had her foot on the first step when a noise like thunder shook the ground. Emma looked up to see someone roaring up the driveway on a large, black horse, its hooves pounding up a choking cloud of dust and gravel that made Emma's eyes water. She assumed it was Mariel, but when she looked again, after the air had cleared, she was surprised to discover that it was Joy riding the horse.

Obviously her crippled leg didn't keep her from horseback riding. Emma knew little about horses, but she could tell that Joy was an excellent rider—confident and in control of her mount. She looked different, too—content and happy, her plain face flushed from the activity, making her look almost pretty.

Emma waved to her and continued up the steps, brushing at the dust that had blown onto her coat. The front door was open, as Jackson had said it would be. Emma stepped inside and looked around. The foyer was empty. Someone had placed a large bouquet of flowers on the foyer table. They made Emma long for spring. Their scent mingled with the smell of furniture polish and the faint odor of horse, which permeated the house. Emma stuck her head in the office. Liz had one of the paintings Emma remembered seeing in the hallway set on an easel with two tall, bright lights on either side. Liz's camera rested on a tripod, and she was squinting through the lens. Emma cleared her throat, and Liz turned around.

"Hey, good to see you." Liz stretched. "I was just going to get a cup of coffee. Want one before you get started?"

"I'll have some tea if there is any."

The kitchen was empty. A large thermos of coffee stood on the center island surrounded by cups and saucers, sugar and a pitcher of cream. There was also a woven basket of tea bags. Emma dug through them until she found a sachet of green tea. She microwaved some hot water while Liz helped herself to the coffee.

Emma was dunking her tea bag in her cup when the doorbell rang.

Heels clicked across the wood floor, and shortly afterward voices drifted into the kitchen from the foyer. Emma and Liz looked at each other.

"That voice is familiar," Liz said.

Emma nodded. "Yes. It sounds like Detective Walker to me." Emma peered around the kitchen door into the hallway. "It *is* Detective Walker."

Liz raised her eyebrows. "I wonder what he's doing here."

"Maybe he's come to ask some questions. It's about time he bothered someone other than poor Aunt Arabella."

Footsteps, two sets this time, clattered back across the wood floor of the entrance hall, and the voices faded away.

Emma and Liz looked at each other.

Emma chewed on a cuticle. "I wish I could hear what they're saying."

"So do I." Liz stirred her coffee thoughtfully.

"I suppose we could eavesdrop."

Liz's face broke into a wide grin. "Let's." She put her cup down on the counter.

They tiptoed out of the kitchen and down the hallway. The voices were louder now and perfectly clear. Detective Walker was talking to Mariel Granger. Emma and Liz lingered in the foyer, keeping out of sight of the living room.

Emma's ears strained to hear both the conversation in the room beyond as well as the sounds of anyone approaching. She certainly didn't want to be caught eavesdropping.

"Did you go out on the terrace to see the fireworks?" they heard Detective Walker ask.

"Yes," Mariel answered.

"And when they ended?"

"I . . . I went back inside with the crowd."

"Your husband was with you?"

"No, no, he wasn't. The party was a bit much for him. He is . . . was . . . in perfect health, but at his age . . ." Mariel's voice trailed off. "He said he'd seen plenty of fireworks in his day and preferred to stay inside and nurse a snifter of brandy."

"So you were alone on the terrace?"

"Hardly alone, Detective. There were dozens of people out there with me."

"When the fireworks ended you came inside, and then someone screamed, is that correct?"

Emma leaned in as close to the door as she dared, but she couldn't hear Mariel's response.

"I'm sorry. I'm sure this is difficult for you. But after the person screamed, someone discovered Mr. Granger's body at the foot of the balcony."

"Yes," Mariel said. Emma thought her tone sounded hesitant . . . as if she were unsure of the answer.

"Do you have any idea why he might have gone up on that balcony? Was he meeting someone?"

"Not that I know of. Perhaps he wanted to get a view of the ballroom from above. That's the sort of thing Hugh would do . . . would have done."

They heard paper rustling, and Walker continued, "As soon as the police arrived at the hotel, we secured the scene."

"What?"

"I mean we locked everything down—all the doors to the hotel were locked, and we had officers stationed at each of them. We obviously couldn't interview everyone that night, but we did get everyone's name and contact information. I have a list of those names."

He paused, and they heard paper rustling again.

"I've gone over the list several times. Your name does not appear to be on it."

"What do you mean?" Mariel's voice had taken on a slightly indignant tone. "There must be some mistake."

"It means," Walker said with exaggerated patience, "that you were not in the ballroom or the hotel after your husband was killed. If you had been, your name would be on the list."

There was a silence that extended for several minutes. Finally Walker spoke.

"Where did you go, Mrs. Granger, and when did you leave? Before your husband was killed or afterward?"

"This is ridiculous." Mariel's voice rose to a near hysterical level. "You can't prove I wasn't there just because I'm not on some list."

Emma could imagine her sitting there fuming, those large, mannish hands clenched into fists.

"Where did you go, Mrs. Granger?" Walker repeated. "That's all we want to know. If you left the ballroom before your husband was murdered, and someone can attest to that, you're one more person we can cross off the list."

"I thought you just said I wasn't on the list." Mariel's voice had a pronounced sneer to it.

Even in the hallway they could hear Walker sigh. "I meant that figuratively, of course. If you have nothing to hide, just tell us where you went and whether someone can verify it. It's as simple as that."

"I'm sorry, but I think it's time you left." They heard the rustling sounds of someone getting up. "I'm sure the mayor would not want to hear that the police have been harassing innocent widows."

Emma and Liz did not hear Walker's response to Mariel's final sally as they turned and scooted back to the safety of the kitchen.

Chapter 10

"WELL that was something," Liz whispered when she and Emma were back in the kitchen, their eavesdropping undetected. They both leaned against the island, panting slightly from their sudden dash.

Emma looked over her shoulder just in case Mariel was headed their way, but she must have gone off somewhere else in the house. "Yes, I find it very interesting that she refuses say where she was when Hugh was killed—especially since it would give her an alibi. Of course, it's also quite possible she murdered her husband and then slipped away before the body was discovered."

"Or"—Liz helped herself to one of the iced lemon cookies from the ceramic jar on the counter—"she didn't murder him, but still can't say where she went." She leaned on her elbows and took a bite of her cookie. "She can't say because she was with someone she shouldn't have been—for instance, that dark-haired man we saw her with in the garden yesterday."

Emma wasn't convinced. "But this is murder. Wouldn't you want to clear your name no matter what the consequences?"

"You're forgetting that Paris is still a very small town," Liz said, echoing Arabella's earlier words. "I would imagine until the estate is settled, she doesn't want *anyone* to know she was playing around. No gossip, no tongues wagging, no being the subject of back-fence chatter. If for some reason, someone decided to contest the will, why give him any ammunition?"

Emma took a sip of her tea, which was now barely lukewarm. She popped the cup into the microwave and hit the Start button. Sixty seconds later the timer pinged. Emma was retrieving it when Joy walked into the room.

"Oh," she said, looking slightly flustered at the sight of Emma and Liz.

"Sorry," Emma and Liz chorused. "We don't want to get in your way. We're just getting something to drink."

"Please, help yourselves." Joy waved a hand toward the provisions set out on the counter. Her face was still flushed from the outdoors, her cheeks pink and her eyes bright. She opened the refrigerator and pulled out a pitcher of sweet tea. She smiled shyly at Emma and Liz. "Riding always makes me thirsty," she said, filling a tall glass to the brim. "Would you like some?"

Emma and Liz shook their heads. The house was always slightly chilly, and Emma was grateful for the warmth of the cup in her hands.

"I saw you riding earlier." Emma tested her tea. It was now too hot so she blew on it briefly, sending ripples across the surface like tiny waves. "I'm always impressed when someone can ride well. I've never gotten the hang of it myself."

Joy's plain face flushed with pleasure, and Emma realized Joy *was* pretty. It was her habitual expression of bitterness that obscured the beauty of her large blue eyes, fine cheekbones and chiseled nose.

"I love riding," Joy said. "My mother had me on a horse by the time I was three years old. I still remember his name—Maximillian. Mother was an expert horsewoman herself." She dashed at the tears that had formed in her eyes. "That was before . . ." She gestured toward her leg. "On a horse, I can forget that I'm . . . crippled." Bitterness twisted her mouth, and the flash of beauty Emma had noticed earlier faded like the setting sun.

Joy turned her back to them and fiddled with the top to the cookie jar. "When I'm riding, the horse becomes my legs, and I can move like the wind, unhampered and . . . free," she said slightly breathlessly. She spun around. "You have no idea how tiresome it is to drag this thing"—she held out her leg—"around all the time."

Joy took a long swallow of her tea and wiped her mouth with the back of her hand. "Riding has many therapeutic properties—it's not just for cripples." Again the bitter half smile, which didn't reach her blue eyes. "Disabilities come in all flavors. It's beneficial for autistic children, those with learning disabilities or with mental health issues." She ducked her head. "Sorry; I'll get off my soap box now."

"No, that's very interesting," Emma said and meant it.

"I'd love to start a therapeutic horseback riding program here at the farm." She shrugged. "It costs a lot of money though. Teachers have to be certified, the horses have to be trained. As I said"—she rubbed two fingers together—"it's expensive."

"It's such a worthwhile project though," Emma said.

"Yeah, well, tell that to the judge," Joy said enigmatically. She picked up her glass of iced tea and headed toward the door. "Please help yourselves to anything you want. I know Molly keeps the fridge well stocked," she called over her shoulder.

Emma and Liz looked at each other for a moment after she was gone.

"She's a very odd girl," Liz said, taking the last sip of her coffee. She rinsed the cup and started to open the dishwasher.

"Oh, please, let me do that for you." Molly bustled into the room, a plain white apron already tied around her waist.

"Thanks." Liz put the cup and saucer down by the sink.

"Did you find everything you need?" Molly asked. She picked up a sponge and began wiping down the counter. Her hands were small but capable-looking, with short square nails.

"Yes," Emma and Liz chorused.

"How long have you been working for the Grangers?" Emma asked.

Molly frowned and put her hands on her hips. She blew out a gust of breath that sent the fine gray hairs around her forehead flying. "Oh, it's been a long time, I can tell you that. How many years though, I'm afraid I've forgotten. Can you believe it?" She chuckled. "I was here when Miss Joy was born, that I know. I'll never forget it; such a pretty baby, and so good, too. She hardly ever fussed, which was a wonderful thing because it was me and Miss Elizabeth alone with her most of the time. Mr. Granger was traveling all over the world, and Miss Joy went from crawling to walking while he was away. Sometimes he hardly recognized her when he got home."

A frown crossed her face. "Some men don't take to babies, and Mr. Granger was one of them. Which was a terribly sad thing when Miss Elizabeth died and Miss Joy had to spend all those months in the hospital, crying for her mother, while they did one surgery after another trying to fix her leg. They did the best they could." Her lips snapped together briskly.

"It was different when Mr. Jackson came along. Mr. Granger doted on him something fierce. It's made Miss Joy a little bitter, if you know what I mean. Not that anyone can blame her. Losing her mother like that, and with a father who took no interest whatsoever. When he married the second Mrs. Granger, I had hopes that she would be like a mother to Miss Joy, but they took an almost instant dislike to each other."

Emma and Liz were quiet, not wanting to possibly staunch the flow of information.

"Recently, Mr. Granger had begun to make an effort. Maybe it was because he was getting on in years and knew his time was limited." Molly gasped and put a hand to her mouth. "Not to say he knew what was coming. I didn't mean that. May he rest in peace."

Molly was quiet for a moment, and Liz and Emma waited with bated breath.

"He tried to take an interest in Miss Joy and what she

was doing. It's just too bad that . . ." Molly stopped abruptly and wrung her hands.

"Just too bad that what?" Emma asked in her most persuasive voice.

Emotions skittered across Molly's face while Emma nearly stopped breathing.

Molly twisted her apron between her hands as if she were trying to wring it out. She gave a deep sigh. "It was right before the big party planned for Mr. Granger's birthday on Saturday night. He and Miss Joy were in the library, talking. I brought them a tray with some sherry. It made me happy to see them sitting there together."

She looked down at the floor, and Emma imagined she was picturing the scene.

She looked up, her eyes large and wet with tears. "I passed the library later on my way to turn down the beds for the night, knowing everyone would come back from the party too tired to do more than slip between the covers. I heard raised voices coming from the library—Mr. Granger's deep voice bellowing out like the preacher's in church at Sunday service, and Miss Joy's louder than I've ever heard it."

"What a shame," Emma said. "What were they arguing about?"

Molly stuck her hands into the pockets of her apron, and Emma could see her clenching the fabric, her fingers curled into fists. "I don't know. I didn't stop to listen. I didn't want to know."

Molly dashed a hand across her eyes where the tears threatened to spill over the rims and cascade down her wrinkled cheeks. "It just makes me so sad, you know?" She looked from Emma to Liz.

Emma put on her most sympathetic look, and she could see that Liz was doing the same.

"I really thought that father and daughter were becoming close, and then this horrible argument on the night he died. I feel terrible for poor Miss Joy. Here the poor man's gone to his grave, and her last conversation with him was filled with anger and strong language. Can you imagine how she must feel, the poor thing? The guilt must be eating her alive," Molly finished with a final wrench of her apron.

Chapter 11

BETTE woke Emma early on Friday morning. Emma sat up, trying to rub the sleep from her eyes. Bette was sitting in front of the door to Emma's apartment, emitting a low-pitched whine that reminded Emma of the drone of a mosquito. It was certainly just as impossible to ignore and definitely as annoying.

Emma reluctantly left her warm bed, pulled on a pair of gray sweats and her fur-lined boots. The boots would be warm enough even without a pair of socks.

"Okay, girl, I'm coming," Emma said. Her eyes weren't quite open yet—they were still sticky with sleep—and she fumbled blindly in her closet for her down jacket, scarf and hat. She had a pair of leather gloves already stuffed in the pockets of her jacket; she would pull those on when she got outside.

Bette's retractable leash was on the wooden table by the front door, half-lost amid a spill of old junk mail and catalogs. Emma made a mental note, as she did every time she retrieved Bette's leash, to clean up the mess and polish the table. She grabbed the leash and called to Bette. Bette mistakenly thought Emma wanted to play and took off running through the apartment. Emma darted after her, swearing softly under her breath.

"Come on, Bette. I thought you had to go out?" Emma stood with her hands on her hips, panting slightly. Bette skidded to a stop in front of Emma, but Emma knew that the moment she reached for Bette, the dog would be off running again.

Instead, Emma headed for the door, ignoring Bette. She was beginning to sweat inside her warm jacket and was actually looking forward to the cold air outside. Bette watched Emma for several seconds, her head cocked to one side, her ears twitching, before scampering after Emma and allowing her leash to be hooked on.

"Let's go, girl."

Emma and Bette ran down the stairs, and Emma pulled open the door to the outside. She recoiled as the first icy blast of frigid air hit her. Suddenly her warm bed with its fluffy down comforter seemed twice as inviting. Bette, however, didn't seem to mind the wintery cold as she scampered across the sidewalk toward the curb. A whiff of some delectable scent had obviously caught her attention because she circled one small spot for what seemed an eternity to Emma who stood there waiting, stomping her feet against the bitter cold.

"Come on, Bette. If you're done, we're going in."

"You're out awfully early."

The voice, coming from behind, startled Emma. She looked up to see Brian striding toward her, his face nearly obscured by an orange and white striped scarf.

"Bette woke me," Emma admitted, tilting her head toward the puppy. "But you're out early, too."

Brian put his hands on Emma's shoulders and drew her toward him for a kiss as Bette wound her way in and out between their legs.

"There are some things I have to get done at the hardware store, and this is the only time I have," he said when he reluctantly pulled his lips away from Emma's. "I'll be on site for a renovation project the rest of the day." He peered at her over the edge of his scarf and sighed. "I've been so busy lately, I haven't had time for anything but work." He slipped his hand into Emma's and squeezed it. "I've missed you."

Emma and Brian had started dating before the summer. Saturday night dinners or trips to the movies had gradually turned into nightly phone calls and sharing takeout or one of Emma's home cooked meals several times a week. But the last week or two Brian had been so busy he'd barely had time for more than a phone call or a cup of coffee.

"I can have some coffee going at the store in under five minutes. Interested?"

"Sure. But can you make that tea?" Emma reined Bette in, and they crossed the deserted street.

"No problem. We're stocked for all contingencies."

Brian pulled his keys from his pocket, inserted them in the lock and pulled open the glass-and-wood front door of O'Connell's Hardware store. He felt along the wall and flipped on a handful of the lights.

Emma followed him inside. The wooden floors creaked

under their weight, and the store had the old familiar smell of lumber and metal. Emma unclipped Bette, and freed from her leash, Bette ran in circles, nose to the ground, enjoying all the new smells.

Brian unwound his scarf and slipped out of his jacket. He moved slowly, and Emma thought he looked tired. Between running the hardware store and his renovation business, he was certainly burning the candle at both ends.

"I gather you and Liz are both working over at the Grangers'," Brian said as he measured coffee into the pot and put a mug of water into the microwave. He turned and put his hands on Emma's shoulders. "Just be careful, okay? There's a murderer on the loose. You're my two favorite girls, and I wouldn't want anything to happen to either of you."

"Don't worry. We won't take any chances."

Emma recounted her and Liz's experience of the day before, eavesdropping on Mariel and Detective Walker. She told Brian how Mariel had refused to reveal where she had gone before the police arrived at the ballroom the night of her husband's murder. She also told him what she'd learned from Molly—how Joy had been overheard arguing with her father hours before his death.

"Interesting," Brian said as he poured coffee into a thick white mug with *O'Connell's Hardware* written on it in green. He handed a similar mug of hot water to Emma, opened a cabinet and rummaged around inside. He handed Emma a box of tea bags. "Of course, Hugh Granger traveled extensively and ran a multimillion dollar business. He was bound to make some enemies along the way."

Emma took a sip of her tea. She was enjoying this moment with Brian. The rest of the world was quiet—probably still sleeping. She shot a glance at Bette—now she was grateful to the puppy for waking her so early.

"Aunt Arabella did say that Hugh traveled an awful lot." Emma was quiet for a moment. "Do you ever get the urge to . . . travel?" she asked. Her hands were still cold, and she wrapped them around the warm mug gratefully. Brian had turned the heat up, but it would take the ancient furnace a while to warm the drafty store.

"Travel? Not really. I'm so busy getting my business off the ground that I don't see how I'd find the time. Maybe someday . . ."

Emma nodded, strangely disappointed. Of course Brian wasn't thinking about travel right now. She had just hoped that he would have sounded more . . . enthusiastic.

"Do you think you'll ever get tired of living in a small town like Paris?" Emma put down her cup.

Brian shrugged. "I don't see why I would. I was born here, and it's my home. My father is here, Liz and the kids are here." He lowered his voice. "And you're here." He leaned over and brushed his lips against Emma's.

It wasn't exactly the answer Emma wanted, but it would have to do.

ARABELLA was already at Sweet Nothings when Emma arrived later that morning. The smell of fresh coffee wafted toward her as soon as she opened the door.

"You're early," Emma said as she unclipped Bette's leash. Bette made a beeline for Pierre, who was lounging in his dog bed contemplating his first nap of the day. Bette managed to persuade him to engage in a brief tussling match before he turned a cold shoulder on her and snuggled down for a couple of winks.

"I absolutely had to get out of the house," Arabella said, her habitual smile absent. Emma could see the muscle in her temple clenching and unclenching repeatedly.

"What's wrong?" Emma grabbed a mug from the cupboard, filled it with hot water from the tap and stuck it in the microwave to heat.

Arabella sighed heavily and walked out into the showroom. Emma followed her.

"What's wrong?" Emma repeated.

"I hate to say this." Arabella stopped in her tracks and turned to face Emma. She clenched her lips as if that would hold the words back and fiddled with the silver and black onyx pendant around her neck.

"Please tell me what it is." Emma put a hand on her aunt's arm.

"Okay." Arabella took a deep breath. "It's your mother."

"Mother?"

"Yes." Arabella nodded briskly. "Quite frankly, she's driving me crazy." She smiled as if to take some of the sting out of her words. "She . . . she . . . *pecks* at me," Arabella said. "It's *Arabella, do you think . . . Arabella, do you really want . . . Arabella, why . . .* all day long!"

"I'm so sorry." Emma hugged her aunt.

"Darling, it's not your fault." Arabella squeezed her back. "Priscilla has always been like that. I remember that when she was little, she would question everything I did as if she were the elder sibling and not me."

Arabella was quiet for a moment, and the only sound was the gurgling of the coffeemaker. "There is one thing, though, where I'm afraid she might have a point." She turned to Emma and looked her straight in the face. Emma noticed her aunt's eyes were wet with tears. "She thinks I'm being terribly selfish keeping you here in Paris helping me with the shop when you could be anywhere doing . . . anything. Something more important or something more interesting, at least."

Emma felt her stomach lurch. She had been thinking much the same thing—not that her aunt was being selfish—but whether or not she was wasting her life staying in Paris.

But she wasn't about to reveal her doubts to her aunt. Not now—this wasn't the right moment. She gave Arabella's arm a squeeze. "Don't be silly. I'm perfectly content here. Why wouldn't I be?"

"I don't know." Arabella looked down at her shoes. "I know there were times when I felt . . . stifled . . . by the small-town atmosphere. Everyone knowing everyone else's business. Nothing changing—or if it did, it took light-years." She looked up at Emma and examined her face as if she were searching for clues. "And I had already traveled the world. I can only imagine how you must feel."

"Please don't listen to Mother," Emma said, grasping Arabella by both arms. "I know what I want, and it's here in Paris."

A twinkle appeared in Arabella's eyes. "I imagine that it's right across the street," she said with a smile.

Emma smiled back. "I think you're right."

But was she really?

LIZ was already ensconced at the Grangers' when Emma got there later that afternoon. Emma stuck her head into the office to say hello. She was sorry that the two of them weren't working together in the same room, but Jackson was right in that it was a lot easier to set up a computer in the art storage room.

Emma was walking down the back hallway toward the storage room's locked steel door when she heard someone behind her clear his throat. She turned around to see Tom Roberts standing at the head of the hallway. He was wearing a tweed blazer, tan corduroy slacks and an open-necked shirt.

"I hope everything is going well," he said hesitantly when Emma turned around. He had a hand in his pocket and was jingling his loose change.

"Very well, thank you."

"You haven't seen my wife, have you? She said she'd be stopping by"—he glanced at his watch—"any minute now."

Emma shook her head. "Sorry, no. But I just got here myself. Perhaps she's in the library?"

"I've just come from there." Tom hesitated. He ran a hand through his hair, disturbing the carefully arranged strands. He smiled at Emma briefly. "I imagine she's on her way. Sabina isn't known for being on time unless it's for a performance." And he drifted away, back down the hall.

Emma opened the storage room and flipped on the lights. It was chilly, and she was glad she'd worn a heavy sweater. She turned on the computer and brought up the custom-designed database she was using to collect information.

She'd already finished entering one section of drawings and was about to start on a group of paintings. She chose the first one—a small watercolor attributed to Cézanne.

Emma examined the label where all the information was filled in save for the date.

Jackson had encouraged her to do as much research as she was comfortable with. She brought up a popular search engine on the Internet and entered the name of the artist and the painting. A long list of articles came up in the resultant search. Emma clicked on the first one. Cézanne was mentioned in the piece, but not the particular work she was researching, but the article caught her interest, and she kept reading. It dealt with works of art that had been stolen, by the Nazis, from Jewish families during the war. Emma was halfway through the article when she realized she was wasting her employer's time. She went back to the search engine to try again.

After a half hour of researching, Emma decided to move on to the next piece. All the information was intact, and she entered the data quickly. She soon became engrossed in the work—each painting or drawing was something new and different. When Emma looked up again, another hour had gone by. She stood up and stretched her arms overhead. The chill in the room was making her feel achy, so she decided to take a break and get a cup of tea.

Emma stopped by the office on her way to the kitchen. "Want a cup of tea?" Liz switched off the bright lights she had trained on the painting resting on the easel.

"Good idea. Make mine coffee, though. Ben had a nightmare last night and woke us up. It was four o'clock in the morning before we got back to sleep." She stretched and yawned.

They were crossing the foyer on the way to the kitchen when the front door opened, and Sabina Roberts walked in.

She was wearing an expensive-looking, full-length mink coat and brown suede boots.

Emma stopped briefly. "Good afternoon. Your husband has been looking for you. I think he's in the library."

"Thanks." Sabina smiled as she pulled off her gloves and tucked them into her pockets.

Liz and Emma watched as she headed down the hall toward the library, then they continued on to the kitchen, where they helped themselves to coffee and tea.

"How is your work going?" Liz cradled her cup in her hands and leaned against the counter as Emma stirred sweetener into her mug of green tea.

"It's going very well. It's a thrill to see so many beautiful works of art."

"I know what you mean. I'm drawing on the colors from this spectacular Matisse painting Jackson showed me for the web site design. You have to ask him to show it to you sometime." Liz sighed. "I guess we'd better get back to work." She glanced at the clock over the kitchen sink. "Matt has an appointment this afternoon so I have to get Alice from ballet class at three."

Emma smiled at the thought of Alice, her goddaughter, with her blond hair and sweet disposition. Alice's brother, Ben, was a few years younger and adored his big sister. Emma felt a pang of jealousy. It would be nice to have her life settled . . . once and for all.

They were heading back to their respective work areas when they heard loud voices coming from the library. Emma and Liz stopped in their tracks and looked at each other. Emma gestured toward the library with her chin. Liz shot Emma a grin before following her down the hall.

They stopped well short of the door to the library. They didn't have to go much closer—the two feminine voices were loud and agitated.

"Sounds like Joy," Liz whispered. "But who is the other?"

"Sabina, I think." Emma listened carefully. "Yes, I'm sure that's Sabina."

They could make out a few words here and there but one phrase rang out loud and clear. It was Sabina speaking. "You know nothing!" she yelled.

Emma and Liz pressed themselves back against the wall as Sabina stomped from the room, her cheeks flushed bright red with indignation, her dark eyes snapping in fury.

Chapter 12

SWEET Nothings was busy on Saturday morning, with one customer coming in as another was leaving. Emma kept a watch on Arabella—she didn't want her to overdo it and get too tired. Sylvia had several bra-fitting appointments, and Emma was keeping an eye on her, too. She was even older than Arabella, and Emma didn't want anything to happen to her. She plunged her hand into her short, dark hair and took a deep breath. Was it time for them to hire some younger help?

It was just after noon when the door jingled again, and Bitsy stuck her head around the edge.

"I've brought you some cupcakes." She held out a white bakery box tied with red and white variegated string and dangled it in front of them. "I'm trying out a new flavor, and I need an opinion."

"You've come to the right place," Emma said.

Bitsy put the box down on the counter, snipped the string with the scissors Emma handed her and lifted the lid. "They're salted caramel with dulce de leche frosting."

Emma lifted one from the box. She'd just had a small salad for lunch and was craving something sweet.

Bitsy watched intensely, her brows drawn together over her enormous blue eyes, as Emma took a bite.

Emma sighed. She could have sworn her eyes rolled back in her head.

"Are they okay?" Bitsy chewed on the edge of her thumb.

"They're . . . they're divine," Emma breathed. "Heavenly and sinful at the same time if that's possible." She laughed.

Bitsy laughed, too. "Phew. I was afraid they were going to be a bust. I started experimenting in the kitchen, and one thing led to another."

"I'd say you've got a hit on your hands."

"You can't be too sure," Sylvia said, reaching into the box. "I think this calls for a second opinion." She selected a cupcake, peeled off the wrapper and took a bite. "Emma is right. These are fabulous—sinfully rich and utterly heavenly. What a combination." Sylvia took another bite and closed her eyes contentedly.

"Aunt Arabella?" Emma held the box toward her aunt.

Arabella smiled. "No, thanks." She patted her stomach. "As Priscilla has pointed out, I've gained a few pounds since she last saw me. Time I started watching what I eat. Francis has corrupted me. We've tried all the new restaurants within a fifty-mile radius, and when we're not eating out, we're cooking wickedly fattening things together."

"I am just so relieved you gals like them," Bitsy said. "They'll be tomorrow's special." She crossed her fingers and held them up. "Here's hoping they'll be a success."

"I know they will be," Emma reassured her.

Just then the phone on Arabella's desk in the stockroom rang. They all jumped. That phone didn't ring all that often. People generally went online to find the store's address, its hours and what exactly Sweet Nothings sold.

Something about the ring set Emma's teeth on edge although she couldn't say what—it sounded just as it always did. She picked it up on the fourth ring, and answered a little breathlessly. "Hello, Sweet Nothings. How may I help you?"

"Emma?" Liz's voice came over the line. It was half question, half sob.

Emma felt the tiny hairs on the back of her neck stand up. "Liz? What is it?"

A groan that turned into a sob was the only answer to her question.

Emma gripped the phone tightly. "Liz! You've got to tell me what's wrong." All sorts of scenarios ran through her head. Was it Matt? Alice or Ben? Emma didn't know how Liz would bear it if anything happened to them.

"It's . . . it's Brian." Liz's words ended on another sob.

Emma felt herself go very still. Everything around her faded into a swirling mist that appeared out of nowhere. All her senses were heightened. She heard each tick of the clock on the wall over Arabella's desk; felt the slickness of the plastic telephone receiver in her hand; tasted the brown sugar in her mouth from Bitsy's cupcakes. "Brian?"

Liz groaned again, and Emma heard her take a deep breath to steady herself. "There's been an accident," she said bluntly, as if all the emotion had suddenly been leached out of her. "Brian . . . Brian fell off a ladder. They've called an ambulance, and the EMTs are there now. At best it's a broken leg. At worst it's . . ." Liz gave another sob, unable to go on.

"What? What is it, Liz?" Emma gripped the telephone receiver so tightly pain shot up her arm and into her shoulder.

"He was wearing his hard hat. He always does, and he makes sure his crew does the same," Liz said all in a rush. "But something happened. The strap broke . . . I don't know how or why. But it slipped off as he fell, and oh, Emma, it's terrible. He's unconscious, and they have no idea when . . . or even if . . . he'll ever come out of it."

Emma ended the call and looked up to see Arabella and Sylvia standing in the doorway. Arabella's face was pale, accentuating the dark circles under her eyes.

"What's wrong?" Arabella asked, her face mirroring her concern. "It sounded bad."

Emma vowed she wouldn't cry. She would be brave and strong and stoic. She had to do it for Liz. But it was so terribly hard. "It's Brian," she managed to get out.

Arabella and Sylvia turned even whiter. "What's happened? Please tell us." Arabella took Emma's hands in hers and squeezed them. "Poor dear, you're freezing."

"According to Liz, there's been an accident." Emma took a deep breath and straightened her shoulders. She had to be brave. "Brian fell off a ladder. He's broken his leg, and there's some concern that he may have a concussion."

Arabella's shoulder's relaxed a tiny bit. "That's terrible, but he can overcome a broken leg, and concussions are a dime a dozen these days."

Emma looked away, not wanting to meet her aunt's gaze.

"You need to get to the hospital right away," Sylvia declared decisively. "I'll drive you. You're obviously in no state to go by yourself."

"Will you be okay?" Emma looked at Arabella.

"Oh, don't fuss about me. I'll be fine. But call me the minute you know anything, okay?"

Emma promised. She allowed herself to be led out to Sylvia's ancient Cadillac and belted into the passenger seat. Arabella tucked Emma's purse in alongside her and shut the door. Emma could see Arabella in the side-view mirror standing at the back door of Sweet Nothings, her arms folded across her chest, as they pulled out of the Sweet Nothings parking lot.

IT didn't take them long to get to the Henry County Medical Center. Emma was so numb she was nearly oblivious to the horns blaring behind Sylvia as they made their way down Tyson Avenue, but she was still relieved when they pulled into the lot. Sylvia maneuvered the Cadillac into a space in the emergency parking area.

"I can get a ride back with Liz, so there's no need for you to stay. Arabella will need you at the shop." Emma jumped out of the car, nearly forgetting her purse in her distress.

"You sure you don't want me to come in with you?"

"I'll be fine. But I don't want Arabella to be alone for too long."

Sylvia nodded, put the Caddy in gear, and slowly backed out of the space, narrowly missing a light stanchion, a parked police car and a large stone planter. Emma could hear Sylvia's brakes squealing in the distance as she pushed open the door to the emergency room.

Two nurses in blue scrubs sat behind the registration desk.

One looked up from putting papers into a folder. "Can I help you?"

"Brian is here," Emma said somewhat incoherently. "I need to see him."

The nurse gave her a practiced smile. "If you could just give me his last name?" Her fingers hovered over the keys of her computer.

"O'Connell," Emma managed. She looked around, praying to spot Liz, but she must have gone through already. "Brian O'Connell."

The nurse tapped a number of keys then looked up at Emma and frowned. "Are you a relative?"

Emma was about to say *no* when she thought better of it. What if they wouldn't let her go back to see Brian? "I'm his wife," she said, crossing her fingers behind her back in the childish gesture they used to make when they were younger.

"I'm so sorry, Mrs. O'Connell." The nurse's eyes strayed to the computer again. "Mr. O'Connell's sister is with him now." She pulled a name badge toward her and reached for a marker from the jar on her desk. "First name, please?" Her hand hovered over the sticker.

"Emma. Emma O'Connell."

The nurse wrote the name down in careful block letters then wrote *Room 15* underneath. She handed it to Emma.

Emma peeled off the backing and waited while the nurse buzzed open the emergency room door.

"Take a left at the end of the hall. Room fifteen is on the right."

Emma took a deep breath and walked through the door. She wasn't squeamish, but she was terrified of what she would find. How would Brian look? Would he be bruised? Bandaged? Would she even recognize him?

Emma got to the end of the hall and hesitated. Had the nurse said to go right or left? She thought left so she headed in that direction. She found room number 15 easily enough and pushed aside the curtain slightly, peering around the edge. Liz was seated in an orange, molded plastic chair beside the bed, her shoulders drooping, chin in her hands.

Brian was on the gurney, eyes closed, his right leg in a splint. He was hooked up to an IV along with various other tubes and wires. Machines beeped and lights flashed dizzyingly. For one moment Emma thought she would faint, but she forced herself to take deep breaths. She needed to be strong for Liz's sake.

Liz must have sensed her standing there. She whirled around. "Emma!" She jumped from her seat and threw her arms around Emma, burying her face in her friend's neck. Emma felt tears pricking the backs of her eyelids and reminded herself she had to stay strong for Liz.

Liz pulled away slightly and fished a tissue from the pocket of her pants. She blew her nose and laughed. "I've already used up the whole box that was in here." She gestured toward an empty tissue box sitting on the bedside tray. She gave Emma another quick hug. "I'm so glad you're here.

Matt is with the kids. One of the guys from the crew was here earlier, but I sent him home." She wrinkled her nose. "He smelled like dirt and concrete."

Emma gave a laugh that turned into a hiccup. She grabbed Liz's arm. "How . . . how is he?" She glanced at Brian lying so still and pale on the bed.

Liz shook her head. "They've done a CT scan, and we're waiting for the results. Apparently he seemed fine at first— apart from the broken leg—but then he lost consciousness. It's possible they will have to operate. The doctor thinks there's some swelling of the brain." Liz gave a sob and buried her face in her hands. "It's all so hard to understand."

Emma felt just as lost. "But he will wake up . . . right?"

"I think so. Once they do the operation to relieve the pressure. The doctor should be back any minute now."

"Can I get you some water or coffee . . . ?"

Liz shook her head. "I'm fine. The nurse brought me some water. I'm afraid caffeine would make me even more jumpy than I already am." She glanced at Emma and gave her a smile. "Hey," she said suddenly, "what's that?" She pointed at the name tag on Emma's shirt.

Emma felt her face turn red. "I was afraid they wouldn't let me in if I wasn't related so I . . . lied."

"Good for you! What did you say? You're his sister?"

Emma ducked her head. "No," she said more to the floor than to Liz. "I said I was his wife."

"Oh, I wish!" Liz cried, jumping to her feet and hugging Emma again. "Brian adores you . . . it's only a matter of time."

Emma felt a deep warmth spread throughout her. She

knew what she wanted—a life with Brian, no matter what that entailed. She looked at his silent form and sent up a fervent prayer.

Suddenly the curtain to Brian's room was pulled aside, the rings clattering against the metal rod, and a woman stepped in. She had on a white coat with a stethoscope protruding from her pocket and a clipboard in her hand. She looked at Emma quizzically.

"This is Brian's wife," Liz explained.

The woman consulted her chart briefly. "I thought . . . the forms said . . ." She shrugged as if it wasn't important and stuck out her hand. "Pleased to meet you. I'm Dr. Mitchell."

Both Emma and Liz looked at her expectantly.

"We've done a CT scan on Mr. O'Connell, and we did find some swelling of the brain. That's normal in cases where there has been a sharp impact to the head. The good news is that we will be able to treat it." She consulted her notes again. "It's a minor procedure that involves draining fluid from the space around the brain." She pointed to her head. "It's generally quite successful."

"What about his leg?" Liz knitted her hands together.

Dr. Mitchell smiled. "I'm afraid you'll have to speak to the orthopedic surgeon about his leg." She tucked her clipboard under her arm. "Transport will be along shortly to take him into the operating room. I'll be able to fix the swelling in his brain, and Dr. Harrison—she's a brilliant orthopedic surgeon—will attend to his leg." She looked at the clock over the gurney where Brian lay, oblivious to everything going on. "I'd suggest you think about going home and getting some rest so you can be here when he wakes up."

Emma and Liz looked at each other. Emma put her arm

around Liz. "You go home. You have the kids to deal with. Arabella will look after Bette. I can stay."

"Are you sure?" Liz had already grabbed her handbag.

"Absolutely."

Liz gave Emma a quick hug and kiss. "Thanks. Call me if anything changes. I just need to make sure that Alice gets her project done for history class tomorrow."

Emma nodded and waved good-bye. She sank into the orange plastic chair and watched as all the monitors surrounding Brian sighed and beeped. She decided right then and there that she didn't care about anything but being with him. Europe could wait. Her career could wait. Right now, Brian was the most important thing in her life.

Emma sat in the chair without moving until the cold began to creep into her limbs. Her right foot had gone to sleep, and she had a minor but persistent throbbing in her left temple. Her eyes were closing, and she was nearly dozing off when the curtains to the cubicle parted and a man in scrubs bustled in.

"Time to take"—he glanced at the chart hanging from the end of Brian's bed—"Mr. O'Connell down to surgery. Do you want me to show you where you can wait?"

Emma nodded. "Please."

He released the brakes on the gurney and began to push it out of the room. "Follow me. There's a waiting room on the surgery floor." He looked at Emma over the rims of his glasses. "You can get yourself a cup of coffee, and there's a snack machine with chips, cookies and granola bars—pretty unhealthy stuff, considering this is a hospital."

Emma picked up her purse and followed him out of the room.

She surreptitiously held Brian's hand as they went up in the elevator. She thought she felt him return her squeeze, but she was probably imagining it. The fellow from transport whistled between his teeth as they waited for their floor. As soon as the doors had swished open, he pushed the gurney out and Emma followed.

"Waiting room is down there." He jerked his head to the right.

Emma gave Brian one last look and headed in the direction the man had indicated.

Three other people were already in the waiting room. Emma chose a chair away from them and near the window. Dog-eared magazines were stacked on a wooden table. Emma glanced through them, chose a women's fashion magazine, and began to flip through the pages. After five minutes, she tossed it back on the table. She couldn't concentrate. All she could think about was Brian and what was happening in the operating room.

She got up for a drink of water, scrolled through her e-mail on her phone . . . anything to pass the time. The hands on the clock moved excruciatingly slowly. Emma was looking out the window, watching the cars come and go from the parking lot, when the doctor came in.

"Mrs. O'Connell."

For a moment, the name didn't register, but then Emma whirled around.

The doctor pulled off her pink surgical cap. "Everything went fine. Mr. O'Connell is in the recovery room, and we don't anticipate any problems. He'll be there for a few hours. You might want to consider going home and getting some rest."

Emma nodded numbly. *Brian was going to be okay.* She felt her face break out into a huge grin, and she realized that her hands were shaking as she gathered up her purse, coat and gloves.

She would call Arabella to pick her up. She pulled her cell phone from her purse and punched in her aunt's number. As soon as she ended that call, she quickly dialed Liz.

Chapter 13

EMMA got to the hospital early on Sunday morning. This time, she wasn't required to have a name badge since Brian had been moved to a regular room, so there was no need to pretend to be Brian's wife. Liz was already there, looking as if she hadn't slept a wink the night before, when Emma arrived. She was sitting in the bedside chair, her computer on her lap, a cardboard cup of coffee on the floor beside her. She looked up when Emma entered.

"Hey. You look terrible. Did you sleep at all?"

Emma shook her head.

"Neither did I." Liz glanced at Brian's still form on the bed and smiled. "He's sleeping. He regained consciousness this morning. The doctor said he's going to be okay." Liz suddenly burst into tears.

Emma knelt at Liz's feet and took Liz's hands in hers. "That's wonderful, Liz. I'm so relieved." She felt hot tears spilling over her own lids and cascading down her cheeks.

"He was only awake for a short time, but he recognized me." Liz pulled a tissue from her pocket and blew her nose. "They've set his leg and drained the fluid that had accumulated around his brain. Both procedures were successful. Hopefully the fracture will heal quickly and he'll be up and around in no time."

Emma looked at Brian asleep in the hospital bed. Her heart swelled to the point where she thought it would burst.

"The doctor said he might sleep for hours," Liz said wiping her eyes with the tissue. "You're welcome to stay, but there's no real need. I can call you when he wakes up. I know he'll want to see you."

Emma nodded. "Okay. I want to check on Aunt Arabella. She's not been herself lately. I don't know what it is."

Emma bent and brushed Brian's lips with hers. She stood for a moment watching him sleep then turned around. "Promise you'll call me if you need me."

Liz held up her hand. "Promise."

Emma left the room with a one last backward glance at Brian. His face was pale, and there were hollows under his eyes, but he was going to be okay. Her spirits rose like a kite in a strong breeze.

She found her way down the hall, into the elevator and back out to the parking lot where she'd left her car.

Emma thought about calling Arabella first, but decided not to bother. Her aunt knew she was coming to get Bette after visiting the hospital. She stopped at Kroger's and picked up croissants, some strawberry preserves and a bouquet of flowers that caught her eye. They reminded her of spring—and the fact that it would arrive sooner or later— and she hoped they would cheer Arabella up.

Priscilla opened the door when Emma arrived.

"Emma, darling." She was already perfectly made up and coiffed and was wearing tan cords and a black V-neck sweater. She took the grocery bag from Emma and peeked inside. "What have you brought?"

"Some croissants, preserves and some flowers for Aunt Arabella."

"Aren't you sweet! We've got coffee going in the kitchen if you'd like a cup."

"I'll take some tea, if you don't mind."

Emma followed her mother out to the kitchen. Francis was seated at the head of the table, the *Paris Post-Intelligencer* spread out around him, a cup of coffee at his elbow. Arabella was at the stove frying some bacon.

"I've brought some croissants and strawberry preserves," Emma announced.

"Wonderful, dear. I've got some bacon going, and I can rustle up some eggs if anyone is interested." Arabella wiped her hands on her apron. "But do tell us how Brian is doing. Has there been any improvement?"

Emma gave a broad smile. "He's conscious according to Liz, although he was sleeping while I was there. But it looks like everything will be okay eventually." She sank down onto one of Arabella's kitchen chairs. Her knees had suddenly become weak.

"Darling, you don't look very good." Priscilla put a hand on Emma's shoulder. "Maybe you should put your head down."

"I'm not going to faint, Mother, don't worry."

"It's the shock," Arabella said as she lifted the crispy pieces of bacon from the pan and placed them on a paper towel–lined plate. "We need to get some food into you."

Emma allowed herself to be fussed over, although she felt slightly guilty since her intention had been to check on Arabella, not the other way around. After a well-buttered croissant, a healthy helping of bacon and a cup of green tea, she felt much better.

Arabella finally joined them at the table, cup of coffee in hand. She made a disgusted noise. "That Detective Walker was around again. He stopped by Sweet Nothings yesterday."

"What?" Emma said.

Arabella nodded and looked around the table. "He keeps asking me the same question—where did I go during the fireworks the night Hugo was killed. I already told him the last time he asked. I was tired and needed a rest. I went out to the lobby, found a comfortable chair and sat down for a bit with my feet up." She looked around the table again. "No crime in that, is there?"

Emma and Francis looked at each other. The last time Arabella had talked to Walker, she'd told him that she'd spent that particular period of time in the ladies' room powdering her nose. Why the sudden change of story?

Francis gathered together the newspaper, grabbed his cup of coffee and prepared to retreat to the small room that Arabella had turned into a study. On his way out of the kitchen, he tapped Emma on the shoulder. "If I could talk to you for a minute?" His dark brows rose up, creating a V above his coal black eyes.

Emma swept up the last of her croissant crumbs and

brushed them into the palm of her hand. She dropped them in the sink before following Francis down the hall.

Francis dropped into the leather swivel chair behind the desk that Arabella had said had been in the family for several generations. She even claimed there was a mark on the left side where a bullet shot during the Civil War had pierced the window and nicked the desk.

The chair groaned as Francis leaned back in it, steepling his fingers under his chin and squaring his jaw. "It's your aunt," he said finally.

Emma leaned forward slightly.

"Walker seems to think she has the strongest motive in Hugh's death. Even though her motive is decades old." Francis snorted in disgust. He fiddled with a letter opener on the desk. "Unfortunately, this isn't my case so my hands are tied." He clenched and unclenched his fists. "It doesn't help that Arabella is giving him conflicting stories about where she went during the fireworks. First she told him she went to the ladies' room to freshen up, then the next time he asks, she's saying she was out in the lobby sitting with her feet up." Francis looked down at his clasped hands. "I don't understand it. It almost as if . . . as if she doesn't actually remember what she did." He looked up at Emma, his face etched with distress.

Emma felt her stomach plummet to her knees. Arabella had always been so . . . *sharp*. She remembered every family member's birthday, never missed an appointment and called all their regular customers by name. Was it possible she was losing her *memory*?

Emma shuddered. It wasn't possible. Not Arabella. It was

stress or fatigue or depression. There couldn't possibly be anything more wrong with her than that. A vacation or some vitamins, and she'd be as good as new.

"What should we do?" Emma asked.

Francis looked even more distressed. He studied his hands as if they held the answer. "I don't know." He looked up at Emma. "Maybe if you can just . . . keep an eye on her? Don't let her work too hard." He shrugged. "Although I know that's nearly impossible. She's put her heart and soul into that store."

"I'll try." Emma nodded her head enthusiastically. "I definitely will. Do you think we ought to call Dr. Baker? He's known Arabella for forty years. Maybe he'd know what's wrong?"

Francis cleared his throat. "I don't want to alarm your aunt. Maybe it's best if we wait and see how things pan out. As long as you can keep an eye on her during the day."

Emma nodded vigorously. "Of course. No problem. I was beginning to think that perhaps we might need to hire some . . . younger help."

"That's an idea." Francis leaned back in his chair. "But I wouldn't bring it up right now. I don't want Arabella to think . . ." He cleared his throat. "Let's just keep an eye on her."

"Absolutely. Perhaps Eloise Montgomery can fill in some more and Arabella can have a break. Eloise won't seem as much of a threat as someone younger might."

"She still won't like it." Francis smiled. "But perhaps if we go about it subtly, she won't notice we're trying to make things easier on her."

Emma laughed. "It's pretty hard to fool Arabella, but I suppose we can try."

"Yes, I imagine that's the best we can do."

EMMA was a little late getting down to Sweet Nothings on Monday morning. Bette had thought it quite a fun game to make Emma chase her whenever Emma got close enough to clip on the puppy's leash. Emma tried to be serious as she ordered Bette to *stay*, but it was impossible to keep from laughing, let alone maintain a straight face, when Bette tilted her head in that cute way she had or when she wagged her tail so hard her entire body shook.

Finally Bette got tired of the game and let Emma fasten the leash, but by then Emma's hair was in such disarray from trying to get Bette out from under the bed or from behind the clothes hanging in the closet, that she had to retreat to the bathroom briefly to run a comb through it and repair the damage.

Emma smelled coffee as soon as she opened the door to the shop—Arabella had obviously already arrived. She was busy removing a gown from one of the mannequins.

"I think this one needs a change. She's been wearing the Olga long enough."

"What did you have in mind?"

"I don't know." Arabella stood in front of the cupboards. She clicked through the hangers. "How about this one?" She pulled out a gown and held it toward Emma.

"That's beautiful. I don't think I've seen that one before."

"I'd almost forgotten about it myself," Arabella said, fingering the delicate fabric. "The colors of robes and nightgowns got rather wild starting in the 1950s. I guess everyone had had their fill of peach, pink and pale blue." Arabella placed the hot-pink and violet gown on the counter. It had spaghetti straps, a ruffled bodice, pink and violet panels in the full skirt and a satin ribbon crisscrossing the waist. Arabella glanced at the label. "Vanity Fair. Excellent condition."

Emma helped her aunt slip the gown over the manne-quin's head. She fluffed out the skirt and stood back to admire the effect. "It won't be long before this sells."

Arabella looked up suddenly. "What were you and Fran-cis whispering about in the study yesterday? I peeked in, and you both looked so serious."

Emma felt her face get hot. She'd never been particularly good at lying. "Oh . . . um . . . we were just discussing the case."

Arabella gave Emma a look that very clearly said she didn't believe her.

"I do wish Francis would stop fussing about it. I told him, and I told Detective Walker, that I went out to the coat-check room. I'd left my lipstick in my coat pocket, and I needed a touch-up."

Emma stood stock still, the skirt of the Vanity Fair neg-ligee clenched in her hand.

"What's wrong, dear?" Arabella looked at her. "If you keep hold of the material like that you're going to wrin-kle it."

Emma swallowed hard. "Arabella." She turned toward her aunt, and she knew she had tears in her eyes.

"You must tell me what's wrong." Arabella's face was scrunched with concern. "Brian is okay, isn't he? You said so. You said the operation was a success. "It's not Brian I'm worried about, Aunt Arabella. It's you."

"Me?" Arabella fiddled with the spill of ruffles on her pale blue blouse. "What on earth for?"

Emma took a deep breath. "The first time Detective Walker asked you where you went during the fireworks at the party, you said you'd gone to the ladies' room." Emma fussed with the skirt on the mannequin and bent to straighten the hem. She didn't want to look at Arabella.

"The next time he asked, you said you'd gone out to the lobby to put your feet up and rest." Emma stood up and looked her aunt in the face. "And just now you told me you went to the coat check."

Arabella's hand's fluttered around her face. "Surely you don't think that I'm lying and I . . . I had something to do with Hugo's death."

"Of course not." Emma put her arm around her aunt. "But don't you see how it looks to Detective Walker? You keep changing your story. You need to tell him where you really went. Then we can get all of this sorted out."

Arabella's face crumpled and she put her hand over her mouth. "That's the problem, dear."

"What is?" Emma asked as gently as possible.

"I don't remember where I went."

"You don't remember?"

Arabella shook her head. "No.

"It was a busy evening," Emma said consolingly. "With so much going on. And on top of the shock of seeing Hugh again after all these years. I'm not surprised—"

"It's not just that. I'm forgetting other things, too. Priscilla noticed." Arabella looked at Emma, her blue eyes wide. "What if I'm losing my memory? What am I going to do?"

"I'm sure it's not that," Emma said trying to convince Arabella as much as herself. She, too, had noticed Arabella becoming more forgetful—little things that she had put down to stress. "I think the first order of business is to see Dr. Baker."

Arabella gave a brave smile and wiped a hand across her eyes. "You're right, dear. I probably need a good checkup. It's most likely just stress. Probably nothing at all to be concerned about."

"That's right," Emma said consolingly.

Neither of them sounded convinced.

Chapter 14

EMMA wasn't sure if Liz would be there when she got to the Grangers', but her station wagon was parked in the driveway as usual.

"You look terribly glum," Liz said when Emma stuck her head into the office to say hello. "I hope you're not worrying about Brian. The doctor was quite positive that everything is going to be fine."

"It's not Brian. It's Aunt Arabella." Emma leaned against the wall and watched as Liz adjusted the lens on her camera. "She's afraid her memory is going. I think it's just stress, but unfortunately, she's told Detective Walker three different stories about where she was during the fireworks when Hugh was killed."

Liz now looked as concerned as Emma felt. "The stress

must be getting to your aunt. We have to figure out who did murder Hugh and put an end to all this," Liz said in a near whisper. "Personally, I'd like to know where Mariel was when Granger was killed. That dark-haired fellow was here again today—the one we saw her sneaking around with on the terrace the other night. I was pulling into the driveway when I noticed him walking across the field toward the barn, where she was checking on her horse."

"It seems strange to me that he never comes into the house."

"Not if they're having an affair. He's probably keeping his distance until everything is settled." Liz stretched her arms overhead. "I could do with some hot coffee. How about you?" She shivered. "It's awfully chilly in here today. Or maybe it's because I'm tired."

"I'll grab some tea before I get started."

The hall was silent, and the foyer was empty. Mail was stacked neatly on the foyer table alongside a vase of fresh flowers. Emma made another mental note to clean off the table in her own entryway. She paused for a moment to enjoy the scent of the flowers as she and Liz went by on their way to the kitchen.

Molly was in the kitchen, vigorously wiping down the counter with a sponge. She was putting some real elbow grease into it, as Emma's grandmother would have said. She nodded at Emma and Liz. "Good afternoon to you."

Emma grabbed a mug, filled it with water and put it in the microwave.

Molly put down her sponge and leaned closer to the kitchen window. She pointed outside. "I think I see a robin. Sure sign that spring is around the corner."

"That would be great. I've had enough of winter." Emma joined Molly at the window and looked out. She didn't notice any birds, but she did spy the man they'd seen with Mariel the other night, picking his way across the rutted and frozen field. The wind blew his dark hair around his face, and he held the collar of his coat closed with one hand.

"Who is that?" Emma pointed toward the fellow, trying to sound completely guileless. "He looks familiar, but I can't place him."

Molly took the bait. She stood on tiptoe and looked out the window again. "Oh, that's Dr. Sampson. He's been treating Mrs. Granger ever since she fell from her horse last year. Apparently the pain still hasn't gone away. Something with her back." Molly put a hand to her own back.

"He certainly seems very attentive," Emma said.

Molly laughed. "Very attentive, indeed." She turned to face Emma, and the look and the wink she gave her said it all.

EMMA and Liz took their drinks back to the office where Liz was working.

"What do you think she was trying to tell us?" Liz asked, taking a tentative sip of her hot coffee.

Emma snorted. "I'm pretty sure her message was that Dr. Sampson is a lot more than just Mariel Granger's doctor."

"It would certainly give her a motive for wanting to be rid of her husband to pave the way for Lover Boy." Liz blew on her coffee. "Of course, she's not the only one with a motive. The daughter, Joy, had a good reason to hate her father—her mother is killed, she's left crippled, and the only person left in her world, her father, rejects her. I can't imagine what it must have been like for her." Liz wiped away a tear that was dribbling down her cheek. She clenched her fists. "Makes me feel like killing him myself, and I never even knew him."

"I know. Joy was one of the people whose contact information the police were missing, according to Francis's sources in the department. Along with Mariel's, and Jackson's, of course."

"Jackson seems to have the least reason for wanting his father dead. He does inherit the business, and now he can run it the way he wants, but I can't see that moving him to . . . murder. Can you?"

Liz looked at Emma, and Emma shook her head. "No, not really. It's terribly . . . extreme."

Emma chewed on a nail. "What about his partner, Tom Roberts?"

"Tom?" Liz tilted her head to the side, considering. "Other than that I think he's kind of creepy and has a beautiful wife, I don't see him in the role." She was quiet for a moment. "I wish there was a way to find out if Mariel left the party before the fireworks started. Maybe she went to meet this Dr. Granger somewhere and that's why she won't admit it?"

"It seems awfully risky considering the party was for her husband, and she was the hostess." Emma had a sudden idea. "What kind of car does she drive?"

"I've seen her running around in a red Porsche Boxster. Why?"

"If she planned on leaving the party for some reason—to meet her lover or to get away after she'd murdered her husband—she probably took her own car to the Beau. They had valet parking that night. And I doubt a lot of people pulled up in a Porsche Boxster, especially a red one. Maybe one of the valets will remember when he brought the car back around for her." Emma stood up. "Do you think you'd have time to run over there after work? Arabella is going to watch Bette for me, and I'll still have time to stop by to visit Brian."

Liz's face broke into a grin. "I wouldn't dream of letting you go alone. I'll give Matt a call and see if he can throw some hamburgers on the grill and get the kids started on their homework."

EMMA worked her way through another section of paintings; glancing at her watch, she realized it was five o'clock. She saved her work, powered off the computer and gathered her things together. She stuck her head into the office. "Will Matt be able to take care of the kids if we go over to the Beau?" Liz looked up, startled. "Five o'clock already?" She turned off her photography lights and began to disassemble them. "Yes, he said it was no problem."

Emma had always been impressed with Liz and Matt's marriage. Their mutual give-and-take kept both of them happy and things running smoothly.

"I'll meet you there." Emma said after Liz had packed up her gear and they were each heading toward their cars.

Emma kept Liz in her rearview mirror on the drive to the Beau. They pulled into the circular drive in front of the hotel, parking just beyond the entrance, where they wouldn't be in the way. The driveway was empty and the valet was not in sight. The tall, ornamental grasses in front of the hotel were wheat-colored now, with feathery fronds on top. They swayed back and forth in the chilly winter breeze.

Emma approached Liz's car. "I don't see anyone. Maybe we should ask inside?"

She had barely finished speaking when she noticed a young man approaching them. He was wearing black pants, a ruffled white shirt and a short white jacket, and was obviously a hotel employee.

"Can I help you?" he asked when he reached Liz's car.

"Are you the valet?" Emma asked.

"Yes. Want me to park the cars for you?"

Emma shook her head. "No. We actually wanted to ask you some questions."

A wary look came over his face, and he smoothed an index finger over his dark mustache. "I suppose that's okay."

"Were you here Saturday night for the big party given by the Grangers?"

"Yeah. Me plus Ricky and Steve. I don't usually work Saturdays. The wife wasn't happy about it. She likes to go out for a drink and maybe a bite to eat on Saturdays, but it was all men on deck for the party." He ran a hand across the back of his neck. "I'm Manny, by the way."

"Are Ricky and Steve here, too?"

"Nah. Weeknights are quiet. I can handle it all by myself." He looked from Emma to Liz. "What is it you want with them? I can give them a message. If there was some damage to your car or something stolen though, you'll have to talk to the hotel manager." He tipped his head toward the entrance to the Beau.

Emma took a deep breath. "We were wondering if any

of you remember parking a red Porsche Boxster that night." Emma looked to Liz for confirmation, and Liz nodded.

The valet whistled. "We don't get a lot of cars like that. Plenty of expensive ones, mind you, but usually dark-colored, late-model BMWs, Mercedes, Audis. Nothing too sporty, you know what I mean."

Emma nodded.

"So yeah, the Boxster really stood out. Ricky parked it. He was really jazzed about driving a Porsche even if he didn't go more than a couple hundred feet in it. He couldn't stop talking about it."

Emma smiled at Manny. "That's very helpful. Now, do you happen to remember when the owner left? Did Ricky bring the car back out?"

Manny nodded his head. "Yeah. There was no way he was going to let anyone else have a chance to drive it." He looked over toward the entrance to the hotel, as if judging whether or not anyone could hear him. He lowered his voice and gave Emma and Liz a conspiratorial look. "Just between you and me—because I can tell you ladies are cool—Ricky said he gave it a little spin around the block. Handled like a dream, he said."

"So Ricky was the one who brought the car back to its owner?" Emma asked.

Manny laughed. "You bet. As I said, he wasn't going to let anyone else drive it."

"Do you happen to have any idea when the owner left the party?" Emma crossed her fingers behind her back.

"Sure. Ricky was about to punch out when the lady who owned the car came out of the hotel. I've never known Ricky to stay even a minute overtime, but he didn't hesitate.

Strolled right up and told her he'd be back in a second with her car."

"This would have been around . . . ?"

"Nine o'clock. Ricky was due to leave at nine, and Chuck was taking the nine to midnight shift. He works at Tom Mulligan's garage days, but he likes to pick up a little extra cash when he can, and he doesn't mind the late hours so Dan—that's our boss—always schedules him for that shift."

Emma and Liz looked at each other.

"You've been really helpful, Manny. Thanks so much."

"Hey, whatever I can do to help out a couple of pretty ladies." He winked at them and strolled, whistling, toward the entrance of the hotel.

Emma and Liz watched him walk away. They remained silent until the revolving door at the entrance to the hotel had swallowed him up.

Emma frowned. "If Manny is telling the truth, Mariel is in the clear. The fireworks didn't start until nearly ten o'clock, and she had already gone by then."

"Looks like she had a rendezvous with someone. And I think I can guess who."

"The good-looking Dr. Sampson," Emma said.

Chapter 15

BRIAN was sitting up in bed when Emma got to the hospital later that evening. His leg was in a cast and had been propped on a pillow. A bedside tray with the remains of dinner was pushed to one side, and he had a paperback book splayed open on the bed beside him.

"You are a sight for sore eyes," he said, his face lighting up as Emma entered the room.

She sat on the edge of his bed, and Brian gathered her into his arms. Emma put her head on his shoulder and tried not to let the tears that were pricking the backs of her eyelids escape. They stayed like that for several minutes.

"I've brought you some things," Emma said, pulling away slightly. "I've got Monday's *Post-Intelligencer*, the latest issue of *Sports Illustrated*"—she brandished the cover at him—"and some fresh fruit."

"You're here. That's what I care about." Brian gave her a big grin. "Tell me what's going on. I hate being trapped here like this." He pointed at his leg. "It's very frustrating."

"You'll be up and around in no time, I'm sure."

Brian laughed. "They had me on crutches today to practice. It's not easy getting the hang of those things." He pointed to the newspaper. "I feel so out of it—getting clonked on the head and losing a couple of days. Has anything happened in the Granger case? Do the police know who pushed Hugh Granger off the balcony at his own party?"

"No . . ."

"The way you said that doesn't sound good."

Emma sighed and Brian took her hand in his. A feeling of contentment washed over her. So what if Brian didn't feel the same urge to travel that she did, or was beyond certain that he'd never grow tired of the small town they'd grown up in? Being with him was all that really mattered. Everything else could be worked out.

Emma wound a loose thread from her sweater around her finger. "Liz and I were convinced that Mariel Granger was guilty. After all, isn't the spouse always the first one the police suspect?"

"It is in the movies."

"She wouldn't tell the police where she'd gone when she left the party, and that alone is suspicious."

Brian raised an eyebrow, and Emma felt her face grow hot.

"Liz and I managed to . . . overhear . . . her conversation

with Detective Walker. We think she may have had a rendezvous with her lover—twice Liz and I saw her meeting this Dr. Sampson. They looked very furtive." Emma's words came out in a rush, tumbling over each other. "It seemed obvious there was more to their relationship than just doctor and patient."

"Sampson?" Brian tilted his head to the side, thinking. "The name sounds familiar." He drew his brows together. "Greg Sampson?"

"I don't know his first name."

"This was before you came back to Paris," Brian said, easing himself up higher on his pillows.

"Do you need help . . ."

"No, I'm fine." Brian settled down again with a slight grimace. "An old fraternity brother of mine did a number on his back playing a game of touch football at a family barbecue. He went to this Dr. Sampson, who recommended the usual stuff—heat then physical therapy followed by an exercise regimen, but he also gave my friend . . . Zack . . . something for the pain. Zack was really hurting so he was glad to have the pills. The only problem was that he became addicted to them. And this Dr. Sampson was more than willing to continue to write prescriptions long after Zack should have stopped taking the stuff. Finally Sampson was busted. It seems Zack wasn't the only one getting pills from him. It was a three-day wonder in the newspaper. He lost his license for a while—obviously he's gotten it back again."

Emma was thinking, putting all the pieces together in her mind. "Mariel hurt her back after a fall from her horse. She made a big show of telling me how she didn't want to take any painkillers because they could be addictive. What if she was lying and this Dr. Sampson is supplying her?"

"Sounds like you've hit the nail on the head. But you said she's already been eliminated as a suspect."

Emma nodded. She caught her lower lip between her teeth. "It does explain where she probably went the night of the party—to beg Sampson for another prescription. I remember when we got there that she looked rather . . . pained."

Brian was fidgeting a bit, plucking at the bedcovers, and moving his head back and forth.

"Speaking of pain, are you okay?"

Brian gave a weak smile. "I think it's time for my pain pills, and I'm not turning them down." There was a slight sheen of perspiration on his upper lip.

"Do you want me to call the nurse?"

Brian shook his head. "I'll be okay. She should be along any minute now anyway." He picked up Emma's hand again and squeezed it. "So, now tell me what's bothering you."

Emma was startled. How did Brian *know*?

"I can tell by the way your eyebrows are scrunched together—just a bit—that something is bothering you."

Now Emma felt contentment seep down to her very core. Brian really *got* her. "Okay," she admitted. "It's Aunt Arabella."

"No." Brian struggled to sit upright. "Nothing's happened to her, has it? Aside from you and Liz, she's my most favorite lady." He gave Emma a lopsided grin that segued into a grimace.

"She's okay," Emma reassured him, "physically anyway.

It's just that she's been forgetting things, which is odd. And when Detective Walker asked her where she was during the fireworks the night of the Grangers' party, she gave him three different answers." Emma's fingers found the loose thread on her sweater again, and she began wrapping it around her thumb. "That's not like Arabella."

"You're right. That's not." Now Brian looked concerned. "Your aunt is usually so sharp. What are you going to do?"

"She's agreed to make an appointment with Dr. Baker. He's known her for ages. Hopefully he can figure out what's wrong."

"Let's hope so." Brian was silent for a moment. "But enough of all that. How about giving me a kiss?"

"DARLING, you're looking a little . . ." Arabella paused, searching for the right word. "A little like a ragamuffin. Don't you think it's time to pay Angel a visit?"

Emma ran her hand through her short, dark hair, disheveling it even more. "I think you're right. I've been putting it off. I've been so busy."

"It's quiet right now, and Sylvia ought to be along at any moment. Why don't you call Angel and see if she has anything open?"

Emma was already pulling her cell from her purse. She punched in the number to Angel Cuts, Angel Roy's hair salon. She clicked off the call with a smile. "She can squeeze me in now before her ten o'clock."

"You go along then. I'll be fine."

Emma grabbed her purse, and Bette, who had been sleeping peacefully in a sunbeam, was suddenly at attention.

"I'm sorry, girl, I can't bring you this time. You stay here with Pierre, okay?"

Pierre opened one eye and twitched his black ear before going back to sleep.

Emma pulled on her coat and gloves and said good-bye to Arabella. Sylvia was just pulling into the parking lot as she slipped out the front door—that made Emma feel better. After everything that had happened, she was a little nervous about leaving Arabella all alone for too long.

Tiny flakes of snow were falling as Emma walked down the sidewalk. She passed the Meat Mart, where Willie, the butcher, was waiting on a customer. Someone came out of the Taffy Pull and delicious smells wafted out with them. Sylvia used to have an apartment over the shop until her children thought it provident that she move to a retirement community. She had nearly burned the building down one time and flooded it another.

Emma pushed open the door to Angel Cuts and was assailed by the perfumed odor of hair spray mingled with the chemical smell of hair dyes. The girl at the reception desk looked up and smiled, motioning toward the sofa with her eyes.

"Emma?" she asked.

"Yes."

"Angel will be with you in a minute. Would you like some coffee, tea or water with lemon?"

Angel had really gone upscale, Emma thought. It hadn't been *that* long since her last haircut, but Angel had replaced the standard-issue chairs with a plush sofa bedecked with cushions. New, framed art decorated the walls. The magazines that were normally strewn across a scarred wooden table were tucked into woven baskets—although it looked to Emma as if the selection remained the same—plenty of gossip rags, one high-fashion magazine and several cooking titles.

Emma pulled a random issue from one of the baskets and settled on the sofa. Angel had made quite the success of her hair salon—managing to compete with the popular chain places at the mall. She had plans to expand, and had even taken some classes to get a handle on how to best run her business.

"Emma!" Emma had barely turned the first few pages in her magazine when Angel came rushing out to the waiting area. She uttered Emma's name in a tone of rebuke, the way hairdressers do when you've waited too long for your trim or to have your roots touched up, or heaven forbid, had actually had the temerity to try another salon.

Angel's hair had undergone a renovation much like the salon had. It was still her trademark fire engine red but instead of being teased high and wide, it was fashionably sleek and layered. Emma couldn't help staring as Angel led her back to the washbasins.

It looked as if the interior of the salon had been redone as well—or at least it was in progress. Emma thought she detected the odor of fresh paint, and all the pictures on the walls had been taken down.

"What do you think of my renovations?" Angel asked as she lathered Emma's hair with shampoo.

"It's very nice. Very chic and elegant."

Angel smiled, pleased. "Do you really think so? I was going for a more big-city, sophisticated look, and you having lived in New York and all, I value your opinion."

Angel wrapped Emma's head in a towel and led her over

to her station. "Speaking of big-city, I heard from your aunt that you're working part-time for the Grangers."

Emma braced herself. Angel was undoubtedly going to pump her for information.

"I heard you were at that big do they had out at the Beau. That Saturday was a killer. I was busier than a one-legged man in a butt-kicking contest. Everyone wanted to come in and get her hair done—even Mrs. La-di-da Granger herself." Angel pulled a comb through Emma's hair. "She told me how she was used to going to places . . . famous places . . . in cities like London, Rome and Paris." A grin spread cross Angel's face. "But she told me she was really pleased with the way I did her hair. I got to tell you, that made my day."

"I can imagine," Emma said as Angel pushed her head forward to trim the back.

"Who knows if she'll come back . . . they're always off somewhere, but of course, now with her husband gone, maybe she'll stick around. That stepdaughter of hers comes in regularly."

"Oh? Joy?"

"Yes. I feel sorry for her being stuck with a name like that. There seems to be so little joy in her life except for those horses of hers. She could be pretty, too, except she won't do anything to bring it out. I've tried to get her to try a different hairstyle or some highlights, but all she ever wants is a trim." Angel opened a drawer and pulled out a blow-dryer. "Then there's the money, of course. She's never been encouraged to go out on her own—her father keeps harping on the fact that she's crippled. Heck, I've seen lots of people with crutches, in wheelchairs or wearing braces who have done just fine for themselves."

"But I imagine she's going to inherit some money now."

Angel snorted and switched on the blow-dryer. She had to raise her voice to be heard above it. "Not according to her. Mariel gets the bulk of it, her brother gets the income from the business along with all the stock, and she keeps the allowance that she's getting now, which, according to her, isn't much. Wouldn't surprise me if she did it herself." Angel switched off the blow-dryer and reached for an industrial-sized can of hair spray. "She hated him that much. Blamed him for her mother's death." Angel lowered her voice. "Some people have said that the accident *was* his fault—he'd been drinking." She sprayed Emma's hair lavishly. "I'm too young to remember, but I do remember my mother and grandmother bringing it up occasionally and speculating about it—chewing it over like it was a piece of fat."

She put down the spray, and Emma let out her breath.

"Of course the rules are different for the rich, you know. Wasn't there something Hemmingway said to F. Scott Fitzgerald? Like Fitzgerald said the rich are different from you and me? And Hemmingway said 'Yeah, they have more money.'"

Emma's eyes widened. Angel certainly never failed to surprise, she thought, as she was spun around so she could see her reflection in the mirror.

Chapter 16

EMMA left Angel Cuts feeling like a new woman. She swiped a hand across the back of her neck and was relieved that all the straggly ends were gone. She also ran a hand through her hair to loosen the viselike grip of the hair spray Angel had used. Emma liked her hair to be soft and touchable. That thought made her think of Brian, and she could feel the color rising to her face.

Arabella had asked her to stop in at the Meat Mart and pick up some pork chops. Emma pushed open the door to the butcher shop. Willie was standing behind the counter, his white apron as pristine as ever. Meat was arrayed neatly on trays inside a glass counter, the aged and well-marbled steaks each splayed out exactly one-quarter inch apart, the crown roast of pork sporting frilly paper crowns on the ends of the Frenched bones, the lamb chops pink and delectable.

"Miss Emma." Willie greeted Emma with a big smile. His round face was almost the color of the huge roll of butcher paper by the counter. "How have you been? I heard from Miss Arabella that you've been doing some work for the Grangers. They're something like celebrities in town. Everyone knows who they are, but they're rarely spotted out and about, traveling as much as they do, but when they are, it's an occasion to be sure." He crossed his arms and stuck his hands in his armpits. "Of course that young 'un, Jackson, we always know when he's around, roaring up and down our quiet country roads in that fancy sports car of his."

Emma smiled and listened patiently. It seemed everyone had an opinion on the Grangers—good or bad.

"Jackson Granger was set to be a real star on the UT lacrosse team, and he was, too, until his grades brought him down. Some people got real mad at his professors for failing him. Thought they lacked school spirit and all that. Apparently Jackson had quite the flair for art, but other subjects like math and history . . ." Willie rolled his round, blue eyes. "Well, they were his downfall." He gave a chagrined smile. "But I don't suppose you came in here to hear me talk. What can I get for you?" Willie's hand hovered over the counter.

"Arabella would like about five nice loin pork chops."

"You've come to the right place." Willie stuck his chest out with pride as he plucked several beautiful specimens from the counter and put them on the scale. "Think that will do her?"

Emma nodded. "Looks good to me."

Willie pulled off a long sheet of waxed butcher paper and stacked the chops on it carefully. He folded the paper just so, fastened it with twine and tucked the package into a brown paper bag. He pushed it across the counter at Emma. "Just be careful, okay? The Grangers always get what they want . . . no matter what they have to do to accomplish it."

Emma left the Meat Mart with Arabella's pork chops as well as very strange feelings. Had Willie been trying to warn her about the Grangers? Certainly it was normal for people of great wealth to think they were entitled to get what they wanted. She didn't anticipate getting in their way, so why should she worry?

MARIEL'S car was in the driveway when Emma arrived later that afternoon at the Grangers'. Another car, a dark, late-model BMW was pulled up behind it. Emma let herself in, as was her custom, and was crossing the foyer when she heard raised voices coming from the living room. She stopped abruptly. One of the voices sounded like Mariel's. The other was a man's. She didn't think she'd ever heard it before. They both sounded angry.

The word *police* caught Emma's ear, and she edged her way closer to the living room.

"That Detective Walker has been around twice now, insisting I tell him where I went the night of Hugh's murder." Mariel's voice softened slightly. "You've got to tell him I was with you. You're my alibi."

Emma heard a rustling sound. "I can't. Not after what happened before."

Mariel gave a high, tinkling laugh that sounded on the

verge of hysteria. "We don't have to tell them the truth. We'll tell them we were having an affair and we agreed to meet somewhere."

Emma stared at the sunbeam that was coming through the window and lighting up the jewel tones in the Oriental rug on the foyer floor.

The man snorted. "And what will my wife say to that?"

"She doesn't have to know. Or, better yet, you can tell *her* the truth. I'm sure she wouldn't want the police to know that you are back in the business of prescribing narcotics." Mariel's voice had taken on a threatening tone.

The man must be Dr. Sampson, Emma realized. She heard his sharp intake of breath.

"I just can't do it. You'll have to come up with something else."

Emma heard footsteps heading toward the door and quickly ducked into the kitchen.

She didn't think Dr. Sampson had seen her; she hoped not.

She heard the front door slam and scurried down the hall toward the storage room, where she quickly set to work.

After two hours Emma was ready for a break. There was one more painting left in the row she'd started earlier that afternoon. She'd plug in that information, and then go out to the kitchen to make another cup of tea.

She lifted the painting from the rack. It was a small Cézanne still life—nothing elaborate, but utterly stunning nonetheless. Emma could almost feel the fuzziness of the blush-colored skin on the peaches and the rough texture of the sharp yellow and green lemons and limes. She stood and admired the painting for a moment. It really was a thrill to be working so closely with so many beautiful things.

She turned the painting over reverently and entered the data into her computer—Cézanne, Paul, 1890, *Still Life*. She added the measurements, took one last lingering look at the work then replaced it in the rack.

She was picking up her mug when she noticed a smudge of green on her finger. She looked at it more closely. It wasn't ink. She hadn't been using any pens, and even if she had, they would most likely be blue or black. She dabbed at the spot. It was damp and looked like . . . paint.

Emma turned around and retrieved the Cézanne from the rack. She held her finger up to the still life—the color of the paint on her finger matched the color of the limes in the painting. She touched the canvas gently and was shocked to find the paint was slightly tacky.

It couldn't be. The piece had been painted in 1890. Emma was truly puzzled.

She wondered if Jackson was around. She headed toward the office, but the room was empty, as was the kitchen. She finally found him in the library, engrossed in a copy of *Art International*. He tossed it onto the tufted leather sofa when he noticed Emma standing in the doorway.

"Good article on the discovery of some paintings that had been snatched from their rightful owners by the Nazis."

"I was reading an article about that online."

Jackson gestured toward the magazine. "Please feel free to borrow any of our books or reading material if you like."

"Thanks."

"Was there something you wanted?" Jackson prompted when Emma didn't say anything.

Emma wasn't sure where to start. "I was cataloging a lovely Cézanne . . ." she finally began.

"They are beautiful, aren't they?" Jackson jumped to his feet. He was wearing a dark blue shirt tucked into what Emma assumed were probably two-hundred-dollar jeans. "He's a favorite of mine." He frowned suddenly. "I hope there isn't a problem?"

"Not a problem, exactly, no." Emma cleared her throat. "But on one of the still lifes, the paint seems to be slightly . . . damp." Emma held out her hand and pointed to the spot of green on her thumb. "See? Some of the paint rubbed off on my hand. I don't know how that could be since the piece was supposedly done in 1890."

For a moment a startled look crossed Jackson's face to be replaced almost immediately by a bland expression. He smiled reassuringly and gave a half laugh.

"It must be one of the pieces that just came back from the restorer. It shouldn't have been in that rack." He frowned. "Sometimes those older works need a good cleaning, and sometimes even a bit of a touch-up. We send them to someone in New York. He's supposed to be the best, but it seems he's gotten careless sending back a painting that was still a bit tacky." Jackson drummed his fingers on the desk. "Did you touch it?" he barked suddenly.

Emma jumped. "Touch it?"

"Yes."

"Just barely. Just to see if that's where this paint came from." She brandished her thumb. "I don't think I've done it any harm."

She had a horrible thought. What if she'd somehow ruined the painting? Would they make her pay for it? It must be worth hundreds of thousands of dollars. Sweat broke out along the back of her neck.

But Jackson just gave another half laugh and waved a hand. "I'm sure you haven't. If you don't mind, could you put it to one side? I'll take a look at it later and see if it needs to be sent back to New York."

BY five o'clock, Emma was more than ready to go home. She turned off the computer, turned out the lights and let the door to the storage room slam shut behind her. She paused in the foyer to slip into her coat and wind her scarf around her neck. She could see forbidding gray skies through the window, and a few light flakes of snow were falling.

The front door opened as she was pulling on her gloves. Sabina bustled into the house, looking warm and comfortable in her fur coat and suede boots. She smiled when she saw Emma.

"How is your project going?" she asked as she pulled off her leather gloves and tucked them into her purse—a large, expensive leather bag that Emma thought might actually be Hermès.

"Very well, thanks."

"I've come to collect my husband." She glanced at her gold-and-diamond wristwatch. "We've got dinner guests tonight, and he's going to need to change." She smiled at Emma again. "When he's among his precious works of art, he loses all sense of time." She sighed. "I'm afraid Tom's missing Hugh terribly. They'd been friends for decades. I'm hoping having some people over will cheer him up and take his mind off it."

She glanced over her shoulder out the window. "Good

thing you've got your scarf. The wind has picked up, and the snow's started again."

Suddenly the front door burst open so hard it slammed against the wall and nearly ricocheted back again. Both Emma and Sabina jumped. Sabina's hand flew to her throat.

A young boy stood there—Emma thought he was the same one who had so conveniently appeared to take care of Mariel's horse the other day. He looked to be around seventeen and had slightly shaggy, dark hair and large, brown eyes. His face was red from the cold, and flakes of snow were melting on the shoulders of his jacket. His boots were muddy and his jacket had a V-shaped tear near one of the elbows. He stared at Emma and Sabina, his eyes round. He opened his mouth, but nothing came out.

Mariel came out of the kitchen just then. She stopped short when she saw the boy. "Peter, what's wrong? Has something happened? Do you need something?"

He looked down at his dirty feet. "I'm sorry about the mud, ma'am, but it's . . . it's . . . Miss Joy, ma'am," Peter managed to stutter finally. "She's hurt, ma'am."

Mariel frowned, deepening the wrinkles in her forehead. "Hurt, how?"

"Thrown from her horse. She was riding Big Boy and something spooked him, ma'am." He stared down at his worn boots.

"Spooked him? What do you mean? Big Boy is very even-tempered. That's not like him."

Sabina began to dig in her purse and pulled out her cell. "I'll call nine-one-one." She put the phone to her ear.

"I know what you mean, ma'am," Peter continued. "But there was a noise, and next thing I know he's throwing Miss

Joy off like she was nothing more than a rag doll. She landed on the ground. It's plenty hard right now on account of being frozen."

"What kind of noise was it?"

"I don't really know, ma'am. But it sure sounded like a gunshot."

Chapter 17

"A gunshot!" Mariel echoed as she yanked open the hall closet and pulled out her barn jacket. "Take me to her right away. Is she conscious?"

The boy looked confused.

"Is she talking?"

"No, ma'am, she's lying there looking all twisted like a bunch of rags with her face all white."

Mariel frowned. "This doesn't sound good," she said to no one in particular.

"Paramedics are on their way," Sabina said. She still held the cell phone pressed to her ear.

Mariel opened the front door and a gust of cold air swept through the foyer. Emma shivered.

"Do you want me to come with you?"

Mariel looked grateful. "If you wouldn't mind. We might have to move her, and another set of hands would be useful."

Emma pulled her collar up around her ears and followed Mariel out the door. The wind momentarily took her breath away, and Emma gasped. Peter led them around to the back of the house, through a gate in the white picket fence, and across a frozen field that was beginning to turn white from the snow that had started to fall.

Emma kept up with Mariel as best she could. She wished she had worn boots instead of shoes. Her foot caught in one of the ruts in the field and she nearly fell. She could feel the snowflakes melting in her hair, and ice cold water dripped down the back of her neck. Mariel seemed oblivious as she marched across the stiff, icy grass, her hair blowing furiously, her coat clutched closed with one hand.

Big Boy stood off in the distance, amid a group of three or four other horses, stamping his feet and snorting clouds of warm air through his nose. Emma saw what looked like a bundle of clothes tossed onto the ground, but, as they got closer, she realized it was Joy. Mariel quickened her pace, and Emma followed suit, nearly trotting to keep up.

Mariel dropped to her knees beside Joy's still body. "She's breathing," she called over her shoulder to Emma. "Joy, can you hear me? Joy?"

Joy moaned and moved her head back and forth. Her face was pale, and the smattering of freckles across her nose stood out strongly. Her eyelids fluttered, and they all held their breath.

"Run and get a blanket." Mariel pointed to Peter.

"You mean the ones we use on the horses?" Peter stood

there, his big hands hanging at his side, his eyes still wide with alarm.

"Yes." Mariel's tone was clipped with impatience. "It doesn't matter. We need to keep her warm." She snapped her fingers. "Hurry."

They stood over Joy, waiting. Emma stamped her feet to try to warm them, and stuck her hands deep into her pockets. Mariel seemed impervious to the cold—still clutching her coat instead of buttoning it, her bare hands turning red from the chill.

Mariel glanced at her watch. "What is keeping the ambulance?"

Peter came running back from the stables with a red and green plaid blanket in his arms. Mariel tucked it gently around Joy's still form. Emma bent and plucked several large pieces of hay from the wool.

Just then they heard the wailing of a siren in the distance, growing louder as it got closer. Emma was past feeling the cold; her hands and feet were numb and prickly.

The ambulance pulled into the driveway. Mariel walked briskly toward the house, waving to them as she went. Two paramedics in black pants and black jackets got out of the front. They opened the back door of the ambulance, pulled out a gurney and lowered it to the ground.

The frozen field made the gurney ungainly, sticking in the ruts and nearly flipping over at one point. One of the men swore, and the word carried on the wind to where Emma was standing. Mariel had come back to join her, and they stood waiting and watching the slow progress of the paramedics.

Joy groaned, and Emma and Mariel leaned over her. Her

eyelids fluttered again, but when they called her name, she didn't answer. Mariel stood up with a hand to her back.

The paramedics had finally managed to maneuver the gurney over to them. They were panting, their breath making huge puffs of vapor in the cold air. One of them grabbed a backboard from the gurney and began setting it up.

The other man squatted down next to Joy. "Has she shown any signs of consciousness?"

Emma and Mariel shook their heads.

"We're going to use the backboard as a precaution. Just in case she's injured her neck or back."

"Okay," Mariel said.

The paramedics removed the plaid horse blanket and replaced it with the clean white one they had brought with them.

"Peter." Mariel looked toward the boy, who stood there with his coat open, seemingly oblivious to the cold that was making Emma shiver. "Can you take the blanket back to the stable? And then come back here, please."

"Yes, ma'am." He tucked the blanket under his arm and took off at a trot.

By the time he returned, the paramedics had strapped Joy to the backboard and placed her on the gurney. They then began their slow journey across the field to the waiting ambulance.

"Peter." Mariel turned to the boy who had finally started to shiver. "You said you heard a gunshot?"

"Yes, ma'am. Least, that's what it sounded like to me."

"Who would be shooting off a gun?" Mariel looked at Emma with her eyebrows raised. "Our neighbors are hardly the sort to go after rabbits or squirrels, and there's nothing much else to hunt at this time of year." She turned to Peter again. "Did the shot sound close?"

"Yes, ma'am. Real close. Otherwise I doubt it would have spooked Big Boy the way it did."

Mariel turned to Emma. "We might as well go back in. I'll follow the ambulance in my car."

She and Emma headed back across the field toward the house. The ambulance had already started down the drive, the siren going and the lights whirling and throwing a kaleidoscope of colors against the white house.

As Emma got into her car, she couldn't help but wonder who had fired off a gun, and whether or not it had been done on purpose to cause Joy's accident.

"I don't like it," Francis said later that evening, when they were all having dinner at Arabella's house. He drew his black brows together. "It sounds to me as if someone spooked that horse on purpose."

"Maybe it was meant as a warning," Priscilla said, taking a delicate sip of her coffee. "Maybe this Joy was getting too close to discovering the murderer."

"That's exactly what I'm afraid of," Francis said helping himself to another slice of pie. "I'm worried about you, Emma. If the murderer gets wind of the fact that you've been snooping around, asking questions, overhearing conversations . . ."

"The murderer might not even be in the house," Priscilla said, arching a brow.

"True." Francis smoothed his mustache with his index

finger. "But they might still find out about it. People like that have their ways."

"I really thought Joy had killed her father herself," Emma said, swiping her fork across her plate to get at the last bit of Arabella's delicious peach pie.

"It sounds as if she hated her father enough," Arabella said.

"We know someone involved has a gun," Francis said, pushing away his empty plate. "Hugh was shot before he was shoved off that balcony. The local boys are still waiting on the ballistic reports." He sighed. "At the rate the lab is going, we'll have the case solved long before we get their results." He turned to Emma and shook a finger at her. "That's why you need to be extra careful."

"How is Brian doing?" Arabella cut in smoothly. She poured herself a cup of coffee and stirred in a spoon of sugar.

They had already cleared the dishes from Arabella's delicious dinner of fried pork chops with gravy, mashed potatoes and collard greens sautéed with bacon. Emma had stacked the plates in the kitchen, and Francis had offered to put them in the dishwasher after dessert and coffee.

"Brian is doing very well. He's being discharged. I'm picking him up in an hour." Emma glanced at her watch.

"That's wonderful," Arabella said, her face glowing. "Such good news. You'd better be off then. He may need help getting his things together."

Emma put down her napkin. "As soon as I freshen up a bit."

It didn't take Emma more than five minutes to wash her

hands, comb her hair—Angel had done a really good job on the cut—and dab on some powder and lipstick.

"Give Brian our best," Arabella called from the kitchen as Emma headed toward the front door.

She beeped open the Bug and got in. She had an ulterior motive in heading to the hospital early. She'd called Mariel to check up on Joy. Apparently Joy had been banged up but aside from some cuts and bruises and a minor concussion, she was going to be okay. The doctor wanted to keep her overnight for observation. But even more important, she was conscious and talking. Emma hoped to sneak in to see her. Maybe she would be scared enough to reveal what she knew. Because Emma was quite certain she knew something— something that had scared the killer enough to spook Big Boy. She didn't know whether they had hoped the accident would kill Joy or whether they had merely hoped it would serve as a warning to her. Emma had to talk to Joy before she put the pieces together and realized that her only safety lay in silence.

Emma pulled into the Henry County Medical Center parking lot and found a space. The woman behind the information desk didn't even look up when Emma asked for Joy Granger. She tapped a few keys on her computer and handed Emma a slip of paper with Joy's room number on it. "You need directions?" she asked, finally looking at Emma. Her slightly protruding blue eyes were crisscrossed with red veins.

"I think I can find it." Emma tucked the piece of paper into her coat pocket and headed toward the elevators.

She got off the elevator, consulted the signs on the wall, and turned left. The door to Joy's room was ajar, and she could hear the television blaring—some ubiquitous game show. "And now, for the grand prize, answer this final question," the host yelled excitedly. Emma peeked around the corner of the door into the room. Joy was snapped into a blue hospital gown, propped up in bed. There was an angry-looking purple bruise on her forehead, and Emma noticed a bandage on her left hand along with an intravenous line leading to a bag suspended from an IV pole next to the bed.

Emma knocked gently and stuck her head into the room.

"Joy?" she called to the figure in the bed.

Joy looked up, her head swiveling toward the door, obviously startled. "Oh, I thought you were the nurse. You're Emma, right?"

"Yes. Do you mind if I come in?"

Joy shook her head, her hair making a swishing sound as it rubbed back and forth against the pillow. She pointed toward the bedside chair where a plastic, hospital-issue basin sat. It was filled with a plastic cup, a tube of hand lotion, a miniature box of tissues and a clean, folded washcloth. "Sorry, you'll have to move that stuff. The nurse left it there."

Emma put the tub on the window ledge and sat down. "I wanted to see how you were doing. We were all so frightened seeing you lying there in the field like that—not moving or talking."

"Fortunately, I don't remember much of anything about it. I didn't come to until I was in the ambulance." Joy winced as she moved sideways on the bed. "I'm a jumble of bumps and bruises, but that's the price you pay when you ride. This isn't the first time I've fallen off a horse."

"You didn't fall, though."

Joy whipped her head around toward Emma. "What do you mean?"

"You were thrown. Someone spooked Big Boy."

Joy's face relaxed. "Horses are spooked all the time—by the strangest things. I've seen a small kitten throw an Arabian a hundred times its size into a tizzy. It doesn't mean anything."

"Peter said he heard a gunshot. Someone shot a gun into the air—on purpose—to spook your horse, hoping he would throw you."

A strange look settled over Joy's face. Emma could see the rapid rise and fall of her chest, and the panicked way her eyes darted about as if she were looking for escape.

"Do you have any idea who would do something like that? Or why?" Emma persisted.

Joy's expression turned mulish, her eyes narrowed and her jaw set. "That's ridiculous." She gave a harsh laugh. "I don't know why someone would do that, let alone who. Besides, being thrown by my horse is hardly going to kill me. Like I told you, it's one of the hazards of the sport. I've probably been thrown a couple dozen times since my mother first sat me on Maximilian."

"Maybe the person didn't want to kill you? Perhaps his intention was just to warn you."

Joy stared at Emma for a moment, her face completely white. Before, her look had been unconcerned . . . even cocky. Something had spooked her horse, and she'd been thrown. No big deal. Nothing out of the ordinary.

Now she looked positively *scared*.

EMMA left Joy's room and headed down the hall toward the elevator. The information about the gunshot had certainly had an effect on Joy. Emma had the distinct impression that the word *warning* had struck a target. And that Joy knew exactly *who* and exactly *why* someone was trying to warn her.

Emma waited impatiently for the elevator. Suddenly she couldn't wait to get to Brian's room—to see him up and about and looking normal. Well, relatively normal. His leg would still be in a cast. Finally the elevator doors fanned open on his floor. Emma exited and headed toward Brian's room. She was already smiling as she neared his door, and she knew she was positively grinning as she walked into his room.

Brian was in a wheelchair parked next to the bed. A stuffed, blue plastic drawstring bag with *Henry County Medical Center* written on it in white lettering sat on the empty bed. A pair of crutches leaned in the corner.

Brian began to grin as soon as Emma entered the room. His broken leg was encased in a cast and stuck straight out, supported by the wheelchair's footrest, and he had a vase holding a bouquet of mixed flowers in his lap.

He held the flowers out to Emma. "These are for you. It seems I missed Valentine's Day while I was out. I'm sorry."

Emma took the flowers and buried her nose in them, absurdly pleased that Brian had remembered, however belatedly. "They're lovely, thanks." She noticed a little red plastic card stuck in the flowers and pulled it out. It read *Get Well Soon.* She showed it to Brian.

Brian gave a crooked smile and shrugged. "I asked the nurse to get me some flowers from the gift shop downstairs. The messages were limited to get well wishes or congratulations on your new baby."

Emma laughed. "They're still lovely."

"I'm glad you like them." Brian gave a devilish grin. "How about a kiss for all of my efforts?"

Emma braced herself on the arms of the wheelchair and leaned in close until her lips met Brian's. They stayed like that for several long moments until the sound of someone passing in the hall made them pull apart.

"It looks like you're all packed," Emma said a little breathlessly, indicating the plastic bag on the bed.

"I'm more than ready to get out of here. Shall we go?"

Emma retrieved Brian's jacket from the cupboard at the foot of the bed and helped him into it. She hung the plastic bag from the handles of the wheelchair, while Brian held the flowers and the crutches in his lap.

"All set?" Emma released the brakes on the wheelchair.

"Yup. Let's blow this place."

She wheeled Brian out of the room and into the hall. A nurse passing by waved, and he waved back. "Good luck," she called over her shoulder before disappearing into a patient's room.

The elevator was large enough to fit a gurney, so Emma had no trouble maneuvering the wheelchair into the space. All the exterior doors were equipped with door openers so that was no problem, either.

"The air feels so good," Brian said as Emma wheeled him onto the sidewalk alongside the parking lot.

She found the cutout and smoothly pushed him down the rows of cars until they came to her Bug. She had just beeped open the doors when the realization struck. How on earth was she going to get Brian into the car?

Brian must have noticed the look on her face. "What's wrong?"

"I don't know how to get you into the car."

Brian laughed. "We'll manage it. If you can give me some support, I can stand on my good leg easily enough, but I think I'd better get in the backseat if you don't mind."

Emma stood by while Brian got himself to a standing position. He put a hand on her shoulder for balance, and at one point, Emma was terrified he was going to fall over. But somehow he managed to get into the backseat. The problem then became what to do with his leg? He couldn't bend it, and she couldn't shut the door the way it was.

Brian started to laugh and so did Emma.

"I should have borrowed Liz's station wagon," she said, wiping her eyes.

"How about if you roll down the window, and I just stick my foot out."

Emma opened the window.

"See," Brian said, "this will work."

The sight of Brian's leg sticking out the window sent Emma into fresh gales of laughter. "We need a red flag to hang on the end of your foot."

"Just don't get too close to any parked cars."

Emma got behind the wheel and slowly drove out of the parking lot. "Are you okay?"

"I'm fine. It's just a little . . . breezy back here."

Emma cranked up the heat. "How are you going to manage at home?"

"I should have told you sooner. Fortunately we're going in the right direction. I'm staying with Liz and Matt for a couple of weeks."

A few minutes later, Emma pulled into the driveway in front of Liz's house. Matt came running out the front door.

"Need some help?" He couldn't help grinning when he saw Brian's foot sticking out the window of Emma's car.

"If you could give me a hand," Brian said.

Matt opened the back door, and Brian stuck his arm out, grasping Matt's. Matt pulled him out of the car and onto his good leg. Brian was standing, albeit unsteadily. He got his crutches under his arms, and with Matt's help began to make his way into the house.

Liz welcomed them all with open arms and led them into the living room, where a fire was burning and spitting in the stone fireplace. She had a bottle of wine open on the coffee table alongside a plate of cheese and crackers.

They got Brian settled in a chair with his leg on an ottoman, and Emma took a seat by the fire, holding her hands out toward the flames. Driving with the back window open had chilled her to the bone.

Suddenly Brian's cell phone rang. He dug in the pocket of his jeans, pulled it out and glanced at the caller ID. "I'm really sorry, but it's John Jasper. We're doing some renovations on his house—very minor, the big projects are already done—but I'd better see what he wants."

"No problem," Liz said as she poured Emma a glass of wine.

They heard a bunch of uh-huhs from Brian followed by a startled exclamation as he half bolted from his chair.

Brian clicked off the call and turned to Emma, Liz and Matt with a startled face.

"That was John Jasper," Brian said. "Well, I guess I already told you that." His face still bore a look of shock and surprise. He turned to Emma. "Do you remember he told us he'd been buying a few pieces from Hugh Granger?"

Emma nodded her head. "Yes. I got the impression that Hugh was helping him build his collection."

"Well it seems that one of the pieces he purchased—the big piece by Mark Rothko, he said—has turned out to be a forgery."

Chapter 18

THEY all sat in stunned silence for a moment.

"I think I know the painting," Brian said. "It's in their living room. It's massive with thick stripes of red, white and a sort of grayish color against a black background." He shifted in his chair. "It's the pride of their collection. He must be distraught."

"I'm surprised," Liz said, nibbling on a cracker. "Hugh Granger has always had a good reputation. At least I've never heard anything against him. There are a couple of paintings hanging in the Memphis Brooks Museum that he donated. I remember seeing them when I was there."

Matt leaned forward and plucked a piece of cheese off the plate. "Granger might not have known it was a fake.

From Brian's description, it doesn't sound as if it would be hard to produce a forgery." He shook his head. "I guess I'm just a country bumpkin. I don't get this modern art stuff. I want to know what I'm looking at when I look at something."

"Perhaps if we could find out where the painting originally came from," Brian suggested. "If it comes from another reputable source, then obviously several people have been fooled."

"You can fool some of the people all of the time . . ." Matt said and laughed.

"You enter all that information into the computer database, don't you?" Liz turned to Emma.

"Yes. The title, date, measurements and what they call the provenance of the painting or where it came from."

"Can you check tomorrow? See where the Grangers got it?"

"Good idea." Emma finished the last bite of her cracker. "Unless they've been holding on to it for a very long time, it can't have come from Rothko himself. He died sometime in the early seventies. I'll need the name of it though, and the year and so forth."

"Let me get John back on the phone." Brian pressed a button on his cell.

John must have answered immediately. Matt handed Brian a piece of scratch paper and a pen. Brian nodded as he wrote down the information. He said good-bye and clicked off the call.

"I've got it all here." He handed the paper to Emma.

Liz looked thoughtful. "Maybe this isn't the first fake

that Granger has sold." She turned to Emma. "Could it be the reason why someone murdered him?"

ARABELLA was late arriving at Sweet Nothings the next morning. Emma stood by the window, a mug of tea in her hand, watching for Arabella's Mini to turn the corner into the parking lot. She wanted to tell her what they'd learned about Hugh's art business before Arabella heard it from anyone else.

Finally, Emma saw Arabella's Mini come down the street, and moments later Arabella herself stepped into the shop.

"Good morning, dear," she called out cheerfully as she unclipped Pierre's leash.

He made a beeline for his dog bed, but Bette had already discovered it and was curled up fast asleep. Pierre gave a low, warning growl that soon had her scampering for safety by Emma's feet. Emma bent down and scratched the puppy's ears consolingly.

"I've got something to tell you," Emma said as Arabella poured herself a cup of coffee and stirred in sugar and creamer.

"Oh? What?"

"Do you remember meeting the Jaspers at Hugh's party?"

"Of course. She was quite beautiful—wearing a very unusual pair of earrings. I would be interested to know where she got them."

"Her husband has bought a number of artworks from Hugh." Emma fiddled with a button on her blouse. "One of them has turned out to be a fake."

"Really?" Arabella stopped with her coffee mug halfway to her mouth. "Do you think that's what Francis and the TBI are after—art forgeries?"

"I don't know. But if he cheated someone else and then refused to give them their money back . . . well, that person might have been mad enough to shoot Hugh and push him off that balcony."

"But Hugh would hardly have invited them to his party."

"It was fairly common knowledge around town that Hugh was giving this party. Even Angel knew all about it. The killer could have just walked into the Beau and waited for the right moment."

Arabella put a hand on Emma's arm. "Now I'm really getting nervous about you going over there."

Emma smiled reassuringly. "Don't worry. I'll be careful."

EMMA had butterflies in her stomach as she pulled into the Grangers' driveway. Today she really would be snooping— not just overhearing conversations or gossiping with Molly. If one of the Grangers was a murderer, she could be in danger.

Emma tried to quell her nerves as she made her way down the hallway to the storage room where she was working. One of the drawings on the wall caught her eye, and she stopped to admire it. She felt her heartbeat slowly return to normal. She was being overly dramatic—she was just having an attack of nerves.

While waiting for the computer to boot up, she went to the rack of paintings and found where she'd left off. She took the piece over to the worktable and turned it over so she could read the label. She entered the data, and then looked around.

She was all alone. At one point she thought she heard footsteps, but no one came through the door. Besides, no one could possibly guess what she was doing, she rationalized, as she sorted the various data in the computer database.

She started by sorting according to the artist's name. Strange, there were no Rothkos listed. Perhaps the information had been entered incorrectly? She clicked a few keys and the database was now sorted by title. Emma went through them carefully but still didn't come up with anything that remotely matched John Jasper's painting. Finally, she sorted by date and was dismayed when she again came up empty-handed.

Emma leaned her elbows on the desk and put her chin in her hands. What next?

She thought about when she'd started the project a couple of days ago. How stupid of her! The very first entries in this database had been hers. Jackson had told her he'd already started taking an inventory, but he had said he'd used the desktop in the library. Obviously the two databases hadn't been merged. Did she dare check out the other computer?

Emma spent another hour logging paintings into the database debating about going into the library and sneaking onto that computer. The house was quiet—she hadn't seen any signs of Jackson or his partner, Tom Roberts. Mariel hardly ever came down this wing. Emma might not get another chance.

Her hands were cold and slick with perspiration. She crept down the hall and across the foyer. Molly was in the kitchen, humming to herself as she swept the floor. Emma wasn't particularly worried about her—Molly had no idea what Emma was doing and wouldn't realize that Emma's job didn't normally take her into the library.

The light was off in the office where Liz usually worked. Emma paused briefly to listen, but she couldn't hear anyone about. She tiptoed down the hall toward the library and peeked in. The room was empty.

She left the lights off as she slipped into the chair in front of the desk. Hopefully she couldn't be seen by someone casually walking by. She powered up the computer and jumped when the light from the monitor came on.

Her hands were damp, and her fingers were clumsy on the keys. Fortunately, the files on the computer were very neatly organized. She found a folder marked *Inventory* and opened it.

A rustling sound from the hall froze her and she held her breath. She listened carefully. Was someone coming? She waited a minute and then let out her breath. False alarm.

Emma clicked a few keys, and the database opened. She had been afraid it might be password-protected but obviously Jackson didn't see the need to go that far. She sorted the information by artist and scanned the column until she came to the *R*s. She gave a hiss of frustration. No Rothko works were listed. Again, she sorted the database in several different ways, but the title of John's painting did not appear. There weren't very many entries—Jackson had obviously quit attempting to inventory the paintings rather quickly.

Emma leaned back in the chair. Did Jackson remove things from the database when they were sold? She tabbed across the page until she came to a column labeled *Sold*.

Names, dates, all the information one would expect was listed there. But no mention of John Jasper or his fake Rothko painting.

Emma closed the file, turned off the computer and sat drumming her fingers on the desk. There was a stack of papers to the right of the computer weighed down by an elegant crystal paperweight. Emma caught the name of a local bank, the Commercial Bank and Trust Company, out of the corner of her eye.

She convinced herself it wouldn't hurt to have a closer look even though she had no idea what she hoped to find. She eased the paper out from under the paperweight. It was a bank statement, and the account was in the name of Jackson Granger. Several large sums had been deposited recently, and the account total was staggering—at least to Emma.

She straightened the papers quickly and had just gotten up from the chair when Jackson walked into the room.

Emma couldn't stifle the cry that came to her lips.

"I'm sorry. Did I startle you?"

"Yes. I didn't hear you coming." Emma's heart was pounding furiously. She was surprised Jackson couldn't hear it.

Had he seen her on the computer? She couldn't tell. She thought he was looking at her rather strangely, but it might be her guilty conscience. The silence lengthened and Jackson raised one eyebrow as if to say *What are you doing in here?*

"I was just . . ." Emma searched frantically for an excuse. She noticed the copy of *Art International* that Tom Roberts had tossed on the sofa, still splayed open to hold his place. "I was just going to borrow this magazine, if you don't mind."

Emma picked it up and brandished it at Jackson. "This article on the Nazis and stolen art looks very interesting."

She couldn't tell if Jackson believed her or not. She didn't care. She bolted from the library for the relative safety of the storage room. She looked at her watch, but she really couldn't justify leaving yet. It might arouse Jackson's suspicions.

Instead, she hauled the next painting out of the rack and began entering the data. She was typing in the information when something occurred to her—Jackson had been lying when he told her that the Cézanne painting she'd found to be slightly wet had been to the restorer. Much more likely it was a fake—one that had just been painted and put into the inventory to be sold to some unsuspecting client.

Chapter 19

EMMA spent the rest of the afternoon looking over her shoulder. She was five minutes away from calling it a day when she heard footsteps in the hallway. They stopped just shy of the door to the storage room. Emma hesitated then swung around in her seat.

Jackson stood there watching her. "Mind if I come in?" he asked politely.

Emma wanted to scream *no*, but instead she smiled and said, "Please do."

Jackson perched on the edge of the worktable and smiled at Emma. She pushed her chair back to increase the distance between them. His hands were spread out on his knees—large hands capable of . . . Emma shook her head. Her imagination was beginning to run away with her.

"I hope you're enjoying the job, and that it hasn't been too difficult for you. I'm afraid I've left you alone. There's been so much to do with my father's funeral, meetings with lawyers and, well, I'm sure you can imagine."

Emma nodded. What was he getting at? Had he seen her snooping in the library? She tried to read the answer in his face, but his expression was bland.

After a few more pleasantries, he went, leaving Emma to wonder . . . had his visit been meant as a warning?

Talking with Jackson had made Emma late. When she checked her phone there was a message from Arabella saying that she was taking Bette to her house, and Emma could pick the dog up there. Emma turned off the computer, slipped into her coat and turned out the lights. She felt the hairs on the back of her neck prickle as she crossed the foyer to the front door. She sprinted to her car and slammed the door shut. Her hands were shaking slightly as she put the car in gear and drove away, churning up gravel in her wake.

Bette was asleep in a sunbeam by the front door when Emma got to Arabella's, but she immediately jumped to her feet to lavish great quantities of affection on Emma, which included licking her face, hands and nearly knocking her over.

"Hello, dear." Arabella came out of the kitchen drying her hands on a towel. "How was your—" she started then stopped abruptly. "Is everything okay? You look as if you've seen a ghost. Come out to the kitchen and get a glass of tea."

Emma followed Arabella to the kitchen, where Priscilla was busy peeling potatoes and Francis was seated at the table thumbing through the newspaper.

"You haven't told me what happened," Arabella said as she retrieved a glass from the cupboard.

"Something's happened?" Priscilla whirled around with the potato peeler in her hand. She had tied one of Arabella's aprons over her tweed slacks and black turtleneck.

"Not really," Emma said, taking a grateful sip of the tea Arabella handed her. "I just did a little . . . snooping, and I'm not sure if Jackson saw me or not."

"Oh dear." Arabella wrung her hands. "Do you really think he might have seen you?"

"I don't know." Emma sank into a chair at the table.

Francis closed his newspaper and folded it up. He smiled encouragingly at Emma. "I hope you found out something for your troubles."

"Oh yes. I tried to find the provenance for the Rothko painting they sold to Jasper. It wasn't in the database I was working on, so I checked one of the other computers. There was a complete inventory on it—except, of course, for the pieces I was cataloging—and the Rothko wasn't there, either."

Francis stroked his mustache. "That's a shame. It would really help to know where the painting came from originally." He absentmindedly ruffled the pages of the newspaper. "Forged art is a tricky business. The FBI may go after the forgers, but, unfortunately, there's no protocol for dealing with the works of art—Jasper will probably be welcome to keep the painting if he wants. And there's nothing to stop him from passing it off as an original a decade or two from now."

"I don't think he would do that," Emma said.

Francis shrugged. "It's happened before."

"But that's not all. Jackson had left his personal bank statement sitting out on the desk. I took a peek at it. The total in the account was astounding, and there were some recent, big deposits."

"To his personal account?" Francis fiddled with his mustache. "That sounds as if his father didn't know what was going on and Jackson had a little side business of his own going."

Arabella bustled over and put a plate of cheese and crackers on the table. "Now, don't eat too many." She shook her finger at them. "There's pulled pork and coleslaw for dinner."

Emma took a cracker and topped it with a piece of cheese. "The other day when I was working, I picked up a painting—a Cézanne—and it was slightly tacky. I got paint on my hand."

Francis's eyebrows rose toward his hairline.

"I mentioned it to Jackson, and he said it had been sent to the restorer and that the restorer had probably sent it back before it was completely dry. Now I'm wondering if it's a fake as well. If it is, it's a very good one. Whoever did it has a lot of talent."

Emma finished her cracker and turned to her aunt, who was standing at the stove. "Have you seen Dr. Baker yet, Aunt Arabella?"

"Not yet, but I have made my appointment. I'm sure it will turn out to be nothing."

Arabella kept her back to them, but Emma could tell by the tone of her voice that she didn't believe what she was saying—she was worried. Emma glanced at Francis, and she could tell by the look on his face that he was worried, too.

LATER, after dinner, Arabella and Francis went into the living room. Francis was going to read his book, and Arabella had her sewing basket and a Lucie Ann negligee she had picked up at a garage sale that needed some mending.

Emma offered to do the dishes. She expected Priscilla to join Francis and Arabella in the living room, but her mother lingered behind, putting away the place mats and wiping off the table.

Emma had the distinct impression that her mother wanted to tell her something but for some reason, she was reluctant. It wasn't like Priscilla to confide in her so Emma was surprised. They made small talk about the weather, which was completely unremarkable, as Emma rinsed the dishes and silverware and put them in the dishwasher.

Priscilla pulled out a kitchen chair and sat down. She twisted her wedding ring around and around, the light over the table reflecting off the diamonds set in the gold band. Emma wondered if she ought to ask if anything was wrong.

Finally, Priscilla cleared her throat. "There's something I have to tell you," she began. "And I just don't know how." She was twisting the ring faster and faster like a person fingering worry beads. "I didn't come up here just because of Arabella."

Emma stopped with a fork halfway to the dishwasher. "Oh?"

"Of course I *was* worried about your aunt. I feel it's my . . . duty to look out for her. I've always been the stable one—the settled one—taking the traditional path in life." She was quiet for a moment. "But now all that seems to be coming . . . unraveled." She choked back a sob.

"Mother, what's wrong?" Emma went over and put her arms around her mother.

"I hope you won't be too disappointed in me . . . in us.

Your father and I both love you very much, and nothing will ever change that. We want the best for you, I'm sure you know that."

"I do. But please tell me what is going on." Emma felt dread settle in the pit of her stomach like an overly heavy meal. Was her father ill? Was that why he hadn't come along?

"Your father and I have decided that it might be best if we . . . separate for a bit. Nothing final, of course. Just to see how things go." She looked up at Emma with tears in her eyes.

Emma didn't know what to say. It was the last thing on earth she had expected. Her parents were . . . her parents. They couldn't separate. They went together like peanut butter and jelly. George and Priscilla. Emma couldn't imagine it any other way.

Priscilla grabbed Emma's hand. "We'll get through this, don't worry."

"Does Aunt Arabella know?"

Again, Priscilla fiddled with her wedding band. "I haven't told her yet. I wanted you to be the first to know." She pulled the ring off, slipped it onto the ring finger of her right hand, then put it back on her left hand. "I'll tell her after you've gone."

"I just can't believe it." Emma felt hot tears pressing against the back of her eyelids. Other people's parents got divorced . . . not hers.

"As I said, nothing is final. It's just a trial . . . to see how we feel."

"Yes. Sure. I understand." Emma turned away, poured soap into the dishwasher dispenser and turned the machine on. She took off her apron, wadded it up and tossed it on the counter. "I think I'd better go back to my apartment. It's getting late."

"Darling, please don't blame me," Priscilla called after her.

Emma stopped in the doorway. "I don't blame you. I just need time to . . . think, okay?"

She grabbed her coat from the closet, and managed to corral Bette and clip on her leash.

She stuck her head into the living room. "Good night, all. Thank you for dinner, Aunt Arabella."

"You're going already?" Arabella started to get up from her seat.

"Please," Emma said, "don't get up. I'll see myself out."

She managed to make it out the front door and to her car before the tears that had been threatening spilled out and ran down her cheeks.

Emma dialed Brian's number as soon as she got home. When anything happened—good or bad—he was the first person she thought to call. Bette sensed that something was wrong and curled up in Emma's lap. Emma found her warmth and steady breathing soothing.

Brian was sympathetic. "I know when my mother died, I felt as if my world had ended. I'm sure having your parents separate must feel something like that."

"It's not as bad as if one of them had *died*," Emma said, "but it still feels as if my life is falling apart. My parents have always just been there."

"You have your own life to live now," Brian said softly. "A life that I hope we will someday build together."

Emma's breath caught in her throat. Brian wasn't exactly

proposing, but he was obviously thinking along those lines. Emma realized he was right—she needed to live her own life now. If her parents divorced, it would be sad. But she had reached the point where she could look forward to building her own family.

By the time she hung up, she was feeling considerably better. She would have to make the best of things no matter what happened.

ARABELLA eyed Emma somewhat warily when Arabella arrived at Sweet Nothings the next morning.

"Would you like something to drink?" Arabella dangled a tea bag in front of Emma.

"Sure." Emma had done the vacuuming as soon as she arrived and hadn't yet had the chance to make herself a cup of tea. She could tell that Arabella was worried about her, which was why she was being so overly solicitous. Emma thought perhaps it would be best if she broached the topic herself.

"Did Priscilla talk to you last night?"

Arabella jerked, and water spilled on the counter. She fussed about, grabbing a paper towel and cleaning it up, her back to Emma. "Yes, she did." Her voice was muffled.

"It's okay. I'm okay," Emma said, and she realized she meant it.

"Are you really, dear?" Arabella put a hand on Emma's arm. "I was so worried about you. It wasn't an easy thing for you to hear."

"I talked with Brian." Emma leaned on the old upright Hoover they kept in the shop. "He helped me put things in perspective." Emma couldn't stop it; a grin spread across her face.

Arabella regarded her, her hands on her hips, head tilted to one side. "The last thing I expected was to see you smiling, so out with it."

Emma ducked her head. "It's nothing really. Just that Brian pointed out that someday we'll be creating a family of our own so I need to look forward."

Now Arabella was grinning, too. "I can see why you're smiling. Do you think he'll surprise you with a ring for your birthday?"

Emma shrugged. "I don't know." And she turned on the Hoover before her aunt could ask any more questions.

The morning went by quickly, and before Emma knew it, Eloise Montgomery had arrived to help out in the shop. She was wearing a beautifully tailored winter white suit with a scarlet, bow-tied blouse. Her white hair was elegantly coiffed as usual, and she wore black peep-toed heels and carried a red designer bag.

She and Arabella immediately put their heads together. Emma left them to it and went upstairs to her apartment to grab a sandwich and freshen up before heading to the Grangers'.

She was very nervous and seriously tempted to throw the whole job over. What if Jackson had seen her snooping? And what if he was the murderer? Maybe Hugh had discovered Jackson's activities and wanted to put a stop to them? Or perhaps he had wanted in on the action? Jackson had expensive tastes and might not have wanted to share the bounty. Although he usually dressed casually, Emma recognized that his sweaters were cashmere and his shoes Italian leather—items he had obviously not purchased locally but in one of the big cities he visited on a regular basis.

Emma found herself driving more slowly than necessary in order to prolong arriving at the Grangers' horse farm. She was relieved to see Liz's car in the driveway when she got there. Joy was back on her horse—Emma could see her out riding in the field just beyond the house, putting Big Boy through his paces. Emma hoped no one would try to spook the horse again, but if someone really determined to hurt Joy and not just warn her, then what was to stop him? She shivered as she made her way up the front steps.

The foyer and front rooms were empty, and when Emma peeked into the kitchen, it was empty as well. The house was eerily quiet, and she was loath to head to the storage room, which was at the end of the back hallway and far from the rest of the house.

A light was on in the office, and she imagined Liz was in there working. Emma decided to procrastinate, and she headed in that direction, wincing at the noise her footsteps made on the wood floor.

"Hey." Liz spun around when she heard Emma. She gave her friend a hug. "Brian told me about . . . your conversation last night. I'm really sorry."

Emma was surprised to feel renewed tears flooding her eyes. She dashed a hand across them impatiently. "I'm more surprised than anything. I never expected my parents. . ." She shrugged. "I'll get used to it, I guess."

Liz nodded sympathetically.

"Have you seen Jackson today?" Emma asked.

"No. It's been strangely quiet, which is fine with me. It lets me get on with my work. I found a babysitter to pick Ben and Alice up from school and watch them for the afternoon."

Emma lowered her voice to a near whisper. "I did a little snooping yesterday."

Liz raised her eyebrows and inclined her head.

Emma explained about researching the Rothko painting, Jackson's bank statement and his nearly catching her out.

Liz drew in her breath and put a hand on Emma's arm. "Be careful okay? Someone's already been killed. I don't want you to be the next victim."

"I will, don't worry," Emma assured her friend. "How is Brian?" she asked changing the subject.

"Much better, although he's still in some pain. He denies it, of course, but I can see it on his face. And he's getting a little frustrated with moving around on crutches. He can't wait till he can graduate to a walking cast. He was actually wondering if he could drive! Said he wanted to go check on one of his renovations."

"I hope you told him not to."

"I most certainly did. He did manage to persuade Bobby Fuller from the hardware store to come by and take him out to one of his sites. I just hope he doesn't do anything foolish and get even more hurt. He gave us a bad enough scare as it was." Liz rolled her eyes.

Emma could certainly agree to that.

"I guess I'd better get to work." Emma wasn't at all anxious to leave the warm, well-lit office. The thought of encountering Jackson creeping about gave her goose bumps.

She reluctantly left Liz to her work and headed down the bare hallway to the storage room.

Emma began working and really got into it—it took her mind off of her parents' impending separation—and was surprised when she glanced at her watch and two hours had gone by. The room was chilly, and she felt cold and cramped from sitting at the computer for so long. Perhaps a cup of tea was in order.

Emma was headed toward the kitchen when she heard the front door open. She stopped and listened. A male voice. Was it Jackson's? She wasn't taking any chances. She walked as silently as possible back down the hall toward her desk.

An hour later, and the house was quiet. Emma was thoroughly chilled by now and longing for some hot tea. She decided to chance it. She was crossing the foyer when the front door opened, sending a frigid breeze through the entranceway. A couple of curling, dried leaves blew in on the wind and skittered across the floor.

Emma stood stock-still for a moment, her heart beating hard and fast, but it was only Sabina Roberts. As usual, she looked comfortably warm in her impressive fur coat. She smiled at Emma as she peeled off her long, leather gloves. She was wearing a scarf that was similar in color to the dress she had worn to Hugh's birthday party.

"It's cold out. Feels like snow," she said in her slightly accented voice. She took off her coat and draped it over her arm.

Emma agreed then scooted into the kitchen. Delicious and tantalizing smells filled the air. Molly was in the middle of putting together a stew—peeling carrots and potatoes and dicing an onion with her small but capable hands. She smiled when she saw Emma.

"I imagine you're after something to warm you up. A

nice cup of tea, maybe? That storage room gets mighty chilly after a while. I told Mr. Jackson that, but he said it was better for the paintings." She turned toward the stove, where cubes of meat were spitting and sizzling in a large pot.

It might be better for the paintings, but it was freezing her hands and feet, Emma thought. "A cup of tea does sound good."

Molly gestured with her head toward the kitchen island. "Help yourself. You know where things are by now." She laid a bunch of parsley leaves on her cutting board, chopped them and scooped them into a small bowl.

Emma grabbed a mug from the cupboard and filled it with water.

"I see herself is here," Molly said as she added the diced onion to the meat browning in the pot.

Emma pushed the button on the microwave and turned around. "You mean Mrs. Roberts."

Molly nodded her head, and her gray bun quivered. "Yes, Mrs. Roberts. Thinks she's such a fancy lady when she's really just a fancy lady, if you know what I mean."

Emma didn't. "I'm sorry, what—"

"Back in my day, a man's mistress was called his fancy lady."

"But I thought they were married . . . Mr. and Mrs. Roberts."

"It's not him I'm talking about." Molly winked at Emma, looking more like a character in a fairy tale than ever.

Was she Jackson's mistress? It was possible. Jackson was in his mid-twenties, and Emma gauged Sabina to be in her late thirties. An age gap in the other direction wasn't unheard of. The movie *The Graduate* suddenly came to mind. Was Sabina playing Mrs. Robinson to Jackson's Benjamin?

Molly stood over the sizzling pot, pushing the cubes of stew meat around with a wooden spoon. She turned to face Emma, the wooden spoon in midair. "It's a wonder Mrs. Granger never found out. Not very discreet, they were."

"Mrs. Granger?" Now Emma was thoroughly confused.

Molly nodded and turned back to the pot on the stove. "Of course, I don't know what all she's doing with that Dr. Sampson. Maybe she didn't care. You know what they say, 'what's good for the goose is good for the gander.'"

Did Molly mean that Sabina had been having an affair with *Hugh*?

"You mean Mrs. Roberts and Hugh . . ." Emma asked.

"Well of course. What did you think I meant?" Molly scooped up the chopped vegetables and added them to the pot. "And poor Mr. Roberts turns a blind eye to everything she does, he's that taken with her. Well . . ." She paused with her hands on her hips. "Why wouldn't he be? She's a beautiful woman. And accomplished, too. Not like some floozy off the streets. That's probably what attracted Mr. Granger to her in the first place."

Emma finished making her tea. Molly had certainly given her something to think about, she realized as she headed back to her desk, mug of tea in hand.

Chapter 20

ONCE again, Emma was glad to leave the Grangers' house behind. Arabella had invited her for dinner again since Priscilla was still visiting. Emma was grateful—left to her own devices, she was either too lazy or too tired to cook for herself and often made do with something in the microwave or a takeout dish.

Emma thought about what she'd discovered as she drove to her aunt's house. What role, if any, might Sabina's supposed affair play in Hugh's death? Always assuming Molly was right. Emma got the impression Molly enjoyed embellishing her stories with just a wee bit of Irish blarney.

As she pulled into Arabella's driveway, Emma could hear Bette's excited bark and Pierre's deeper one. She smiled to herself. She could always count on the dogs for a passionate greeting.

Emma had to shoo them both away from the front door so that she could slip inside. She still had to be careful about Bette getting out. She hadn't yet learned to come when called, and Emma was considering enrolling her in the local puppy training classes.

"Hello?" she called from the foyer. The house was strangely silent. Emma stood listening, staring at the dust motes dancing in the light coming in the window.

For once, Arabella didn't bustle down the hall offering a drink of sweet tea before they even reached the kitchen. Emma sniffed. No tantalizing smells coming from the kitchen, either. That was strange. Usually Arabella had dinner going by the time Emma arrived.

She walked out to the kitchen and was surprised to find it empty. The lights were out, nothing was on the stove and the table wasn't set. Perhaps Arabella was planning on a late dinner?

Emma walked back to the hallway and peered into the living room. No sign of either Priscilla or Arabella. Now she was beginning to worry.

"Hello. Anybody home?" she called up the stairs.

Priscilla appeared on the landing. She looked surprised to see Emma.

"Hello, dear," she said as she came down the stairs. "I was just sitting in my room reading. I didn't expect you."

"But . . ." Emma said, looking around. "Where is Aunt Arabella?"

"I think she's getting ready. At least she was, twenty minutes ago."

Emma was more confused than ever. "Arabella invited me for dinner tonight. If that's not convenient, I can . . ."

Now Priscilla looked confused. "Tonight? But Francis is taking her out to dinner tonight. I planned to heat up some soup for myself. I've been eating way too much good food lately." She patted her stomach. "Are you sure Arabella said today?"

"Yes, I'm positive." Emma thought back to that morning, when she'd talked to Arabella. She was certain she didn't have it wrong.

Emma followed Priscilla into the living room. Priscilla perched on the edge of the needlepoint chair she favored, and Emma plopped on the sofa.

"This is very worrisome, coming on top of those other instances where Arabella couldn't remember where she was or what she had been doing. I think the stress of this whole situation is getting to be too much for her."

The front doorbell pealed, and both Pierre and Bette jumped to their feet and ran toward the foyer. Emma followed them.

She pulled open the front door to find Francis standing there. He smiled when he saw Emma. She held the door wider, grabbing Bette's collar in the nick of time. "Come in. Mother said you're taking Arabella out to dinner tonight." Emma took Francis's coat and hung it in the hall closet.

"Yes. I've got a reservation at Ruggero's Italian Bistro at the Paris Winery." Francis was wearing gray slacks, a navy blazer and a crisp white shirt. He glanced at his watch. "We'd better get going. Is your aunt ready?"

Just then Arabella came down the stairs. She was wearing a pair of old, stretched-out yoga pants Emma knew she kept to clean the house in, and a tattered white shirt with stains on the front.

"I'm sorry. I must have fallen asleep. Emma, Francis, what are you doing here? Not that I'm not glad to see you . . ."

"You invited me for dinner," Emma said.

"I'm taking you out to dinner," Francis said almost at the same time.

Arabella looked utterly bewildered. She sat down on the stairs and rubbed her forehead. "That's strange because I don't remember either." She looked up with troubled eyes. "What's wrong with me?"

Francis joined her on the step, putting his arm around her. "I'm sure it's something that's easily fixed. When is your appointment with Dr. Baker?"

"Tomorrow. At least I think so. It seems I can't trust my memory for anything anymore," Arabella said sharply, sounding almost like her normal self.

"No harm done," Francis said consolingly. "What say we all order a pizza? I saw some cold beer in the fridge."

Emma noticed Priscilla's lip curl ever so slightly, but she didn't say anything.

"That's done then. Let's not worry anymore. Dr. Baker will undoubtedly be able to sort things out."

EMMA was relieved to see that Arabella was in her usual good spirits when she arrived at Sweet Nothings the next morning. It was almost as if the previous evening hadn't happened. Was that because she had put it out of her mind or because she just didn't remember it? Emma wondered.

They had a slow morning and had been open for business for an hour when Priscilla walked in.

"I just wondered," she said to Arabella, "if you want me to come with you to see Dr. Baker."

Emma saw Arabella's spine stiffen. "That's very kind, but I'm perfectly capable of getting myself there and back. There's no need to worry."

"But I *do* worry," Priscilla said. "I can't help it. It's just the way I am." She smiled sadly at her sister. "If you're absolutely sure . . ."

"I'm positive," Arabella said with conviction.

"Well, then, I'll be going. I'm having coffee with a woman I worked with at the hospital. It will be fun catching up."

She left, closing the door quietly behind her.

Arabella blew out a puff of air. "I'm sure she means well, but sometimes . . ." She let the sentence hang in the air.

The rest of the morning went by quickly, and just before noon Sylvia arrived. They heard, rather than saw, her Cadillac pulling into the parking lot in back of Sweet Nothings. Eloise Montgomery had come with her, and she looked slightly shaken up as they entered the shop. Her hat was askew, and her eyes were wide.

"Stupid cop," Sylvia said to no one in particular as she took off her coat.

"You did run a red light," Eloise remarked.

"So maybe I did." Sylvia turned around to face them. "We didn't hit anything, did we? It was an honest mistake. Forgive and forget, that's what I always say."

"I don't think that policeman is going to forget anytime soon," Eloise said, taking off her hat and putting it behind the counter.

"Did you get a ticket?" Arabella asked, her eyes twinkling with amusement.

"Yeah. I tried to charm him out of it, but he was having none of it. Never mind there's not a single blemish on my record. You'd think that would count for something."

Emma supposed it did, but it was only by sheer luck that Sylvia hadn't been ticketed before. She had ridden with Sylvia once and that was enough. She was beginning to wonder if from now on she shouldn't offer to pick Sylvia up and then deliver her safely back to Sunny Days when her shift was over. Certainly she doubted Eloise would relish riding with her again anytime soon.

Arabella came out of the back room with her coat on. "I'll be off now to Dr. Baker's," she said as she pulled on her gloves and wound her scarf around her neck. "Wish me luck. I'm a little nervous. It's one thing to be told you need to take pills for your cholesterol or your blood pressure and another to think that you might be going . . . " She didn't finish the sentence.

"I'm sure everything will be fine," Emma said, but she crossed her fingers behind her back just to be sure. "Maybe you should have let Priscilla go with you?"

"No. I can manage on my own. She would make me even more nervous." She gave Emma a quick hug, said, "Wish me luck," and disappeared out the door.

Sylvia looked at her watch. "I guess you'd better get going, too, kiddo. Eloise and I can hold down the fort while you're gone. No need to worry."

Emma quickly ran up to her apartment to eat a container of yogurt and run a comb through her hair. She dreaded going back to the Grangers'—what if Jackson was there?—but she

213

had to see this through. She pulled on her coat and sprinted down the stairs to her car.

The wind had picked up, and Emma could feel the Bug rocking from side to side. The sprinkling of snow they'd gotten the other day had melted, but there were still icy patches here and there on the road.

She pulled up in front of the Grangers' house and got out. Jackson usually pulled his car around back to their enormous five-car garage, so she had no idea if he was at home or not. Liz's station wagon was there along with a strange black car. Emma glanced at it as she walked by— some sort of official shield was propped in the front window. That was curious.

Emma opened the front door and stepped into the foyer, glad to get out of the cold. She peeked into the kitchen. Molly was peeling a pile of potatoes, and good smells were coming from the stove. Perhaps she could persuade Molly to tell her what was going on.

"It's freezing out there," Emma said, rubbing her hands together. "I thought I'd make myself a cup of tea to start."

"Help yourself." Molly jerked her head toward the tea canister. "I'm putting together a nice shepherd's pie for dinner. On a bitter day like today, they'll be wanting something warm and comforting in their bellies." She deftly cut each of the potatoes into quarters. "There's a show I want to see on the telly tonight, so I'm getting things ready now. All that will be needed will be to pop it in the oven for half an hour."

Emma took her time selecting a tea bag and filling a mug with water. "I saw a strange car outside," she began, hoping Molly would take the bait.

"The black one pulled up just beyond the front door?"

Emma nodded. She slid her mug of water into the microwave and pushed the Start button.

"They showed up about an hour ago. Two men in black suits. Looked like undertakers but they said they were with the FBI. What the FBI could be wanting with Mr. Jackson, I can't imagine."

"They didn't say what they wanted?" The microwave pinged, and Emma retrieved her mug.

"No, but I've heard raised voices coming from the library. And here Mr. Jackson is usually so even-tempered. It took me by surprise."

"I don't suppose you heard what they were saying."

"I did indeed. I didn't like the way they were talking to Mr. Jackson so I stopped outside the door to listen. Something about a forged painting." She shook her head as she filled a large pot with cold water and dropped in the potato quarters. She set the pan on the stove and turned the burner to high. "The Grangers have been in the art business for decades and not a whisper of scandal, and now this. I'm sure they'll soon discover it's all a big mistake."

"I'm sure you're right." Emma picked up her tea and headed down the corridor. At least Jackson was occupied with his visitors. Hopefully their paths wouldn't cross. She stuck her head into the office to say hello to Liz. She was staring through the lens of her camera at a spectacular Renoir painting.

Emma didn't want to scare her so she cleared her throat. Liz turned around.

"Hi, when did you get here?"

"Just now."

"Can you believe it?" Liz whispered. "The FBI is here. They showed up over an hour ago and have been in the library with Jackson ever since."

"I talked to Molly, and she said it had to do with a forged painting. I wonder if the Jaspers called them about their Rothko."

"I don't know, but Jackson did come in here at one point. He was frantically going through some files and muttering under his breath. Something about 'an impeccable provenance,' I think he said."

Emma took a sip of her tea. "Perhaps he's trying to prove that some work is real. Or at least that he got it from a reliable source."

"You're probably right."

Liz had just finished talking when they heard the squeak of a door opening and footsteps, muffled by the Oriental runner, coming down the hall. The two men in black suits, who Molly claimed were with the FBI, passed by the open door to the study. Jackson was trailing them and had a file folder under his arm. His expression was serious but not necessarily worried.

They could hear voices coming from the foyer, then the door closing and finally footsteps heading back down the hall. They stopped outside the door to the study.

Jackson walked in, nodded at Liz and Emma and tossed the folder he'd been carrying onto the other desk. Emma looked at it longingly, dying to know what was inside.

Jackson ran his hands over his face and rubbed his temples. "Long day," he said curtly before walking out again.

Liz and Emma looked at each other and, without a word Liz went to stand guard at the door while Emma approached the desk and the folder Jackson had left sitting out. She touched it tentatively with the tips of her fingers, pulling it closer until she could see the writing on the tab. It read "Rothko, 1950, oil on canvas." It had to be the Jaspers' painting.

Emma eased the folder open carefully. She looked up at Liz for confirmation, and Liz gave her a thumbs-up. The coast was clear.

Emma glanced through the papers—letters, copies of e-mails, an invoice and a black-and-white photograph of a painting. She turned the photograph over. The painting's details were written on the back in black ink in a strong hand. Also written on the back were the words, *This certifies that this is an original work by the hand of Mark Rothko.*

Emma quickly glanced at Liz again, and once again Liz signaled to go ahead.

Emma scanned the letters and e-mails. They all related to the sale of the painting. She flipped over the invoice and nearly gasped when she saw the price. She thought she saw something out of the corner of her eye and looked up to find Liz waving at her frantically. She shut the folder and pushed it back to its original position.

She had seen enough—the papers indicated the painting had come from the Wasserman Gallery in Memphis. Emma planned to call them the next day to see if they were willing to verify the sale.

Chapter 21

EMMA and Liz had both scooted back to their original positions by the time Jackson walked into the room. Emma's heart was pounding furiously, and judging by the color in Liz's cheeks, hers was doing the same.

Jackson didn't seem to notice anything amiss.

"Emma," he said suddenly, and she tried not to jump or look too guilty. "I'm wondering if you'd be willing to do me an enormous favor?" He turned his most persuasive look on her. He was an attractive young man, and Emma supposed he often used that to his advantage. He was obviously used to getting his way.

"Yes . . ." she said somewhat tentatively.

"Sabina's painting has come back from the restorer. She really wanted to have it today for an important dinner party she's giving tonight." He smiled apologetically. "Would it be too much of a bother for you to run it over to her? She's only about ten minutes from here. I'd do it myself, but I have an appointment in twenty minutes."

"Of course. I wouldn't mind at all."

"I'll just get the painting then." And he bolted from the room as if he was afraid Emma would change her mind.

He returned moments later with a bubble-wrapped package. Emma was relieved to see it was relatively small—there wasn't much room in the Bug for hauling anything very large.

"Here's the address." Jackson handed her a slip of paper. "Do you have GPS?"

Emma shook her head. "No, but I know where this street is so it's not a problem."

Emma tucked the slip of paper into her purse and put on her coat. Jackson thanked her profusely once again and left the room.

"I'll see you later," she said to Liz.

Liz leaned her elbows on the desk and propped her chin in her hands. "How about coming over for dinner soon? It would cheer Brian up. He's been moping about and driving me crazy. I guess not being able to get around is driving *him* crazy."

"Of course." Emma felt a pang of conscience. She should have stopped in by now to see Brian. "Call me, okay?"

"Will do." Liz bent her head over her laptop.

The kitchen was empty and clean when Emma went past. Molly must have finished her dinner preparations.

She carried the wrapped painting out to her car and stowed it carefully in the backseat. She put the slip of paper with the address on the passenger seat next to her so she could refer to the house number. The street was the same one that an acquaintance of hers and client of Sweet Nothings, Deirdre Porter, lived on. It was an exclusive, gated community with large houses on even larger plots of land.

After slightly more than ten minutes, Emma turned onto the street Jackson had indicated. She stopped at the redbrick gatehouse and gave her name to the attendant. He picked up the phone, dialed a number and spoke briefly.

"You can go on through."

The wrought-iron gates swung open and Emma entered the prestigious enclave, where everything was perfect and nothing was out of place. She scanned the house numbers until she came to Sabina's house. It was in a contemporary style, low and sprawling, with enormous windows along the front.

Emma shivered as she stood on the front step and rang the bell. It pealed melodically inside the house. The painting was tucked securely under her arm. She didn't know what it was, but it was bound to be expensive.

A maid in a light gray uniform opened the door and led Emma into a two-story, cathedral-ceilinged foyer. Emma immediately felt dwarfed by the enormity of the space. There was a dining room on one side with a modern-looking glass table. On the other side was the living room decorated with contemporary furniture including an orange Eero Saarinen chair Emma recognized from the Museum of Modern Art in New York. Vivid and colorful modern paintings adorned the all-white walls.

The maid spoke briefly into an intercom next to the front door.

"If you'll come this way." She led Emma into the vast living room and indicated she should have a seat. "Would you care for a cup of tea?"

"No, thank you," Emma said knowing she wasn't there on a social visit—she was merely acting as Jackson's gofer.

"Mrs. Roberts will be with you shortly," the maid said and left the room.

Emma looked around in wonder. It was like sitting in a museum. There was a spare white table along one wall covered in silver-framed photographs. Curiosity got the best of her, and she went over to examine them.

Most were family photographs—Sabina or her husband posed against various exotic backdrops: beaches with impossibly blue water, snow-capped mountains or foreign-looking cities. There was one black-and-white photograph among them. Emma looked around, but Sabina had yet to appear. She picked the photo up for a better look.

Pictured were a couple sitting together on an old-fashioned, wood-framed velvet sofa in what looked like a formal living room. The woman had closely permed gray hair and was wearing a plain dress with stout, black lace-up shoes. The man was balding and had on a tweed suit and a pipe clenched between his teeth. Next to the sofa was a round draped table with a stained glass Tiffany lamp.

Behind them, and just visible, was part of a colorful painting of the blue sea seen through open shutters. It looked like a work by Matisse—Emma had seen very similar paintings in her art history textbook in college.

She was about to put the photograph back when a voice came from behind her.

"My grandparents," Sabina said. "That was taken before

the war, in their house on Friedrichstrasse in Berlin. They had to leave it all behind when they fled to England."

Emma jumped, and her face flushed crimson. "I'm sorry. I didn't mean to pry."

"Don't be silly. The photographs are out in order to be seen."

Sabina was as elegant as usual in a pair of well-fitting jeans and a long, cashmere turtleneck, her dark hair flowing around her shoulders.

Emma handed her the painting.

"Thank you for bringing this. I hope it wasn't too much of a bother. Its absence left a space on the wall in the dining room. I didn't want to rearrange all the paintings to cover it. Too tedious." She started to pull off the bubble wrap. "I hope the restorer has done a decent job."

She pulled the painting from its wrappings and held it up to look at it. It was an abstract with splashes of bright blues, reds and yellows. Emma didn't recognize the artist.

Sabina was examining it closely when she suddenly looked up at Emma. "I'm sorry. Would you like a cup of tea to warm up? I can hear the wind even in here."

Once again, Emma turned down the offer of a drink. "I should be going."

Sabina walked her to the door. "Thank you again. It was very kind of you to make the trip. I've been up to my neck in preparations for tonight's dinner party."

Emma gave Sabina a last smile and headed toward her car. She thought about the photograph of Sabina's grandparents as she headed back to the Grangers'. What must it have been like to have to flee, leaving everything you owned behind, in order to save your life? She couldn't imagine it.

She had sold a lot of her things before leaving New York—no point in paying to ship furniture she'd picked up in secondhand stores or found discarded on the edge of the sidewalk. Some of the things had been difficult to part with—the overstuffed armchair Guy had helped her wrestle up the stairs to her third-floor walk-up, the wobbly kitchen table where they'd shared many meals and bottles of wine, the lamp her next-door neighbor had kindly rewired for her. It had been hard enough leaving her old life in New York behind, but she had known she would have a warm welcome from Arabella. She couldn't imagine arriving in a foreign country, knowing no one, possibly not even understanding the language. What strong people they must have been.

Emma decided not to go back to the Grangers'. Instead she ran some errands, and by shortly after five was heading to Arabella's house. She was anxious to hear about her aunt's appointment with Dr. Baker. She had hoped that Arabella would call her, but when she checked her phone there were no voice mail messages or texts. Arabella was very proud of her new iPhone and had even had Emma show her how to take photos and use the calendar function as well as how to text.

Francis's car was in Arabella's driveway when Emma got there. Bette and Pierre were making their usual racket before Emma even closed her car door. She smiled as she went up the walk. She could see the two of them in the glass alongside Arabella's front door—glass that was now covered with dog nose prints.

The door was open, as it often was, so Emma walked in, stepping carefully to keep the excited dogs from tripping her. Bette wound in and out of Emma's legs, wagging her tail so hard it almost disappeared. Pierre was slightly more sedate, rolling onto his back to invite a tummy scratch. Emma scratched Bette behind the ears with one hand and Pierre on the stomach with the other.

"Now that's enough, you two," she said, standing up and heading toward the kitchen. Both dogs galloped after her, sending the hall rug bunching up behind them.

"What smells so good?" Emma walked into the kitchen, where Priscilla was taking a turn at the stove, and Francis and Arabella were nursing drinks.

Priscilla turned around with a spoon in her hand. "I'm doing chicken divan. It's always been your father's favorite." Her voice caught slightly, and she quickly turned back to the stove.

Emma bit her lip. It was hard to know how to comfort her mother when she felt in need of comfort herself.

"Is that sweet tea you're drinking?" Emma pointed to the tall glass in Arabella's hand.

"No, honey, Francis made his famous recipe for Tennessee tea. There's more if you'd like some."

"You know, I think I might."

"We're celebrating," Arabella said, smiling at Francis.

"Celebrating what?"

"Good news from Dr. Baker. Get yourself a drink, and I'll tell you all about it. I'm sorry I didn't call you as soon as I got back from my appointment—I know you've been worried about me although you've been pretending not to be—but we were run off our feet this afternoon at Sweet Nothings. It seems the Junior League had decided to organize an excursion to our little shop. Very profitable for us." Arabella raised her glass in a toast.

Emma retrieved the pitcher of Tennessee tea—a concoction of Jack Daniels, triple sec, sweet-and-sour mix and cola—and poured herself a glass. She perched on one of the stools around the island and had a big sip, savoring the taste as it slid down her throat.

"Just what I needed after a long day. And to top it off, Mom's chicken divan. And"—she turned to Arabella—"good news, I gather?"

Arabella's face was quite pink—whether from the warmth coming from the stove or from the drink in her hand, Emma didn't know.

"Yes. Remember when Dr. Baker put me on that cholesterol medication?"

"And told you to cut out fried foods, if I remember correctly," Francis added.

Arabella pretended to pout. "Give up fried chicken? Never. But I have cut back. I really have. But anyway, that's not the point. The point is that one of the side effects of the medication is memory loss. Which explains why I can't remember where I went during the party the night Hugh was killed," she finished triumphantly. "I'm not losing my mind after all. Dr. Baker is switching me to another pill to see if that will lessen the side effects."

Francis cleared his throat and looked at Arabella over his steepled fingers. "Unfortunately, it still doesn't answer Detective Walker's question. Rumor around the police station is that you're still prime suspect number one."

"You've got to be kidding," Arabella burst out.

"How could anyone think Aunt Arabella would . . . murder someone?" Emma said.

"It is absurd," Francis agreed. "But the police are floundering and want to grab on to something . . . anything. The murderer was extremely clever picking the time and place that he did. With so many people milling about, all he had to do was mingle with the crowd. From what I've heard, the police have questioned numerous people already, and no one seems to have noticed anyone going up the stairs to that balcony. Apparently no one even saw Hugh himself head up there."

A flash of a memory streaked through Emma's mind, but although she tried hard to grasp it, it eluded her as surely as a wisp of fog.

Priscilla turned around and paused with a whisk in her hand. "You know what they say, *cherchez la femme*. Look for the woman."

Emma had another sip of her Tennessee tea and then put the glass down resolutely. It was beginning to make her head spin. "But Mariel has an alibi, so that rules her out."

"Didn't you tell me there was a mistress?" Arabella said.

"Yes, the wife of Hugh's partner. Sabina Roberts."

"The one in the orange . . . excuse me . . . tangerine gown?" Francis said with a twinkle in his eye.

"Yes." Arabella patted his hand.

"Maybe they had a falling-out? Or, he'd taken up with someone new." Priscilla removed a box of frozen broccoli from the microwave and dumped the contents into a bowl. "Men like that often do. Women mean nothing to them."

Emma glanced at Arabella. A shadow passed over Arabella's face. Was she regretting the time she'd wasted on Hugh Granger, Emma wondered? Somehow she didn't think so. Arabella wasn't the type to regret things—even her mistakes.

"Anyway, the FBI were there today."

"So the Jaspers have made a fuss about the painting. That must mean that the son refused to give them their money back."

"I think he's insisting it's real." Emma finished her last sip of tea. "He showed the FBI something in a folder, and afterward I managed to sneak a peek at what it was. It was a collection of letters, e-mails and even an invoice for the painting along with a black-and-white photograph with a certification on the back from the Wasserman Gallery."

Francis shrugged. "Don't know it."

"It sounds familiar," Arabella said. "Out of my price range though, I'm afraid."

"I'm going to call the gallery tomorrow and see what I can find out about the Rothko. If they sold it to the Grangers then Jackson or Hugh must have bought it in good faith, and that's the end of that trail."

"What about this Jackson?" Arabella asked. She got up and began getting place mats and napkins out of the cupboard. "I should imagine he's going to come into a lot of money now that his father has died. Could he have been tempted to hasten it along? Maybe he has debts, or gambles?"

"Their housekeeper loves to talk," Emma said. "I'll see what she can tell me."

"Just be careful." Francis wagged a finger at Emma. "A lot is at stake for the Grangers. And someone has killed already."

WHEN the last of the chicken divan had been scraped from their plates, and the last drop of the Tennessee Tea drunk, Emma collected the dishes and offered to do the cleaning up. As she loaded the dishwasher, she heard Arabella bidding Francis good night followed by the sound of her footsteps on the stairs. Pierre was asleep on the rug under the table, and Bette was curled up at Emma's feet, occasionally twitching and making little mewling noises. Emma wondered what she was dreaming about. She hoped it was a good dream and not a nightmare.

She wiped down the counters, checked that everything was in its place and turned out the lights. She woke Bette, who immediately sprang to her feet as if she had never even closed her eyes.

Emma clipped on Bette's leash and headed down the hall toward the front door. She glanced into the living room and was surprised to see her mother sitting there alone with the light from a small lamp across the room barely piercing the darkness. She wasn't reading or knitting and didn't have the television on. She seemed to be simply sitting and staring at . . . nothing.

Emma unclipped Bette—who made an immediate beeline for the kitchen—dropped her leash on the foyer table and stood in the entrance to the living room. She cleared her throat, and her mother spun around.

"Are you going?" she asked.

"Soon." Emma walked into the room and took a seat opposite Priscilla. "What are you doing in here all alone?"

Her mother dabbed at her eyes with a balled-up tissue. "Thinking." She looked at Emma. "Trying to figure out what I'm going to do. Where I'm going to go."

"What happened between you and Dad?" Emma asked softly.

Priscilla shrugged. "I guess you could say we grew apart.

It's such a cliché, but it's true. We were both used to working hard, and then all of a sudden, that was over, and we had time to spend together. Unfortunately, we didn't know each other anymore. We're like polite strangers inhabiting the same house."

"But couldn't you"—Emma twisted her hands in her lap— "get to know each other again?"

Her mother didn't answer.

"Was this . . . Dad's idea?"

Priscilla shook her head vehemently. "No, I'm afraid it was mine. I don't know what got into me or why I did it. I wish I hadn't." She pressed the tissue to her eyes, and Emma could see her shoulders heave.

She touched her mother's arm. "Maybe if you called him?"

"It's too late now," Priscilla sobbed. "He was so . . . hurt. I don't know if he'll ever forgive me."

"You won't know if you don't try," Emma said, quoting a saying she had heard dozens of times from Priscilla herself. "Why don't you try?"

Priscilla raised her chin. "Maybe I will. You're right. I won't know unless I try."

Chapter 22

ARABELLA was extremely chipper when she arrived at Sweet Nothings the next morning. Emma was putting out some new stock—she'd purchased a few racier things for Sweet Nothings, items their younger clientele had been asking for, like satin garter belts and lacy bustiers. They would be displayed discretely, of course, so as not to offend the sensibilities of their more mature customers.

"What did you say to your mother last night? She was looking decidedly more cheerful this morning." Arabella poured herself a cup of coffee from the carafe sitting on the heated coil.

"It seems that this whole separation thing was her idea, not Dad's. She's been thinking twice about it, but she's afraid to call him. I convinced her to give it a go."

"I've felt the whole thing was a mistake from the beginning. They've been together too long to split up now."

Emma put the last of the new garter belts in one of the drawers behind the counter. She held up one of the satin-and-lace bustiers.

"Do we dare display this on a mannequin?" she asked her aunt.

Arabella frowned. "I don't know. This is still a small town with small-town ways. Perhaps it's best if we keep that under wraps, so to speak."

Emma nodded. "That's what I thought." She found a spot for the bustier on one of the shelves in the armoire. If anyone asked, she could guide them to it.

A cacophony of horns blaring outside announced Sylvia's arrival. She burst through the door with her usual verve, hung up her coat, stowed her purse and joined Arabella behind the counter.

"So what's new?" Sylvia asked with a gleam in her eye.

Arabella nodded her head toward Emma. "Emma's on the trail of a forged painting. Are you still going to call that gallery?" Arabella asked.

Emma nodded. "Potentially forged. I suppose I should give Jackson the benefit of the doubt."

"Forged painting?" Sylvia asked eagerly.

Emma was filling her in on the latest when the door opened and a customer walked in. They scrambled like spilled marbles—Arabella approaching the customer and Emma and Sylvia busying themselves with straightening the stock.

A half hour later, Emma left Arabella and Sylvia in charge and went to sit at the desk in the stockroom, where it would be quiet and she could take notes if necessary. She had all the details about the painting on a slip of paper in her pocket. Her hand hovered over the telephone receiver. She'd thought out what she was going to say, but she was still nervous.

Finally she picked up the phone and without allowing herself to think about it any more, dialed the number in front of her.

"Hello, Wasserman Gallery," a very cool voice intoned.

"Hello. This is Emma Andrews," she said with what she hoped sounded like conviction. She'd decided to use her mother's maiden name just in case anyone tried to trace the call back to her. She twined the phone cord around her finger nervously. "I'm with Granger Art here in Paris, and I have a question about the provenance of a painting that was purchased from you." She tried to emulate the cool, slightly snooty tones of the woman answering the phone.

"I will transfer you to the gallery director. One moment, please."

Emma clasped the phone tightly. So far, so good. But would the director be as easy to fool?

"Hello?" a cultured-sounding male voice drawled. "This is Henry Dubois. How can I help you?"

Emma identified herself, almost forgetting that, for the sake of this conversation, she was Emma Andrews and not Emma Taylor. "I have a question about the provenance of a painting that Granger Art in Paris purchased from your gallery."

"I hope there isn't a problem."

"Oh, no," Emma reassured him. "I'm just checking a few

details." She thought she heard a sigh of relief whisper over the phone wires.

"In that case, I'd be more than happy to help. Can you gave me the details, please?"

"It's a Rothko painting." Emma added the date, size and inventory number she'd copied down from the file on Jackson's desk.

"One moment, please." She heard the clicking of computer keys.

"Hmmm . . ." Henry said. "We don't seem to have that painting in our records. Let me look for that title. Is it possible the inventory number is wrong?"

"It's . . . it's possible."

More clicking of computer keys. "No, I'm sorry, that painting doesn't come from us. There must be some mistake."

"Yes, I imagine there is. Thank you for your time." Emma hung up quickly.

So the Rothko hadn't come from the Wasserman Gallery—which meant that Jackson had faked those papers she saw in that folder. Which meant the painting didn't have a provenance—it originated with Granger Art.

Therefore it must be a fake. She wondered how long it would be before the FBI discovered the same thing and made a return trip. She was surprised it hadn't happened already, but then they obviously had more than just one case to work on at any given time.

Arabella pounced as soon as Emma emerged from the stockroom. "So what did you find out?"

"It's a fake," Emma said bluntly.

Arabella bit her lip. "I can't believe that of Hugh. I *don't* believe it! He would abhor forgeries on principle—the same way he hated ugly, or as his daughter called them, *broken things.*"

"I'm putting my dollar on the son." Sylvia came over and leaned on the counter. "I'm betting his father found out about the fakes and that's why he had to kill him." She drew a finger across her throat dramatically.

"I don't like it." Arabella shook her head, and her bun quivered as if with indignation. "It makes me nervous, you being there. If this Jackson finds out you've been snooping . . ." Arabella let the rest of the sentence hang.

Emma gave her aunt a quick hug. "I'm heading over there now." She looked at her watch. "And don't worry. I'll be careful."

EMMA felt slightly uneasy as she headed toward the Grangers'. She hoped Jackson was out—she felt as if her newfound knowledge was written on her forehead. She'd never been particularly good at keeping a poker face. She was relieved to see Liz's station wagon already pulled up in front of the house. At least she wouldn't be alone.

Emma opened the car door and shivered as the brisk wind snaked its way down the back of her neck and up the sleeves of her coat. Despite the bitter weather, someone was out riding. She was far out in the field and heading toward the house. From this distance she was a mere speck, and Emma couldn't tell whether it was Mariel or Joy.

Emma supposed the horses needed exercise no matter what the weather. She'd never cared for riding herself. Her grandfather had sat her on a pony once when she was around four years old. It was one of Emma's earliest memories. The pony had reared up for some reason, and Emma had promptly fallen off. She'd never been particularly keen to try it again.

Emma found Liz in the office, as usual. Emma perched on the edge of the desk.

"Have you seen Jackson?"

Liz shook her head, and her blond hair swished back and forth. "Not yet."

Emma looked around then leaned her head close to Liz's and whispered, "I called that gallery that was listed in the papers in that folder—the Wasserman Gallery—and found out that the Rothko painting sold to the Jaspers is a fake."

Liz looked startled. "Really?" she squeaked.

"The gallery knew nothing about it."

"That means that Jackson . . ." Liz sank into the nearest chair and put her head in her hands. "I don't know if I can keep working on this knowing that . . ."

"You have to," Emma pleaded. "He can't know what I've discovered."

"But it's . . . it's criminal."

"Murder is even worse. I think Jackson may have killed Hugh. Arabella is convinced his father wouldn't condone selling forged paintings. My guess is that Hugh found out, they argued and Jackson plotted to kill him. Francis said Jackson wasn't on the list of names collected by the police after the murder. He must have fled right afterward."

Liz shivered. "This whole thing is giving me the creeps."

"I know." Emma slid off the desk and headed toward the door. "I'd better get to work. Believe me, I wouldn't stay on if I weren't trying to find out who was responsible for killing Hugh Granger. I have to, for Aunt Arabella's sake."

"Be careful," Liz whispered after her.

Emma headed toward the kitchen. She wanted to take some tea back to the storage room with her since it was always slightly chilly back there. The kitchen was empty but as she was heating up her water, Molly bustled in with a grocery bag in each arm. Her cheeks were bright red from the cold, making her look more like a gnome than ever.

She clunked the bags down onto the kitchen table and pulled off her gloves. "Oooh, that wind would skin you alive, it's that cold out." She unbuttoned her tweed coat. It had large buttons up the front and looked as if it had been in style forty years ago.

"Someone was out riding," Emma said, taking her mug out of the microwave. "She must be freezing."

"Probably Miss Joy. She goes out in all kinds of weather. I think it's the only time she's truly happy." Molly opened the pantry and began stacking cans on the shelves. "Mrs. Granger has been going out in all kinds of weather, too," Molly said, her voice slightly muffled with her head in the closet. "I suppose it's her way of coping with Mr. Granger's death." She turned around, her hands on her hips and her lower lip stuck out defiantly. "The police were around again, asking questions, but no nearer are they to solving the case. It's a crime—someone getting away with murder."

Molly shook her head and *tsk-tsk*ed under her breath. "That Detective Walker even came around asking me questions, as if I would know anything about it. I wasn't even at the party. Mr. Granger did ask me, but what on earth would I do at an event like that? I'd only be comfortable if they let me help wait tables or peel the vegetables for dinner. Besides, my only good dress isn't fancy enough—it's fine for Sunday morning at church but the ladies would all be in long gowns, not a ten-year-old polyester shirtwaist."

Emma stirred some sweetener into her tea. "What did Detective Walker want to know?" She looked away so Molly wouldn't see how eager she was for the information.

"He wanted to know how everyone in the house got along and who might have had a fight with whom." She folded up one of the grocery bags and tucked it into a corner of the pantry. "I had to tell them the truth. Miss Joy argued with her father, like I told you, and Mrs. Roberts did, too."

"Sabina?" Emma paused with her mug of tea halfway to her mouth.

Molly put her finger alongside her nose. "Lovers' quarrel, I should imagine. And terribly fierce it was. Mr. Granger was rather quiet, but I could hear herself all the way out to the kitchen, she was that mad."

"Maybe he was ending the affair?" Emma suggested. "Or had found someone else?" Would that have made Sabina mad enough to kill? Emma didn't think so.

"I only heard the few words—something about *give it back*. What, though, I can't imagine."

That was more food for thought. Emma headed back to the storage room, her mind whirling with possibilities. Although she doubted Sabina and Hugh's lovers' quarrel had anything to do with his death. *Give it back*—that didn't make any sense. Probably Molly had heard wrong.

Joy's quarrel with her father, on the other hand, made her a very good candidate for her father's murder. She had good reason to hate him—he was responsible for the car accident that crippled her and killed her mother. And he'd taken little interest in her—unlike Jackson whom he had taken under his wing and brought into the art business. That must have further cemented Joy's hatred.

EMMA had been working for two hours when her computer froze. She tried every trick she knew—admittedly not many—to get it going again. She crossed her fingers—hopefully she wasn't going to lose the afternoon's work. She tapped several keys, but the screen didn't change. Maybe Liz would know what to do. As a web site designer, she probably knew a lot more about computers than Emma.

Emma was crossing the foyer when she heard raised voices coming from outside. She peered through the glass alongside the front door, which gave her a partial view of the driveway. She could see the back end of Mariel's red Porsche and Mariel herself, her ash-blond hair blowing across her face, which was red from the cold. She was gesturing at the car and yelling, her expression clearly indicating that she was angry about something. Emma couldn't hear what she was saying nor could she see the person Mariel was yelling at.

The front door opened, startling Emma. She backed away from the window quickly. The open door let in a blast of wintery air along with the deep tones of a masculine voice. Jackson's?

Joy moved awkwardly into the room. She slapped her gloves and riding helmet down on the foyer table and unbuttoned her red, quilted paddock jacket. She was wearing black and tan boots and khaki breeches with suede patches at the knee. To Emma, she looked far more comfortable in these clothes than the long, burgundy satin dress she had worn to her father's birthday party.

The red jacket brought some color to her face, and her light brown hair was becomingly tousled by the wind. Once again Emma thought that with very little effort she could be an attractive woman.

"I saw you out riding," Emma said, trying to be friendly. "You must have been freezing." Emma wrapped her arms around herself. Just the blast of cold air from the open door had sent the temperature in the foyer plummeting.

Joy looked at Emma, a quizzical expression on her face. "Cold? No, I didn't really notice it. I never do when I'm out on Big Boy. I let him have his head, and we galloped across the back fields. It's exhilarating. I don't notice much except his motion, the sound of his hooves and the scenery speeding past. I guess I concentrate on the ride and don't notice how I'm feeling, one way or the other." She gave a tiny half smile.

Emma darted a glance toward the window alongside the door. Mariel was still out in the cold, gesturing furiously at her car. Her companion moved slightly, and Emma caught a glimpse of Jackson. He wasn't dressed for the outdoors— wearing only a turtleneck sweater and no jacket—and was staring stony-faced at his mother.

Joy jerked her head toward the door. "Mariel is absolutely furious with Jackson. That doesn't happen often. I'm tempted to pull up a chair and watch the show." Her lip curled sardonically.

"Why? What's happened?" Emma looked openly out the window now. Mariel was pointing to a spot on the car. Jackson shrugged his shoulders.

"Mariel seems to think he scratched the front bumper of her Porsche. It's barely visible—she only just now noticed it. But she's mad for that car." Joy shook her head. "I don't see what difference it makes, but to each his own, I guess." She joined Emma by the window.

"Doesn't Jackson have his own car?"

"Yes, of course. A brand-new BMW Z4. His birthday gift." Again her lip curled in what looked like a sneer. Her resentment of her brother was obvious.

"So why borrow his mother's car? Was his already in the shop? A brand-new car?"

Joy shook her head. "No, he didn't take his car. We all went over together. Father organized a limo to drive us." She paused. "Except Mariel, of course. She went over early in her own car to check on things."

"When was this?" An idea was forming in Emma's mind, but it couldn't possibly be right.

"The night of Father's birthday party, of course. We're not in the habit of all getting together on a regular basis. This was quite an exception."

"So Jackson went with you in the limo . . ." Emma was quickly putting two and two together. "And then Jackson left in his mother's car."

Joy looked at her like a teacher whose slowest pupil has finally caught on. "Yes, and apparently he nicked the bumper or something. She's only just noticed it, and she's furious. It's the only time she's ever let him borrow the Porsche. And obviously the last."

"Then how did Mariel get home? Did she ride back with you?"

"Yes. When the police finally let us go, Mariel was

nowhere in sight. The driver waited a good fifteen minutes . . . it was awful . . . I was exhausted and horrified, as you can imagine. I just wanted to get home to a cup of tea and a hot bath. With Father . . . dead . . . and Jackson already off someplace, it was just me in the car. We were about to pull away from the hotel when Mariel suddenly appeared."

"She came out of the hotel?" Emma asked, trying to picture the scene.

"No, I don't think so. I don't think that's possible. I remember staring at the front door, willing her to appear. I would certainly have seen her. All of a sudden, she appeared out of the darkness and was banging on the car window demanding I let her in."

Mariel hadn't been in the ballroom when the police took down everyone's contact information. Emma doubted she'd been inside the hotel at all or surely she would have been at her husband's side. Unless *she* had murdered him, and had then arranged to disappear. Had Dr. Sampson been waiting to drive her away from the scene?

Joy looked at Emma with a peculiar expression on her face—one Emma couldn't read. "I can see the wheels turning in your head," Joy said dryly. "You're wondering if my stepmother murdered my father." She stared Emma straight in the face. "Frankly, so am I. Father was upset by her increasing drug use. It started with painkillers for her back when Roy threw her—and ended with addiction, as it so often does with those pills. Father wanted her to go to rehab—some swanky place in Arizona with a spa, yoga instructors and gourmet food. Sounds like a vacation to me." She gave a bitter laugh. "But Mariel refused. Said it was all nonsense and that she could stop anytime she wanted to, and there was no harm in it. Of course she had Dr. Sampson wrapped around her finger, writing her prescriptions presumably against his better judgment." Again, that bitter laugh.

Emma was hardly listening. All she could think about was the fact that Mariel didn't have an alibi for Hugh's death. She hadn't left the Beau early in her very memorable red Porsche as Emma had thought. Jackson had been the one to collect the sports car from the valet. Jackson hadn't been at the hotel when Hugh was killed, but Mariel had.

Chapter 23

EMMA was dying to tell Liz what she'd discovered, but Jackson had come back inside—slamming the door behind him and dislodging a small, early Miro sketch from the wall. The drawing hit the floor, shattering the glass. Jackson swore as he picked up the drawing and kicked the shards of glass out of the way.

"Molly!" he bellowed from the hallway.

Emma heard Molly scurrying down the hall, her footsteps sounding like the scratching of a field mouse.

Emma herself scurried back to the relative isolation of the storage room. The screen saver had come up on her computer—a whirling ball that moved from one side of the screen to the other. Emma jiggled the mouse, and her spreadsheet appeared, still frozen with her last entry only half-complete. She would have to turn the machine off and back on again and hope that that solved the problem. The last thing she wanted to do was to go to Jackson for help. He was obviously in a foul mood after the encounter with his mother.

Turning the machine off and then on again seemed to have done the trick. Emma glanced at the data apprehensively, but all her work was there except for the last entry. Thanks heavens for auto save. She decided she was done for the day. She was going to Liz's for dinner and wanted to go home and freshen up. She felt her spirits rise. She would be seeing Brian soon.

Emma drove home, her mind only half on the road, contemplating the information she'd gleaned from Molly and then Joy. She barely missed going through a red light and forced her concentration back to her driving.

Arabella had offered to keep Bette for the evening. The pup still needed regular bathroom breaks, so Emma didn't want to leave her alone for too long.

She breathed a sigh of relief as she put her key in the lock of her apartment. It was good to be home. She rolled her shoulders forward and back. Being at the Grangers' always made her tense. She was constantly aware that she was there under false pretenses. She would be glad when she could quit.

Emma had enough time for a few yoga poses. She did a half-dozen sun salutations and rested in child's pose for a few minutes. By the time she was done, she'd gotten the kinks out of her body.

She washed her face, redid the minimal makeup she wore and worked some product through her hair. Dinner's at Liz's was always a casual affair, but Emma wanted to look nice for Brian. She chose a pair of cropped denim pants, a pale pink angora turtleneck and flats. By six forty-five she was ready to go.

Liz and her family lived fifteen minutes out of town in the house that had belonged to Liz's parents. She and Matt had completely renovated the place, including turning two rooms into a family-sized kitchen and adding a separate family room.

Emma pulled into the driveway right on the dot of seven o'clock. Fragrant wood smoke curled up from the stone chimney, and Emma stood for a moment enjoying the scent.

Brian answered the door when Emma rang. His face was already lit with a broad smile that put crinkles around his blue eyes and brought out his dimples. He was standing upright with only one crutch for support.

He hugged Emma fiercely, holding her close against his broad chest. Emma felt herself relax even further in the circle of Brian's warm embrace.

"I wanted to take you out to dinner," Brian murmured against Emma's hair, "but I hated to ask Liz or Matt to drive us since I don't fit in your Bug. Hopefully my leg will heal even faster than the doctor's predictions, and I can get rid of this cast."

Emma followed him out to the kitchen. Liz was at the stove, stirring something that smelled heavenly, and Ben and his sister, Alice, were at the table eating bowls of macaroni and cheese. Ben was rhythmically kicking the table leg until Liz turned around and gave him a look that clearly said *stop*.

Alice had her blond hair in a neat ponytail, and Ben's

slightly darker blond hair was cut short though not short enough to eliminate the cowlick that gave him a strong resemblance to Dennis the Menace.

"Aunt Emma." Alice jumped up from the table and threw her arms around Emma. Emma hugged her back.

Ben scowled at them both as if he found this feminine display of affection distasteful. Emma had to laugh. Ben was turning into a real boy.

"Where's Matt?"

Liz jerked a thumb toward the French doors that led to a large deck. "He's firing up the grill, believe it or not. He says it's never too cold for a barbecue."

Emma rubbed her hands together. "A barbecue in February. How wonderful. What is he cooking?"

"He got a butterflied leg of lamb from the Meat Mart." She gestured to the pot on the stove. "I'm doing creamed spinach and garlic-roasted potatoes to go with it."

"My stomach is growling already."

"Brian"—Liz pointed at the refrigerator—"can you get Emma something to drink? There's a bottle of white wine chilling and a pitcher of sweet tea if you'd rather that."

"I can get it—"

"Please, let me." Brian hobbled toward the refrigerator on his crutches. "It makes me feel useful. I've been doing nothing lately but lying around reading."

"That's not true." Liz turned around. "You've been to several renovation sites with Bobby Fuller. You've been working on the hardware store books, and you've kept the kids occupied while I got some work done." She turned back to the stove and stirred the pot. "I *wish* you would get some rest."

Brian pulled open the refrigerator. "And I wish you would stop worrying. The doctor said I'm doing fine, remember?"

Emma almost laughed. They sounded so like brother and sister—like Ben and Alice when they squabbled with each other.

"Which would you like? Wine or tea?" Brian stood poised in front of the open refrigerator.

"I'll have some wine."

He brought out the bottle of pinot grigio and pivoted on his good leg just enough to set it on the counter. Leaning on one crutch, he maneuvered himself closer, pulled open a drawer and retrieved the corkscrew. The cork gave a festive pop as he pulled it out. Brian reached for a wineglass from the rack overhead, poured Emma a glass and handed it to her. He reached for another glass and poured one for himself.

"We're done. Can we be excused?" Alice and Ben chorused from the table.

Liz glanced over and checked their dishes. Both were empty. "Okay, go ahead."

Before she could say another word, they had bolted from the room.

"Now, I'd suggest you two"—she pointed to Emma and Brian—"go and sit in the living room and get out of my way."

Emma heard the smile in Liz's voice and knew exactly what she was doing. Normally she and Liz would hang out in the kitchen and chat while Brian helped Matt with the barbecue. She was giving Emma and Brian a chance to be alone.

"Can you manage?" Emma asked Brian. "I can carry your glass if you'd like."

"Thanks, that would be great." He handed the wine to Emma.

Emma matched his slow steps as they made their way down the hall and into the living room. A fire was burning in the stone fireplace—the wood crackling, popping and spitting as the flames licked the logs.

Brian plunked down on the sofa, and Emma curled up next to him. He put his arm around her, and she snuggled closer.

Brian smiled and kissed the top of Emma's head. "This is heaven, don't you think?"

"Mmmm," Emma murmured.

"I've been thinking," Brian said, swiveling slightly so he could see Emma. "I had this idea."

"Oh?"

"I realize that living in Paris is a bit of a letdown after New York City. And working behind the counter at Sweet Nothings can't compare to the career you had in New York."

Emma sat up straighter. Had Priscilla been talking to Brian? Emma went to protest, however feebly, but Brian held up his hand to stop her.

"There's no need to deny it. I understand. A future in Paris isn't nearly as bright as your future in New York would have been. That's why I had this idea."

Now Emma was more curious than anything. "What idea is that?" She turned, too, so she and Brian were facing each other.

"The way you renovated Arabella's place has really had people talking."

No, Emma thought, *it was the murder at Sweet Nothings last spring that had them talking,* She shuddered as she remembered finding the body of her ex-boyfriend on the floor of the shop. But she didn't say anything.

"More than one of the shopkeepers I've spoken with has said that they would like to spruce their place up, too."

Emma nodded. "Angel already has. I almost didn't recognize Angel Cuts when I walked in."

"Exactly," Brian said triumphantly. "And there are others as well. Who wants to go to some dusty old store when they can shop at the mall? Shop owners are beginning to recognize that they have to keep up with the times now that they have competition."

"So what is your idea?" Now Emma was really curious.

"We go into business together. You design the interiors, and I'll do the work. You know how to make a little money go a long way in terms of decor. You did it for your aunt. And that's important, because our clients certainly wouldn't have huge budgets. The jobs won't be that big, so I can keep on with my renovation business. Eventually we could branch out to other towns. Once word gets around, my guess is we'd be pretty busy." Brian had been sounding more and more excited, but now he looked down at his hands. "Sorry, I guess I got carried away." He looked up at Emma. "But what do you think?"

"What about Arabella?" Emma couldn't desert her aunt now.

"My guess is you'd still have time to help at the shop. I know you do the bookkeeping for Arabella and all the buying, but there's no need for you to spend your life behind a counter. Arabella has Sylvia, and now I've noticed this other woman is helping out."

"Eloise Montgomery."

"And there must be other people who would like a part-time job."

Was Brian doing this just to make sure she stayed in Paris? Emma wondered. No matter, it was a wonderful idea. It would give her something more challenging to do—that ought to please Priscilla. And it would mean she and Brian would be doing something together.

"I think it's a great idea."

Brian's entire body relaxed. "You do? That's wonderful. I've been talking to Willie at the Meat Mart. He's interested in some small renovations—he wants to add space to carry some gourmet products like fresh cheeses, imported olive oil and things like that."

Emma was already picturing the inside of the Meat Mart. It was as basic as a butcher shop could get. She could imagine adding some baker's racks, a few framed posters . . .

Liz's voice brought her back with a start. "Dinner's ready."

The table was already set, and Matt was coming through the French doors with a platter of meat when they got to the kitchen.

"Do you need any help?" Emma felt guilty for sitting while Liz did all the work.

"No, everything's ready." She brought two white serving bowls to the table.

Brian slid into his seat and propped his crutches in the corner. Emma took the chair next to him.

Liz looked from Brian to Emma and back again. "You two are up to something. I can tell. What gives?"

Emma helped herself to some creamed spinach. She looked to Brian since it was his idea.

Brian explained the idea he had just laid out to Emma.

"That's a wonderful idea," Liz exclaimed when Brian finished. She looked at Emma suddenly. "I'm sorry. I just assumed you thought so, too."

"I do," Emma reassured her. "Although I'm a little nervous about what Aunt Arabella's reaction would be."

"I don't think she'd mind a bit." Liz forked up a bite of spinach. "You've already been working part-time, and she's managed just fine."

Emma realized that was true, and the thought made her a little sad. Arabella had been completely dependent on her when she first arrived back in Paris. But Brian's idea was the answer to some of the questions that had been plaguing her recently about whether she would be satisfied spending her life helping Arabella at Sweet Nothings. Now she would have something challenging and interesting to do as well. And she and Brian would be building something together.

Matt put down his knife and fork and picked up his wineglass. "Here's to your new venture." He raised his glass to Emma and Brian.

"Now, tell us if you've discovered anything new about the Grangers," Liz said as she touched her napkin to her lips.

Emma swallowed her bite of lamb and recounted what she'd learned that afternoon from Molly and Joy.

"So Mariel is back in the running with no alibi," Liz said. "And Jackson is out."

"And Sabina had an argument with Hugh a few days before his birthday. We can't forget her."

"So Sabina, Mariel and Joy are still in the running." Liz ticked them off on her fingers.

"And don't rule out some angry collector—if the painting Jackson sold to the Jaspers was fake, I'm sure there were others," Matt said. He leaned back in his chair, and it gave a loud creak. He turned to Liz. "I hope his operation isn't shut down before you get paid. You've already put in a lot of time on this project."

"I did get half up front," Liz reassured him.

Matt grunted.

"According to Molly, the police were around again asking questions. I hope that means they're no longer considering Arabella as a suspect," Emma said.

Matt laughed. "The very idea is ludicrous."

"Tell that to Detective Walker." Emma pushed her empty plate away.

Emma helped Liz clear the table and put out dessert plates and cups and saucers. Liz cut them each a piece of apple pie, adding a dollop of vanilla ice cream to the top.

They chatted amiably as everyone finished their coffee and desserts. The sounds of canned laughter came from the family room, where Ben and Alice had retreated to watch television.

Matt glanced at his watch. "I think it's time the rug rats got ready for bed. I'll go get them in their pajamas."

Liz cleared the rest of the dishes, and Brian hobbled alongside Emma to the door.

"I'm so glad you like my idea," he said. "I couldn't take a chance on your becoming bored with life in Paris and possibly going back to New York." He grinned at Emma, then bent his head and kissed her gently. The move put him off balance, and Emma had to grab him to keep him from falling.

"You know one thing I'm really looking forward to," Brian asked with a gleam in his eye.

"No, what?"

"Getting this blasted cast off! It's really cramping my style," he said as he lowered his lips to Emma's again.

Emma drifted home as if on a cloud. She barely remembered steering the car, but suddenly there she was in the Sweet Nothings parking lot. She was getting out of the Bug when she noticed a magazine on the backseat. She didn't remember tossing it there. She pulled it out. It was the issue of *Art International* she'd taken from the Grangers' library to cover up the fact she had actually been in there snooping.

She thought she might as well glance through it before returning it just in case Jackson asked her about it. She tucked the magazine under her arm as she walked up the stairs to her apartment.

It felt strange without Bette to greet her. She hoped the puppy was having fun at Arabella's. Pierre wasn't always interested in playing but occasionally Bette could persuade him into the canine version of tag or hide-and-seek.

Emma changed into her usual around-the-apartment attire—a pair of yoga pants that had seen better days, and a sweatshirt that had as well. She grabbed a mug from the cupboard, filled it with water and popped it into the microwave.

When the microwave dinged, she grabbed a tea bag from the box on the shelf and dunked it several times before tossing it in the trash. She took her tea over to the sofa, and with a groan, stretched out with her magazine.

She leafed through it marveling at all the different sorts

of things that constituted *art* these days. Some of the works were beautiful and evocative, others . . . looked as if preschool children had splashed paint willy-nilly onto a canvas.

Emma turned the pages, her eyes starting to feel heavy and nearly closing, until she came upon the cover article about artwork that had been stolen by the Nazis from Jewish families during World War II. The accompanying picture had her sitting bolt upright on the sofa nearly knocking her tea over in the process.

The picture was of a Matisse painting, and Emma could have sworn it was the same one that was in the picture of Sabina's grandparents sitting on the table in the Robertses' living room. A glimpse of an old-fashioned parlor was visible, and Emma thought she recognized the table from the old black-and-white photograph.

She began to read the article. The Matisse painting in question had belonged to a Mr. and Mrs. Jacob Meyer of Berlin. The Meyers had fled with their family to England leaving everything behind, including their elegant home on Friedrichstrasse and all its contents. They had owned dozens of works of art as well as antiques, silver, china and jewels, all of which had been looted by the Nazis.

Emma continued reading the article. Some of the artwork stolen from the Meyers had surfaced in the years after the war and had been returned to the family. Others, like the Matisse painting, the jewel of their collection, had gone underground never to be seen again. According to the article, there were plenty of unscrupulous collectors who would be more than willing to purchase the piece even though it meant being very careful how it was displayed and to whom it was shown.

Emma closed the magazine. She was quite certain the Matisse pictured in the article and the one in the photograph in Sabina Roberts's living room were one and the same. She wondered if Sabina had seen the article. It must be very painful to realize all that had been lost by her family because of the war.

Emma tossed the magazine onto the coffee table. She would take it back to the Grangers' and leave it in the library. Her stint there had certainly proved fascinating. She had a feeling though, that it was coming to an end.

Chapter 24

SATURDAY was a busy day at Sweet Nothings. Not that Emma was complaining, but she was exhausted by the time she locked the door shortly after five o'clock. She leaned against it for a moment. Her feet and back ached, and she was longing for a hot bath. She could only imagine how her aunt must feel.

"Am I glad tomorrow is Sunday," Arabella said as she put away some stock. "Did your mother tell you she plans to leave on Monday?" She turned toward Emma, one of the store's vintage bullet bras in her hand.

"Don't aim that thing at me." Emma laughed.

Arabella glanced at the piece of lingerie in her hand and she, too, laughed.

"No, Mother didn't say she was leaving." Emma was

about to spray glass cleaner on the counter but stopped abruptly. "What is she going to do? Where is she going to go?"

"I don't know. I tried to persuade her to stay longer—I have plenty of room—but she feels she's in the way." Arabella tucked the bra into one of the drawers.

Emma spritzed glass cleaner on the countertop and wiped it down with a paper towel. She stood back to see if she had removed all the fingerprints from the glass. "I don't think it's that. I think she wants to get home to talk to Dad. Although she's afraid she's hurt him too much for him to be willing to reconcile."

"That doesn't sound like your father at all," Arabella said. "I'm going to have to talk to Priscilla and see if I can persuade her to call George before this goes any further. I'm sure he'd be more than willing to take her back. He must be suffering, poor thing."

"I'm sure he is." Emma conjured up a picture of her father. He'd been a crackerjack attorney, and was a better than average golfer and a whiz at trivia. The one thing he hadn't been was a cook. "Dad can't even heat up a can of soup without help. I can't imagine what he's doing with Mom gone."

Arabella gave her a sharp look. "I wouldn't worry about his being fed. I'm sure all the widowed or divorced ladies in the community are lining up to bring him casseroles," she commented dryly. "It was the same when Francis's wife died. He said his freezer was stuffed full of tuna noodle casseroles, turkey tetrazzini, one-dish chicken noodle meals and other delights."

"Really?" Emma said doubtfully.

"Your father is still a very good-looking man." Arabella

sighed. "Why do men get better looking as they age while no one calls *our* wrinkles and gray hair *distinguished*? It isn't fair."

Emma was now worrying in earnest. "I'm going to have to convince Mom to call him before anything happens."

"Excellent plan." Arabella nodded approvingly. "Come for dinner tomorrow. You can talk to her then and see her off. I've promised her another batch of fried chicken. I'll make some extra for her to take on her trip."

Emma couldn't imagine her mother eating fried chicken in the car. She was the only person Emma knew who never picked it up with her hands to get at the meat closer to the bone. Priscilla insisted on using her knife and fork as her grandmother Andrews had taught her, she would always say when encouraged to pick up food in her hands.

"Oh." Arabella turned around as if the thought had just occurred to her. "I've asked Brian, too. Liz said she'd be more than happy to run him over in her station wagon since he doesn't fit in your car."

Arabella smiled coyly, the picture of innocence.

EMMA spent Sunday puttering around her apartment. It was a luxury she didn't often have. She cleaned out her closet, washed the kitchen floor and took Bette on several long walks, bundling up against the cold wind that was blowing. It was snowing lightly—but not sticking—and Bette was entranced with trying to catch the flakes that melted as fast as they fell.

Emma spent a good part of the day mulling over Hugh Granger's death, and everything she had learned in the meantime. Jackson now had an alibi whereas Mariel didn't. Sabina had argued with Hugh shortly before his death and so had Joy. It went around and around in her head but by the time she was ready to leave for Arabella's she still had not come to any conclusions.

By the time she clipped on Bette's leash and went down to her car, she'd nearly given herself a headache. Her spirits lifted as she approached her aunt's house. *Brian will be there* ran through her head like some sort of musical refrain.

Priscilla was sitting in Arabella's living room, staring at the cell phone in her hand, when Emma arrived. Her suitcase was already packed and was at the ready by the front door. It was a somber black but with a bright red pompon on the handle, which her mother had put there to identify the bag whenever she and Emma's father traveled. For some reason, the sight of it made Emma inexplicably sad.

Emma unclipped Bette, who made a mad dash for the kitchen to see if Arabella had any treats. She hung her coat in the closet and hesitated on the threshold to the living room.

Her mother turned around. She gestured to the phone. "I called him, but there was no answer."

Emma sat on the ottoman opposite her mother's chair. "Did you leave a message?"

"Yes. But I doubt he'll call me back."

Emma squeezed her mother's hand. "I think he will."

Just then the bell rang. "I'll get it," Emma called to her aunt in the kitchen. She pulled open the front door. It was Brian standing rather unsteadily on the front steps, leaning heavily on his crutches.

Emma felt the grin spread across her face. She held the door wide as Brian made his slow and awkward way into the foyer. He gave Emma a lingering kiss then struggled out of his jacket and handed it to her. He was wearing a blue plaid flannel shirt, which brought out the color of his eyes, and a pair of jeans with one leg partially cut off to accommodate his cast. Emma noticed that both Ben and Alice had already left their signatures on the plaster—Alice having dotted the *i* in her name with a heart.

Brian took a deep breath. "It sure smells good in here. Is that Arabella's fried chicken?"

Emma smiled. If the way to a man's heart was truly through his stomach, Brian was going to end up marrying Arabella. The thought gave her pause for a moment—perhaps she ought to cook a nice meal for Brian. Not fried chicken; she couldn't compete with Arabella on that front. She hadn't cooked much of anything of late beyond grilling a piece of meat or throwing together an omelet. Perhaps it was time she brushed off her skills. When she was dating Guy, he'd done most of the cooking. She shuddered remembering the prodigious amounts of butter and cream he had used that never seemed to put an ounce on his sinewy frame.

Priscilla came out of the living room. "Brian, how nice to see you again." She held out her hand.

Her mother was a true Southern gentlewoman, Emma thought, never letting her feelings or emotions get in the way of good manners. She had plastered a smile on her face, albeit a slightly stiff one, and risen to the occasion.

They all trooped into the kitchen, where Arabella was lowering chicken pieces into the pan sizzling on the stove. Priscilla went to the pantry and got out the place mats and napkins, and Emma began to fill the water glasses.

Brian looked chagrined. "I wish I could help."

"Don't be silly," Arabella said as she turned a piece of chicken over with a pair of tongs. "You sit and rest that leg of yours." She turned and pointed a finger at Brian. "But as soon as that cast is off, we'll put you to work, don't worry."

Brian laughed. "It's a deal."

"Where's Francis?" Emma asked.

"At some kind of departmental meeting. He's going to be so sorry he missed this meal." Arabella began moving the chicken pieces to a large white platter.

She had been using that same platter for years. Emma remembered Arabella serving fried chicken on it when Emma was a child. As far as Emma knew, it wasn't used for anything else.

Finally Arabella had hustled everything over to the table, and they all sat down.

"Everything looks delicious," Brian said as Arabella handed him a bowl of succotash.

"Has there been anything new at the Grangers'?" Arabella asked Emma as she helped herself to a biscuit. She spread it with butter, drizzled it with honey and took a bite.

"Liz is very upset by what is going on over there," Brian said, putting down his fork. "I'm not so sure it's a good place for you to be, either." He reached out and put his hand over Emma's.

Emma noticed her mother watching them.

"I don't feel as if I'm in any danger," she reassured Brian. "I'm hoping to get to the bottom of things very soon."

"Can't you leave that for the police?" Brian still looked concerned.

"The police have been too busy barking up the wrong tree to get anywhere," Arabella said acerbically.

"What about that Jasper fellow?" Priscilla pushed a bite of chicken around on her plate. Emma noticed she'd barely touched her dinner.

"John Jasper? What about him?" Brian looked wary.

"Well, you told us that the painting he purchased from Granger Art turned out to be a forgery. What if he'd found that out a lot earlier than he admitted? Maybe he approached Granger and demanded his money back. Granger refused so he"—she swallowed delicately—"did away with him."

Brian was already shaking his head. "No, no, John would never do something like that. It's impossible."

"Besides"—Emma put down her fork—"John bought the painting from Jackson, not his father. Arabella doubts Hugh knew anything about the forgeries."

"That's right. It wouldn't be like Hugh at all to sell fake artwork," Arabella interjected.

"Then why kill Hugh? Why not Jackson?"

Priscilla shrugged. "You're right. It wouldn't make sense under those circumstances."

The sudden sound of a cell phone ringing made them all jump.

"That's mine." Priscilla fumbled in her pocket. "I'm so sorry. I meant to turn it off. It's just that I thought maybe . . ." She glanced at the caller ID and jumped up from her chair, banging the table in the process and nearly upsetting her water glass. She put out a hand to steady it. "It's George," she said with a note of wonder in her voice.

"Well, don't just stare at the phone," Arabella admonished, "answer it."

"Hello?" Priscilla said breathlessly as she bolted from the room.

"Keep your fingers crossed," Arabella said to Emma.

Brian looked confused.

Emma put her hand over his. "I'll fill you in later."

They were all quiet while Priscilla was out of the room. Emma strained to hear her mother's conversation, but all she could hear was the low, indistinct murmur of her voice. Suddenly her appetite deserted her. What if her father refused to reconcile? It was unthinkable.

They were still eating silently when Priscilla burst back into the room, her usual decorum put aside for the moment.

Three heads swiveled in her direction.

"Well?" Arabella said.

Priscilla let out her breath in a whoosh that fluttered the edge of her napkin. "Everything is going to be fine!" She beamed.

"Wonderful," Arabella and Emma chorused at the same time.

Brian looked from one to the other of them, then shrugged and reached for another biscuit.

Priscilla smiled at everyone and then, much to Emma's complete amazement, picked up her chicken leg in her fingers and began to nibble it.

They took their dessert and coffee into the living room and were just finishing up when they heard a car horn toot followed by the ringing of the doorbell.

"It's me," Liz said when Emma opened the door. "I hope I'm not too early."

Brian had struggled to his feet and was making his way to the door. He smiled at his sister. "I'm afraid I'm becoming a real bother to you."

"Don't be silly," Liz admonished. "You've been a great

help with the kids. They're ecstatic to have their uncle Bri around. Giving you a ride is the least I can do to repay you for keeping them occupied."

Brian stuck his head into the living room. "Arabella, thank you for another delicious dinner." He patted his stomach. "And Mrs. Taylor, it was a pleasure seeing you. Have a safe trip home tomorrow."

Brian brushed Emma's lips with his then took Liz's arm as they descended the stairs to the sidewalk.

Emma turned around to find her mother standing in back of her, a thoughtful look on her face. She put her arm around Emma's shoulders and gave her a squeeze.

"I know what I said earlier—about whether it was wise of you to stay in Paris and about your young man's plans for his career." She gestured toward the door through which Brian had just departed. "Forget what I said." She smiled. "Don't let Brian go. He's a keeper."

Chapter 25

WHEN Emma left that night to go back to her apartment, her mother gave her a real hug good-bye. Emma was surprised to see Priscilla had tears in her eyes.

"You've been a wonderful support to me," she said as she squeezed Emma tight.

Emma hugged her back. "Say hello to Dad for me."

"Next time, we'll both come. And as soon as you can take some time off, come down to Florida. And"—she winked at Emma—"bring your young man with you."

"I will," Emma promised. Emma found her own eyes tearing up as she waved a final good-bye and headed down the steps toward her car.

The clouds parted, and a broad beam of light from the moon illuminated Emma's drive home. She pulled her car up under the sodium light in the parking lot, got out and beeped it closed. Her cell phone rang just as she reached the top step and was fumbling for the keys to her apartment.

She finally found them, got the key in the lock and pushed open the door. She dumped the contents of her purse onto the sofa and retrieved her phone.

"Hello?" she said somewhat breathlessly.

It was Brian.

"Hi. I just called to make sure you got home okay and to say good night."

A feeling of warmth and contentment coursed through Emma.

"I wish I could come over there right now."

"I wish you could, too," Emma said, smiling.

"It feels like I've been in this cast forever."

"Hopefully soon . . ."

"I see the doctor tomorrow. I'm hoping he can give me some good news." Brian was quiet for a moment. "I wish you didn't have to go back to the Grangers'."

"It'll be fine," Emma reassured him. "Besides, I'm almost finished with the project." She sighed. "I'm afraid I didn't discover much of anything."

"Is Detective Walker still bothering Arabella?"

"She's still on his list, although she did explain to him about the pills she was taking causing temporary memory loss. He seemed slightly mollified by that. I fear he doesn't have any other ideas at the moment."

"What was that all about with your mother?"

"Oh, that. She'd gotten up the nerve to call my father

earlier, but he was out. He returned her call and said he was more than willing to take her back."

"Let's not let that ever happen to us—where we grow apart," he said, his voice husky.

"We won't." Emma's voice was a whisper.

"Promise?"

"Promise."

The warmth Emma felt from hearing Brian's voice stayed with her as she got ready for bed and slipped between the covers. The sheets were icy cold, and she wished that Brian were there to keep her warm. She had to be content to snuggling up to Bette instead.

EMMA was a little late leaving Sweet Nothings on Monday afternoon. Sylvia's ancient Caddy had refused to start, and Emma didn't want to leave Arabella alone. Finally, they heard the familiar belching that heralded the arrival of Sylvia and her automobile.

"Don't bust a gasket, I'm here," Sylvia said, barreling through the door. She had a paisley scarf, which had slipped slightly askew, tied over her hair.

Emma noticed raindrops on the shoulders of Sylvia's coat. "Is it raining?"

"Yeah, it's coming down pretty good." Sylvia pulled off her kerchief and shook it out. "But if the temperature drops any lower, we'll be getting some more of that white stuff."

Emma groaned. "I'm ready for spring."

"Me, too," Arabella said.

Sylvia looked at the clock. "You'd better get going, kid."

* * *

EMMA pulled on her coat, gave Bette one last scratch behind the ears and headed out the door. Although it wasn't too long after noon, the dark skies made it look and feel much later. An icy, slanted rain splashed into the puddles that had already formed in the parking lot's ruts. Emma skirted one carefully. She looked back at Sweet Nothings, where mellow light poured from the window in the back door. She was tempted to turn around and go back but instead she beeped open the Bug and got in.

Rain drummed on the roof of the car, sounding a staccato beat that matched Emma's heart rate. She switched on the windshield wipers and pulled onto Washington Street. As she drove she tried to put her finger on what was causing her sense of unease, but there was nothing in particular that she could think of. She shook her head. She was just being fanciful. She forced herself to think about Brian, but the warm glow she'd experienced last night failed to materialize. She shivered and reached out to crank up the heat.

Emma pulled into the driveway in front of the Grangers' house and parked off to the side. Mariel's red Porsche was in front of the door. Emma wondered if she had just gotten in or was about to go out.

The rain had turned to fat drops of snow that melted almost as soon as they hit the ground. Emma started up the front steps, and her foot slipped on the slick surface. She grabbed the railing just in time to avoid falling, but the incident left her heart pounding.

She opened the door and stepped into the foyer. No lights were on, and the house seemed unusually chilly. Footsteps clattered down the hall, and Molly came around the corner. She had her coat on, a long, knitted scarf around her neck and a serviceable black purse hanging over her arm.

"You're here," she said when she saw Emma. She grabbed Emma's arm in a tight grip. "Those men were here again—the ones in the black suits. Mr. Jackson has gone off with them. I'm worried." She tightened her grasp on Emma's arm. "Do you know who they are?"

Emma shook her head. "Not for sure. But I think they might be with the FBI."

Molly's face turned pale. "What would they be wanting with Mr. Jackson?"

"I'm afraid I don't know," Emma said although she thought she could guess. Was Jackson under arrest? she wondered.

Molly twisted the handle of her purse. "I don't know what the world is coming to, that's for sure."

"Are you going out?"

"Yes. We'll be needing some milk and some butter. I'll just have a quick run to the grocer's."

"Is Joy home?"

"What do you think? She's out riding. She can't stay away from those horses." Molly started toward the door.

"Be careful," Emma warned. "It's getting slippery out there. I almost fell coming up the steps."

Before Molly could open the door, Mariel came down the hall, her high-heeled boots tapping against the wood floor.

"Molly," she called, "are you going to the store?"

"Yes. To Kroger's."

"Would you pick up a couple of bottles of club soda?

We're all out, and Jackson will want his scotch and soda tonight."

Molly fiddled with the top button on her coat. Emma thought the thread looked loose and hoped Molly wouldn't pull it right off.

"Mr. Jackson has gone with those men," Molly said. "The ones in the black suits who were here the other day."

Now Mariel's face turned pale. "When did they leave?"

Molly consulted her watch. "About fifteen minutes ago."

Mariel yanked open the door to the hall closet and pulled out a coat. "I've got to go out. I don't know when I'll be back." She flew out the door without even bothering to button her jacket.

Molly continued to twirl the loose button on her coat. Emma felt sorry for her. So much had happened lately, it had obviously left her reeling.

"I guess I'll be going then," Molly said somewhat reluctantly.

"Be careful," Emma said again as the door closed in back of the housekeeper.

The house was extremely quiet—so quiet Emma could hear the ticking of the clock on the mantel in the living room. She felt like making some noise just to break the silence. She cleared her throat loudly but when the sound died away, it was as quiet as before.

Perhaps if she got to work, she would get lost in the task—it had worked before. Seeing all the beautiful pieces of art was absorbing.

She headed down the hall toward the storage room, her footsteps echoing on the wooden floor. She opened the door and was about to let it close behind her when the thought gave her a chill. She didn't want to be locked in the room all by herself. She looked around for something with which to prop open the door. She finally pulled over the extra chair and stuck it in front of the door, but the door was heavy, and it pushed the chair out of the way. Emma tried again—this time she angled the chair so that it was wedged between the door and the jamb. She stood back and examined it with satisfaction, then began to laugh. If anyone saw it, they would think she was crazy. But she felt considerably better being able to see into the hallway and, more important, to hear if anyone was coming.

Emma had marked the spot where she'd left off on Friday. She pulled out the next work in the rack—a small Giacometti drawing—and turned it over. The details on the label were sketchy. Emma didn't mind—she enjoyed researching. Jackson had been quite pleased with some of the information she had unearthed for him.

Emma pulled up her favorite search engine and was soon engrossed in the task, forgetting her earlier nervousness. Before she knew it, an hour had gone by, but she was pleased to be able to fill in a little more of the drawing's history.

Emma carried the drawing to the storage rack and put it back in its place. She was pulling out the next piece when something clattered to the floor. She gave a little cry and jumped back.

When she looked around she saw it was a cane—although she supposed it would be more appropriately called a walking stick. It was very elegant—ebony in color with a horn handle tipped with a hammered silver cap. It reminded her of the walking stick her aunt had used when she sprained her ankle. The handle of the cane had come off in the fall.

Emma picked up both pieces and tried to fit the silver-tipped handle back onto the stalk but it refused to stay. She took it over to her chair so she could sit and examine it more closely. Something was preventing the handle from screwing back onto the base. She peered at it carefully. The cane itself was hollow, and something had been rolled up and stuffed inside. Whatever it was, was sticking out of the very top and was getting in the way. It looked like a piece of canvas.

Emma stuck her finger into the cane and tried to push the item farther inside so she could screw the handle back on, but she merely succeeded in pulling it out more. It *was* a piece of canvas, with a bright splotch of blue paint at the edge.

Curious, Emma tried to tease it out of the cane. She thought she heard a noise and whirled around to look behind her, but the hallway was empty and quiet. Emma very slowly pulled the rolled-up canvas from the inside of the cane. She put it on the desk and very carefully unrolled it.

She couldn't imagine what it was doing inside the cane or why it had been put there. As she unrolled it, a scene slowly came into view—the blue of the sea, bursts of red from two pots of geraniums sitting on a small balcony and the soft green of painted wooden shutters open to the view.

Emma stood back and gasped. It was the Matisse painting she had seen in the issue of *Art International*—the same one she was almost certain had been in the photograph on the table in Sabina's living room—the painting that had been stolen by the Nazis from Sabina's grandparents.

What on earth was it doing rolled up and stuffed into a cane in the Grangers' storage room? Maybe she was mistaken, and it wasn't the same one after all. Emma had left the copy of the magazine in her car. She quickly rolled the painting up again and tucked it out of sight. Her heart had taken up a staccato beat, and she was terrified that someone would catch her snooping.

She peered into the hallway, but no one was there. She crossed the foyer quickly, conscious of the noise her shoes made against the wood floor. The blast of cold air made her gasp when she opened the front door. Gripping the railing tightly, she made her way down the slick and slippery steps. The sharp wind immediately cut through the fabric of her pants and top. Emma shivered and sped up to a trot.

She beeped open her car and grabbed the magazine from the backseat, clutching it to her chest as she dashed back toward the house. She pulled the front door closed in back of her with a feeling of relief.

As soon as she reached the storage room, Emma began thumbing through the magazine. She missed the story on the first go-round and had to start again from the beginning, flicking through each page until she found it.

She spread the magazine open on the desk. Unless she was very much mistaken, the painting pictured in the article was the same as the one she'd just found hidden inside the hollow cane. She retrieved the canvas and unrolled it alongside the copy of *Art International*.

The works *were* the same. Emma examined both closely, but every detail in the photograph matched the painting in front of her. Emma felt her breath catch in her throat. If she was right, she was looking at a Matisse painting that had been missing since World War II.

Emma suddenly realized she had no idea what to do. Should she roll the canvas up again, put it back in the cane and pretend she'd never seen it? Should she say something to Jackson? Was it possible he didn't know it was there? Or was he the one who had hidden it?

Emma's hand automatically went toward her purse and her cell phone. She would call Brian and ask him what he thought. She dug around in the depths of her handbag, occasionally glancing toward the hall to make sure no one was coming.

She finally pulled out her phone and hit the speed dial number for Brian. One ring, two rings, *come on, pick up* Emma intoned to herself. Just as Brian's voice came over the line, Emma heard footsteps coming down the hall. She clicked the phone off without answering and tossed it in her bag. She was trying to roll up the canvas when she heard someone enter the room.

"Well, well, well. What do we have here?"

Emma spun around to find Sabina looking over her shoulder. She still had her coat on, the collar pulled up against the chill.

Sabina's eyes glowed as she looked at the painting. "You found it for me," she breathed. "I should thank you. You've saved me a lot of trouble."

"Is this the same painting—"

"As the one in the photograph that so fascinated you? Yes. It belonged to my grandparents and was stolen by the Nazis."

"But how . . ."

"When Hugh was in the air force, he was assigned to a task force investigating art stolen by the Nazis. There were plenty of unscrupulous dealers more than willing to make their money selling other people's property. Of course it had to be done very discreetly—and sometimes that meant waiting many years, after the trail had gone cold, to make a sale. Hugh always did have a lot of patience." She fumbled with the clasp on her purse with one hand.

Emma's cell phone rang. It was probably Brian wondering why she'd hung up on him. If the call had been dropped, she would certainly have called back by now. Emma's hand instinctively went toward the phone.

"Don't answer it," Sabina commanded in a sharp voice.

Emma withdrew her hand as if it had been slapped.

"How did you know about the painting?"

"Hugh showed me a picture of it. He said it was the crown jewel of his collection. I recognized it immediately. At first I assumed he didn't know it had been stolen, but it turned out he knew perfectly well. I asked that it be returned to my family." She gave a small shrug. "He refused, of course." She laughed. "I told him I would steal it back. He said it was hidden where I'd never find it." She leveled a glance at Emma. "He was right. I certainly tried, but it never occurred to me he would take it out of the frame and hide it that way."

Emma's mind was reeling. She thought back to the night of Hugh's party. She and Brian were making their way to the terrace to see the fireworks, but someone—a woman in a tangerine dress—was moving against the crowd. She was the only person there wearing that color. And she was slithering through the crowd and into the ballroom toward the stairs leading to the balcony.

"You did it." The words burst from Emma before she could stop them.

"Killed Hugh, you mean?" A very smug look came over Sabina's face. "Yes, I did. It was very satisfying to see the look on his face when I pulled the pistol from my purse."

"I can understand your anger . . . but murder?"

"It was more than just the painting. I grew up listening to my grandparents' stories about the Holocaust and what had happened to the Jews. It made me angry, and every time I heard a new tale, that anger built. This was a way of getting at least a crumb of justice for them."

"But Hugh didn't have anything to do with—"

Sabina shook her head violently. "He knew the work was stolen, and he still refused to return it to its rightful owner. He even bragged that he'd bought and sold other paintings that had been ripped from the homes of those who had been herded into the concentration camps."

A thought occurred to Emma. "And you used that same pistol to spook Joy's horse." It was a statement not a question.

"Yes. It was meant as a warning, but if something worse had happened . . ." Sabina shrugged nonchalantly. "She saw me heading up to the balcony after Hugh during the fireworks and followed me. She tried to blackmail me." Sabina threw her head back and laughed, showing her long, slender column of a neck. "I told her it would have been her word against mine."

Sabina's hand had been in her purse and just then she pulled it out. "And now I'm going to use that same pistol to get rid of you."

Emma's eyes widened as she stared at the gun in Sabina's hands. It was small, but she had no doubt that it was deadly.

"Why don't you just take the painting? That's what you want, after all. I won't say anything . . ."

Sabina laughed again. "Of course I'm going to take the painting, but I'm hardly going to keep you around as a witness." She shook her head. "No, you are going to have an unfortunate accident."

"A gunshot is hardly an accident." *Keep her talking*, Emma thought. Maybe Mariel or Molly would return, or Joy would come in from horseback riding. Perhaps Brian was wondering why she'd hung up so abruptly and wasn't answering her phone and was already on his way. Emma thought about the plaster cast on his leg, and her hopes fizzled. There wasn't much Brian could do in the condition he was in. But maybe he would call the police? She realized it was a forlorn hope even as the thought crossed her mind.

"It's time we went outside." Sabina motioned toward the door with the pistol.

"Outside?" Emma reached for her coat.

"Leave it," Sabina commanded.

Emma tried to drag her feet as much as possible but then she felt Sabina press the muzzle of the gun into her back and knew she meant business.

Chapter 26

EMMA crossed the foyer with Sabina's gun still pressed into her lower back. The house was quiet, the only sound the ticking of the clock in the living room. Emma hesitated at the front door.

"Open it." Sabina pressed the gun a little farther into Emma's back.

Emma pulled open the door and shuddered as the blast of cold air chilled her instantly. She instinctively wrapped her arms around herself. Light snow was falling again, leaving wet blotches on Emma's sweater and pants. She wished she'd worn her boots and not a pair of thin-soled shoes. She shot a glance at Sabina, who was warm and snug in her fur coat and suede boots.

"Across the field." Sabina gestured with the gun toward the stables behind the house.

Emma began the torturous journey across the rutted field. The grass was frozen and slowly turning white from the falling snow. Emma was shivering violently now as she slipped and slid her way toward the barn. At one point she fell, crying out as her bare hands hit the hard ground.

"Get up," Sabina demanded, waving the gun around where Emma could see it.

Emma stayed on her hands and knees for a moment, trying to catch her breath before heaving herself to her feet again. A strange feeling was coming over her. She was past being scared. Now she was mad. The surge of adrenaline propelled her forward, and she no longer felt the biting cold.

"Where are we going?" Emma had no idea where Sabina was taking her, but as long as they were out in the open field, there was still a chance that Molly or Mariel would see them. Emma risked a glance back toward the house and the driveway, but no cars had pulled in yet. For a moment she imagined that she saw Brian's bright red pickup truck parked in the circular drive, but when she blinked again it was gone— merely an illusion or wishful thinking on her part.

Sabina marched her steadily toward the stables. They were close enough now to hear the occasional whinnying and snorting of a horse.

Emma suddenly remembered an article she had read in the paper—about how it was actually very difficult for an amateur to shoot a moving target and that when faced with someone with a gun, your best bet might be to run away. Her stomach knotted up at the thought of running while

Sabina was firing at her. Emma had no idea how good a shot the woman was.

They were almost to the stables now. Was Sabina planning on shooting her there, where the noise would be less obvious? Emma decided she didn't want to wait to find out. She took a deep breath and took off at a run across the slippery field.

"Stop," Sabina commanded, but she didn't fire.

Emma's feet, in their thin-soled shoes, slipped and slid on the snow-covered grass. She kept her eyes on the ground, fearful of putting a foot wrong on the uneven terrain. A tuft of grass hid a deep rut in the frozen earth, and Emma caught her foot in it, slamming to the ground with enough force to knock the wind out of her.

In seconds, Sabina was leaning over her, the gun pointing threateningly at Emma's head.

"Get up."

Emma tried to stand up, but her hands slipped, and she landed on her knees again. Sabina prodded her with the gun. Finally Emma was on her feet and moving once more.

"Don't try that again," Sabina warned.

Emma risked another glance over her shoulder, but the driveway was still empty.

Emma was beyond chilled to the bone by the time they reached the stables. Sabina pulled open the door and shoved Emma inside.

The sudden comparative warmth felt glorious. The smells of hay and horse filled Emma's senses, and she heard pawing and snorting from various stalls as if the horses were surprised by their sudden visitors.

A row of stalls ran down either side of a wide aisle lit by

hanging overhead fluorescent lights. The stall doors were wood on the bottom with metal grills on top and over each was a metal plate with the horse's name on it. Emma noticed that Big Boy's stall was empty. Joy must still be out riding.

The horses moved around restlessly, perhaps wondering if Emma and Sabina had come to feed them. One large black mare named Pretty Girl snorted loudly and banged against the door of her stall with her rump, startling Emma and making her jump.

Emma's mind was racing trying to think of a way to escape from Sabina. Sabina had approached Pretty Girl's stall and was fumbling with the latch, her gun still trained on Emma. She finally unlocked the door and grabbed Emma by the arm.

"What are you doing?" Emma tried to resist, but Sabina waved the gun in her face.

"You're going in there," Sabina said, pointing to the horse's stall. "And when I shoot off my gun"—she brandished it in Emma's face—"the horse is going to go crazy. You won't be able to get out of her way, and it will all look like a terrible and unfortunate accident."

"No," Emma protested. The mare was stomping and snorting in earnest now as if she was angry at the intrusion into her territory. Emma watched as more than one thousand pounds of horseflesh slammed into the sides of the stall. If Emma went in there, she would be crushed for certain.

She decided to take her chances. She yanked her arm from Sabina's grasp and began to run, zigzagging across the stable floor. She was out the door before Sabina was able to respond but it was mere seconds before Emma heard footsteps pounding behind her followed by the sound of the gun being fired.

She flinched but kept running, changing direction repeatedly so that she would be harder to hit. Another shot, then another, but she was still running, her breath rasping in her ears, her heart feeling as if it would burst.

A thunderous noise came from behind Emma. She turned around and glanced over her shoulder quickly. Joy was galloping across the field, standing out of the saddle, a look of intense concentration on her face. Big Boy was kicking up clods of mud behind him as he flew across the grass.

Sabina raised her gun in the air, and Emma held her breath. If Big Boy spooked now, Joy could be seriously injured. Sabina pulled the trigger but . . . nothing. No sound, no bullet. She swore loudly, throwing the gun on the ground. She turned around and looked at Emma then back at Joy.

Joy and Big Boy were headed straight for Sabina. Sabina hesitated like a deer caught in a car's headlights, then she began to run. Joy and Big Boy easily overtook her, the huge horse knocking her to the ground. Joy pulled on the reins and Big Boy slowed and finally came to a halt, his chest heaving and clouds of vapor streaming from his nose. Joy dismounted and both she and Emma made their way toward Sabina, Joy suddenly clumsy now that she was no longer on Big Boy's back.

Sabina lay on the cold grass, her face white and her body still.

"Is she breathing?" Joy asked, her own breath coming in gasps.

Emma, who had begun to shiver uncontrollably, knelt and felt Sabina's neck. She looked up at Joy. "There's a pulse."

"Time to call nine-one-one." Joy pulled a cell phone from her jacket pocket and punched in the numbers.

Just then they heard the sound of a car engine, and they both turned toward the house. Brian's red pickup truck was barreling down the drive. Emma couldn't help the smile that spread across her face. The truck came to a stop in a spray of gravel and both doors flew open.

A man—Emma thought it was Bobby Fuller—was sitting on the driver's side as Brian slid out of the passenger seat, swinging his crutches after him. He began to make his slow and laborious way toward Emma.

Emma began to run, cold, stiff and limping slightly from all the times she had fallen. She reached Brian about two-thirds of the way across the field and threw her arms around him, burying her face in his chest. Brian whipped off his coat and wrapped it around Emma, holding her tight against him. She began to cry, and he stroked her hair gently.

"How did you . . . why did . . ."

"Sssh," Brian said softly. "When you hung up on me earlier and then didn't answer your phone, I had a strange feeling. I didn't like it. I convinced Bobby to drive me over here to check on you. We were already out looking at a job."

"It was Sabina," Emma said somewhat incoherently, gesturing toward the field. "She was trying to kill me."

Brian tightened his arms around Emma. They both heard the faint wail of a siren in the distance. Emma twisted in Brian's embrace. She looked back toward the field. "I'd better go help Joy. If Sabina wakes up . . ."

But before Emma could move, a police cruiser had pulled into the driveway and the two occupants were running toward the figure lying in the field, their guns drawn.

"Let's get you inside. You're freezing," Brian said.

Another siren blared in the distance getting louder and

louder until it cut off abruptly as the ambulance pulled into the driveway.

"They'll take care of everything," Brian said, gesturing toward the police and the EMT crew who were pulling a gurney from the back of the ambulance. He began to lead Emma back toward the house. "It's all over."

Chapter 27

EMMA let Brian lead her back inside the house. Mariel still hadn't returned, but Molly was in the kitchen staring out the window. She gasped when she saw Emma. "What's happened? You look terrible. I saw the police cars and the ambulance. I couldn't imagine what was going on."

Emma looked down at the mud on her knees. There was a small hole in her right pant leg, and the elbows of her sweater were equally dirty.

"A cup of tea—that's what you need." Molly bustled about the kitchen, retrieving a mug from the cupboard and the tea bags from the pantry. Her forehead was creased in worry, and she made soft *tut-tut*ting sounds under her breath as she filled the mug and placed it in the microwave. When the microwave pinged, she added a tea bag and a heaping spoon of sugar and handed it to Emma. "Drink this. It'll do you good. I put plenty of sugar in it."

Emma wrapped her hands around the warm cup. The shivering had finally stopped, and now she just felt unbearably weary. Brian watched her, his eyes narrowed in concern.

Molly twisted her apron between her hands. Finally she could no longer contain her curiosity. "What is going on? Why are the police here?"

Emma took a deep breath and began to explain about Sabina and the painting. Molly stared at her, her mouth open in a round O.

"Well, I'll be," she said when Emma had finally finished. "I did tell you I heard Mrs. Roberts and Mr. Granger arguing that day. It must have been about the painting."

"Yes." Emma took a sip of her tea. "You said she said something like 'give it back.'"

"It makes all the sense in the world now." Molly took another mug from the cupboard and began to fill it. "But what about Miss Joy? She had that big blowup with her father shortly before he—"

Her words were cut off by the sound of the back door opening. Joy came into the room bringing with her the scent of cold, fresh air mingled with horse and hay. Despite the chill, her hair was damp with perspiration around her temples, and she had her jacket open and her scarf undone.

"I can tell you what the argument was about." Joy shot Molly a sharp look.

Molly looked down at her feet.

"I told him I wanted to start a therapeutic horseback riding program here on the farm. I've been saving up the money for it. Riding has done so much for me; I wanted to help other people, too." Joy's eyes filled with tears. "But he wouldn't hear of it. He said he didn't want all these cripples crawling all over the farm. I told him that riding also helps people with mental problems, and he said that was even worse."

"Are you going to do it now?" Emma asked.

Joy lifted her chin. "Yes. Mariel is fine with it and so is Jackson. I've been in touch with a certified instructor. Gordon said he would do anything to help me get things off the ground."

A very becoming blush rose from Joy's collar to her hairline, and she turned away abruptly. Emma looked at her curiously. It seemed as if Gordon might be a little bit more than simply a riding instructor.

Suddenly Emma just wanted to go home. She caught a flash of light as the ambulance made its way back down the driveway.

Emma turned to Joy. "Was Sabina badly hurt?"

"She was regaining consciousness. They'll run a million tests, of course, but I think she's going to be okay."

"You saved my life." Emma put her hand on Joy's arm.

Joy looked embarrassed. "It was nothing. Besides, I never could stand that woman. She's contributed very nicely to my new enterprise, though." Joy grinned. "I saw her go up the balcony stairs after my father the night he was killed. I didn't follow them—I assumed it was some planned rendez-vous. But then when the police discovered my father had been shot, I put two and two together. Sabina was desperate to keep me quiet. When spooking Big Boy didn't work, she resorted to giving me money. I knew the police would figure things out in the end with or without any help from me."

"But they almost didn't," Emma protested. "And Sabina almost killed me."

"I am sorry about that. I never meant for that to happen."

Emma was shocked. Was it the background of immense privilege she'd been surrounded by her whole life that made Joy think that was morally acceptable?

Emma wasn't going to stick around to find out. She put her mug down on the counter and turned to Brian. "I'm ready to go now if you are."

"Will you be okay driving or do you want to ride with me and Bobby and come back tomorrow for your car?"

Emma didn't want to go back to the house . . . ever. "I'll drive. I'll be fine."

"Okay." Brian put his free arm around Emma, and they made their way to the door and out into the cold air.

EMMA loved lazy Sundays. This one was cold, but the skies were clear and a brilliant blue. She bundled up, snapped on Bette's leash and they set off for a long walk through town. Emma peered into the window of the Toggery, where there was a mannequin sporting a baby blue cashmere sweater. It would look good on Brian, Emma thought. Bette tugged on her leash as if to say *let's get moving*.

Emma continued down the block past Angel Cuts, where the flowery odor of hair spray and the chemical smell of hair dye lingered in front of the shop even though it was closed. Finally Bette began to tire, and they headed back home.

Arabella had invited Emma, and Bette, too, of course, for brunch. Bette jumped into the car and took up residence in the front passenger seat as soon as Emma opened the door. Emma made a mental note to clean the window—Bette's nose and paws had left a collage of prints all over the glass.

The door was unlocked when they got to Arabella's house. Emma stepped into the foyer, where a welcome rush of warm air greeted them, and took off Bette's leash. Bette went flying down the hall to find Pierre, Emma following behind.

Francis was at the stove managing to look completely masculine despite the frilly apron tied around his waist. His sleeves were rolled up, and he was flipping pancakes on a hot griddle.

Brian was seated at the table, his leg stretched out in front of him. His face broke into a smile when he saw Emma. "Pardon me if I don't get up."

Emma went to him and brushed his lips with hers. She turned around to find Arabella smiling at them.

"I just had a call from your mother," Arabella said brightly. "She and George are planning a vacation—it sounds more like a second honeymoon to me. Apparently their time apart has given them both a new appreciation for each other and a new perspective on things."

Emma felt her heart lift at that news.

Francis carried a platter piled with golden brown pancakes to the table. "Do you have the bacon, dear?"

"I'm keeping it warm in the oven." Arabella grabbed a pot holder, opened the oven door and pulled out a pan of crispy, fried bacon.

The kitchen table was already set and a sweating pitcher of orange juice was set out along with a beaker of warm maple syrup and a carafe of coffee. Emma slipped into the seat next to Brian. He reached out, grabbed her hand and held it, intertwining his fingers with hers.

Finally Arabella and Francis sat down, and they were ready to eat.

"Has there been any news about the Granger case?" Arabella asked.

"More like cases. Plural." Francis poured syrup over his towering stack of pancakes and added two pats of butter. "Jackson Granger immediately hired some expensive New York lawyer in an Armani suit, and the lawyer is already making a racket about the charges. Claims that the paperwork from the Rothko painting came from the seller and how was Jackson to know they were false? Of course, Jackson has yet to produce the previous owner of the painting. But all the legal wrangling will keep the case going for years while Jackson's out on bail making even more money."

Francis shook his head. "Looks like the apple fell close to the tree. The father wasn't above selling stolen paintings— the FBI found several works that had been taken from their rightful owners and which hadn't been seen in years—and the son took it one step further and sold fake paintings." Francis lowered his gaze and looked over the tops of his reading glasses. "Which he painted himself apparently. They found several works-in-progress in his house."

"He was very good," Emma said thinking of the faux Cézanne. "He could have been an artist in his own right."

"Too much trouble," Brian said. "He struck me as someone who wanted to take the shortest route to the most money." He took a sip of his coffee. "Jasper is suing Jackson for the return of the money he paid for the fake Rothko. And he's doing the right thing—he's destroying the painting so that it doesn't fall into some other unscrupulous hands and get passed off as real again."

"Good for him," Francis said.

"But what about Hugh's murder?" Arabella said softly, and Emma had the impression that while Arabella had certainly stopped caring about Hugh a long time ago, his murder had brought back a lot of memories.

"Sabina Roberts has an extremely expensive lawyer, too." Francis reached for the carafe and poured himself a cup of coffee. "But they found her gun in the field after they arrested her, and while Walker is still waiting on some tests from ballistics, he's quite certain it will prove to be the one used to shoot Hugh Granger."

Arabella shuddered. "She's an evil woman."

"Some good has come of all this at least." Emma dipped a piece of her pancake in the syrup that had pooled on the side of her plate.

"I can't imagine what that would be!" Arabella said with some asperity.

"Joy is starting her therapeutic riding school. It's going to be a wonderful resource for a lot of people."

"She ought to be locked up for withholding information and obstruction of justice," Francis said, slamming his coffee cup down for emphasis. Some of the brew sloshed over the edge onto his place mat. "We'd never be able to prove it, of course. But if she had come forward with her information in the first place . . ."

"No harm has come of it, really," Emma said trying to placate him.

"No harm?" Brian's voice rose nearly to a squeak. "You

could have been killed." He turned toward Emma with a look of horror on his face.

"Thanks to Joy coming along when she did, I wasn't."

"If Joy had spoken up in the first place . . ." Francis sputtered to a stop. "That's water under the bridge now, I guess."

The conversation turned to other topics as they finished their meal. Emma helped Arabella clean up while Brian flipped through the paper.

Finally, Brian glanced at the clock above Arabella's sink. "Liz will be here for me any minute now. She's picking me up on her way back from church." He reached for his crutches and struggled to his feet. He jerked his head toward the plaster encasing his leg. "I should be getting this off very soon and graduating to a walking boot. I have to tell you, I can't wait."

"I can imagine," Arabella said, patting Brian on the back.

A car horn sounded in the driveway. "I told Liz she didn't have to come to the door. No need to unbuckle Alice and Ben and then have to get them all situated again two minutes later."

"I'll walk you to the door."

Emma held Brian's hand as they made their way down the hall to the foyer. Emma glanced into the living room to see both Bette and Pierre asleep in a weak sunbeam that slanted through the bay window, both snoring softly. The sight made her smile.

Emma retrieved Brian's coat from the closet. He had to lean his crutches against the wall and balance on one foot as Emma held it out for him.

He looked at Emma, suddenly quiet. "I have something to ask you," he said finally.

"What?" Emma felt her heart beat faster.

Brian looked down at his feet, then looked around Arabella's foyer. He shook his head as if saying *no*.

"This isn't the right place. It should be somewhere more romantic—somewhere memorable—with candles and champagne." His eyes were sparkling. "How about if I make a reservation at L'Etoile for Saturday night? If I get this thing off"—he gestured toward his cast—"I should be able to drive. I'm sure Liz will lend me her station wagon."

Emma wasn't sure if she could speak so she just nodded.

"I'll see you then." Brian bent his head toward Emma's and gave her a soft, lingering kiss.

After Brian left, Emma leaned against the closed door and tried to catch her breath. She thought she knew what Brian was going to ask her, and she already knew what her answer would be.

How was she going to get through the whole week until Saturday night?

*Someone takes decorating for
Halloween to a deadly level...*

FROM NATIONAL BESTSELLING AUTHOR

B. B. HAYWOOD

TOWN IN A
PUMPKIN BASH

A Candy Holliday Murder Mystery

Halloween is on the way, and Cape Willington is busy
preparing for the annual Pumpkin Bash. Local blueberry
farmer Candy Holliday is running the haunted hayride
this year, hoping to make some extra cash. But her hopes
might be dashed when she discovers a dead body near
some fake tombstones. Now, as Candy uses her keen
eye for detail to unearth secrets, she'll discover that
not all skeletons hidden in this small town's closets are
Halloween decorations . . .

"A savory read, which brings the people
of coastal Maine to life."
—*Bangor (ME) Daily News*

INCLUDES DELICIOUS RECIPES!

hollidaysblueberryacres.com
facebook.com/HollidaysBlueberryAcres
facebook.com/TheCrimeSceneBooks
penguin.com

M1373T0913

FIRST IN THE *NEW YORK TIMES* BESTSELLING SERIES BY

SHEILA CONNOLLY

Buried in a Bog

A County Cork Mystery

Honoring the wish of her late grandmother, Maura Donovan visits the small Irish village where Gran was born—never expecting to get bogged down in a murder mystery. When Maura realizes she may know something about the case, she fears she's about to become mired in a homicide investigation and has a sinking feeling she may really be getting in over her head . . .

Praise for the County Cork Mysteries

"A captivating tale—sweet, nostalgic, and full of Irish charm."
—*The Maine Suspect*

"The setting and local personalities are cleverly woven into two mysteries . . . A very promising start to a new series."
—*Booklist*

sheilaconnolly.com
facebook.com/TheCrimeSceneBooks
penguin.com

M1376T0913